STRANGELY FUNNY IV

STRANGELY FUNNY IV

SARAH E GLENN
EDITOR

MYSTERY AND HORROR LLC
TARPON SPRINGS FL

Strangely Funny IV
Trade Paperback Edition

Sarah E. Glenn, Editor

Copyright © 2017 by Mystery and Horror, LLC
Published by Mystery and Horror, LLC

ISBN: 978-0-9981132-3-4

TABLE OF CONTENTS

The Hortons

By Bennie L. Newsome

"Daddy. $3x^2 - 2xy + c$. Solve for 'x'."

Mr. Horton paused. His gloved hands held a plate beneath the warm, soapy dishwater like a serial killer who favored drowning his victims. He looked over his left shoulder. His eyes appeared to look up at nothing, but Mr. Horton was working the equation out on a mental chalkboard. He held that posture for a full thirty-two seconds. The constants and variables faded in and out of his recollection, making the process more difficult. At length, Mr. Horton said, "Repeat the question."

Amanda returned her gaze to the Algebra One textbook opened before her. She found the equation beneath the index finger of her right hand – a fleshy place marker – and read, "$3x^2 - 2xy + c$. Solve for 'x'."

Mr. Horton looked off into the distance, seeing that mental blackboard again. The equation blinked in and out like twinkling Christmas lights.

"Hold on," Mr. Horton growled, obviously frustrated with being bothered.

He let the plate drop. It sunk through the dirty water and thumped against the sink's bottom. The rubber gloves he wore were removed and placed on the counter. Mr. Horton—wiping his naked hands on the apron that proclaimed him "King of the Kitchen" — walked over to where his daughter sat at the kitchen table. He peered over Amanda's shoulder. She pointed at the equation in question: $3x^2 - 2xy + c$. Solve for 'x'.

After a moment, Mr. Horton said, "They're supposed to provide you with a number to plug in for 'x', ain't they? Then you solve the equation."

"No sir. You're supposed to solve *for* 'x'." Amanda pointed to the scratch sheet of paper that lay atop her five-subject notebook. "I already subtracted 'c' on this side of the equal sign, then did it on that side. That's easy enough. When it comes to $3x^2$ and $-2xy$, do you divide the entire grouping or do you break it up into parts and divide it then?"

Mr. Horton looked from the textbook—chock full of instructional paragraphs and step-by-step examples that simplified nothing—to his daughter's illegible notes. He shook his head at the absurdity of it all. "You know what? There's no need for me to pretend. I'm a mailman. The only numbers I deal with are addresses, and I get those right only half the time. Can't you just find the answer in the back of the book?"

"The back of the book only has answers for even numbers. Ms. McFarland assigned us the odd numbered equations."

There was a moment of silence as Mr. Horton considered their options.

"Well, you have a smartphone," he said at last. "See if it lives up to its name. Google the problem."

"That's not a bad idea," Amanda told her departing father's back. He donned the yellow rubber gloves, then fished the sink for his latest victim. "But I have to show my work."

"Tell Google to show its work."

"Ooh! You know what? They might have an app for that."

"There you go."

Sitting amidst the scattered sheets of loose leaf papers and half a dozen pencils was Amanda's purse. She reached into the Nine West and removed a mobile phone. While she searched the internet for an app that could do her homework, a chime filled the house—*beep, beep!* The sound alerted them to the fact that someone had entered through the front door. And sure enough, Missy walked into the kitchen seconds later.

"Good evening, peeps."

Mr. Horton and Amanda both gave a dry "Hey" in response.

An unfazed Missy frantically waved her hand in Amanda's peripheral vision. Amanda looked away from her phone to find her older sister grinning moronically. Scowling was Amanda's initial reaction to Missy's apparent happiness. She hated her sister's smile. Or maybe it was the joy behind the expression. Who was she kidding? Amanda hated both. Fifteen-year-old Missy was Amanda's senior by two years. Despite the age gap, the sisters had been mistaken as twins for most of their lives – dark skin, same "cute as a button" noses, and almond-shaped eyes. That all changed a year ago when Missy's breasts and buttocks exploded from their confines like airbags during an automobile collision. Amanda, on the other hand, looked as if she had inherited Mr. Horton's flat chest and the late Mrs. Horton's (God rest her soul) lack of rump.

Amanda unwittingly stared at her sister's torpedoes. *Does she have to show so much cleavage?*

Meanwhile, Missy (who currently wore so much makeup that she and Amanda barely looked like they had the same parents, let alone twins) held up a cardboard box. Amanda's eyes shifted from the Rocky Mountains to the package. The rectangle container was bound by black tape that repeatedly read, "Amazon Prime." Free two-day shipping, movies, television shows, and free music streaming was also advertised on that well-known strip of tape. Such a sight could only mean good news.

Amanda's eyes widened. *Is that it?*

Missy answered with a nod of her head; a gesture that was accompanied by the toothy grin Amanda had come to loathe. She would tolerate it for the moment, however. The package had arrived. Missy pointed the box in the upstairs direction. They both looked to their father. Mr. Horton continued going about his business of dipping food-stained dishes into the sudsy water, then bringing them up sparkling clean. The towering stack of dirty dishes to Mr. Horton's left promised to occupy him for some time.

Amanda jumped to her feet. She abandoned her cellphone that showed Google listings for mathematical apps. The mess of homework responsible for the search was left behind as well. "$3x^2 - 2xy + c$. Solve for 'x'" remained unsolved.

The girls quickly made their way through the Horton house, a beautiful two-story brick home located in the Mountain Brook area of Birmingham. It was a typical lavish home with the circular driveway that showcased at least one – sometimes three, depending on who was at home – luxury automobile. The mailbox stationed at the end of the driveway snagged the attention of every passerby and informed them that "The Hortons" lived there. What the mailbox did not say was that the Horton household was one member short and had been for two years. Although the mail receptacle sported a magnetic breast cancer awareness decal, it did not say those living under that roof were made aware through firsthand experience. The mailbox was tightlipped when it came to the issue of Mr. Horton not being able to afford the mortgage with his postal income alone, or how Missy would sneak out of the house late at night and jump into the passenger seat of a car whose tag read, "MUAHAHA." There was a lot the mailbox did not reveal.

Lack of transparency was huge in the Horton household. Mr. Horton kept the pending foreclosure of their home a secret from the girls. Missy kept her late-night outings a secret from both her sister and father, and together, the girls were hushed about the Ouija board that now lay between them.

The Amazon box had been torn open and tossed aside. It lay atop Missy's bed along with the board's container — a pink box that read, "Ouija: for Girls." The spirit board was the same color as its packaging: mostly pink with purple corners. The writing (also purple) was done in a seventies font. Instead of the typical phrases — Yes, No, and Goodbye — Ouija: for Girls gave spirits the option of answering with Definitely, As If, and TTYL (talk to you later).

They studied the Ouija board by flickering candlelight. "What should we ask it first?" Amanda asked.

"We have to make contact first."

Missy lightly placed her painted fingertips on one end of the Ouija board pointer, or planchette. Amanda — her fingernails gnawed beyond the tips of her fingers — did the same, making sure to keep clear of the device's plastic eye. "Are there any spirits here?" Missy asked.

The girls watched the Ouija board with wide eyes. Their hearts beat rapidly from anticipation.

Nothing.

After seconds of waiting for a response and not seeing anything, Missy repeated her question. "Are there any spirits here?"

"Maybe you should—" Amanda never got a chance to finish her statement. The planchette went into motion as if it had a mind of its own, swiftly guiding her and Missy's fingers across the board. Its plastic eye halted on "Definitely."

Missy and Amanda looked at one another. Missy's eyes were wide and full of wonder, while her younger sibling's eyes were narrowed slits of accusation. "You moved it!" Amanda cried.

"I did not! I swear!"

"Yes you did! I felt you move it!"

"You felt it move, but it wasn't me moving it!"

Amanda, still wearing that look of mistrust, examined her sister. She watched for the slightest twitch at the corners of Missy's mouth — a telltale sign that big sister was struggling not to smile. Amanda studied Missy's eyes for a twinkle of mirth. There was no humor in the expression Missy wore; at least none that Amanda could detect. In the end, Amanda accepted Missy's denial of manipulating the Ouija board. But if Missy was not responsible (and Amanda knew *she* did not move the planchette) that could only mean one thing: they made contact.

The girls scanned the candlelit room, inspecting dark corners and second guessing the shifting shadows. "Maybe we should leave this alone," Amanda said, her frightened eyes still searching the room.

"There's no turning back now. We already woke something up."

Missy returned her gaze to the board. For the second time since they began their dangerous task of contacting the spirits, Amanda studied Missy's expression. Her older sister was a bit shaken, and understandably so, but Missy's overall demeanor was one of calmness. Amanda drew strength from Missy's resolve and was able to resume her part in their fellowship with the departed – dearly or otherwise.

"Are you still there?" Missy asked.

The planchette moved in a small circle before landing back on, "Definitely."

"Who are we talking with?" Amanda wanted to know before the conversation went any further.

The Ouija board pointer took off again, seemingly on its own. "M," the girls said, reading aloud. "O... M... M... A."

"Momma! I knew it!" Missy exclaimed.

Amanda smiled. The gesture was false, however. She had more than a few doubts about the ghost's identity. The Ouija board instructions were still inside the box – so Amanda was not one hundred percent sure about the rules of spiritual engagement – but she did not think there was a law stating the departed had to properly identify themselves. Would not a fiend say anything for an invitation?

Missy, on the other hand, was not bothered by the worries that plagued her sister. "Momma," Missy said just as casually as she had prior to the discovery of the cancerous lump nestled in Mrs. Horton's right breast. "We haven't been able to find your jewelry. I'm not talking about the costume jewelry you kept in the mirror chest. We can't find the pearls and diamonds—"

"Told you Daddy probably gave it to his girlfriend," Amanda mumbled.

Missy opened her mouth to refute her sister's logic, but the planchette moved unexpectedly. The girls read along. "W... H... A...

T.... What. G... I... R... L... F... R... I... E... N... D.... Girlfriend. What girlfriend?"

Amanda looked to her sister who wore a disapproving frown. Amanda shrugged; a gesture that meant, *how was I supposed to know she* (a dead woman) *would care?* She did not voice this thought, however. What Amanda said was, "I didn't know she could ask *us* questions."

The planchette moved again.

"W... H... A... T.... What. G... I—"

"What girlfriend?" Missy finished. "There's no girlfriend, Momma. Amanda's running her mouth 'bout something she doesn't know."

Amanda scoffed.

The Ouija board's pointer rushed up the board, the girls' fingers simply along for the ride. The device's eye stopped above the phrase "As If." Then the planchette made its way back down to the twenty-six letters.

"W... H... A... T.... What girlfriend?" Missy sighed. "Momma, a lot of things changed since you've been gone. Daddy's been dating this lady from his job – Janice. Me and Amanda can't stand her. She's stupid. And Daddy's not the same now that you're dead. He doesn't spend time with us and he's not as fun to be around anymore." As an afterthought, Missy said, "Amanda's flunking out of school."

"Am not!" Amanda exclaimed. "I got F's in two classes, but I'll have them brought up by report card time. It's not like anyone around here helps me with my work anyway. And what about you?"

"What about me?"

"You're pregnant!"

Missy's mouth fell open in shock. It was not a "How dare you tell such a lie?" expression, but more of a "How did you know?"

Amanda smirked. "I found your pregnancy test in the trashcan. Congratulations."

Missy removed her hand from the Ouija board. Amanda, knowing things were about to get physical, abandoned the spirit board as well and scrambled to her feet. *Hit first, hit hard, then run,* Amanda coached herself. Flutter away like a butterfly after stinging like a bee. Before the clash could take place, however, a whooshing wind – warm and foul smelling – blew through the room. The tiny flames atop all six candles sputtered before vanishing altogether. The room went pitch black. A strong, lavender scent masked the stench that accompanied the blast of air.

"Missy!"

"I'm here. Going to turn on the light."

Moments later, the overhead light fixture emitted a radiance that was much brighter than the candlelight to which they had become accustomed. Missy stood by the on and off switch located near the closed bedroom door. Amanda remained near the Ouija board. "What was that?" the younger of the two asked about the wind that blew through the room. They both looked to the window to verify what they already knew: it was closed.

"Let's get out of here."

Missy grabbed the doorknob. It turned easily within her hand. She yanked the door open and caught a brief glimpse of the hallway before the door slammed shut on its own – boom! Missy let out a small cry. Panic began to build in her chest, a pressure-like sensation akin to having a tiny sumo wrestler plop down atop her. Missy took ahold of the doorknob a second time, her hands trembling with fear, but the brass fixture did not cooperate. She planted her feet and called upon every muscle in her body to fight in that tug-of-war with the door. But like the civil right activists of the 1960's, it would not be moved.

"What are you doing?"

"It's not me!" Missy cried as she attempted to kick down the door. Every impact echoed throughout the house. "It won't open!"

The bedroom light flickered for two or three seconds then held steady. Missy stopped stomping the door with the reluctance of a cop who wanted to execute that search warrant. She glanced around the room. Stuffed animals were everywhere. The glassy eyed critters were total contradictions to the posters of shirtless hip-hop artists. Amanda moved closer to her sister; the two of them crowding near the bedroom door. Their glances (eyes wide with fright) ricocheted around the room like hard thrown bouncy balls. The girls' breaths were labored from increasing anxiety. And when the closet door creaked open on its own, their chests rose and fell even quicker.

The door was ever so slowly pushed open until its knob touched the adjoining wall. A strident creak accompanied the door's movement – a ghastly trumpet announcing the arrival of a fallen angel. Amanda and Missy, their backs pressed firmly against the door, stared at the closet's dark interior. Initially, they saw only hanging clothes and a mess of shoes covering the carpeted floor. Then she materialized from the darkness.

Mrs. Horton staggered from the closet; her jerky movements akin to that of a faulty robot. Leading the way before her was a badly oxidized IV pole from which hung a bag of black fluid. Clear tubing (filled with the disgusting liquid) connected the IV bag to her emaciated right arm. Mrs. Horton's entire body seemed to have withered, from her bony legs covered in torn flesh to her face with its sunken cheeks. The worst sight of all was the woman's soulless eyes. They were as black as the tar-like substance fueling Mrs. Horton's body, and the girls found themselves paralyzed within that frightening gaze.

"Momma," Missy groaned. Aside from two years of decelerated rot, Mrs. Horton looked as she had just before she died. Her misshapen head was bald from months of chemotherapy radiation. Her attire consisted of a filthy open back hospital gown and a pair of equally dirty socks.

Amanda's heart quickened at the sight of her resurrected mother, then she saw the switch (a long, slender stick removed from shrubbery) held in Mrs. Horton's left hand. Amanda's heart nearly jackhammered its way out of her chest. The charred branch's leafy tip forever burned like the end of a cigarette, emitting tendrils of smoke. If Amanda did not know better, she would have sworn that her mother snapped the switch from Moses' legendary burning bush.

"Daddy!" Amanda screamed as she pounded on the door. "Daddy!"

Missy joined her sister. The two of them screamed as loud as they could – "Daddy!" – while beating on the door with their hands and feet. At the same time, Mrs. Horton lurched closer. One of her shoulders rose higher than the other. The undead woman's neck was held at a crooked angle. *Squeak, squeak, squeak* went the rusty wheels of the IV pole. Soon, Mrs. Horton got within a few feet of the girls. They were ramming the door with their bodies by that point. Their screams no longer held any semblance to a language.

"Daadeeeeeeeeeeeeee!"

Eight feet of distance became six feet, then three. The whole time, Mrs. Horton moved like a marionette doll – her movements spasmodic, almost comical. Once she was in striking distance, Mrs. Horton pulled the switch back like a tennis player preparing to return a serve. "Momma, no!" Missy cried out; her left leg raised and hands held out in defense. Amanda cowered behind her sister. There was no mercy in Mrs. Horton shriveled heart for either of them. No pity. She brought the switch forward, fast and hard – *Whip!* The barbaric process was repeated over and over again. *Whip! Whip! Whip!* Mrs. Horton, that avenging angel, cut down her girls with that bizarre version of a flaming sword. The switch shredded jeans and reduced shirts to tatters; however, the girls' skin produced only crisscrossing red welts. Perhaps Mrs. Horton did possess a smidgen of mercy. Then again, the girls' ear-piercing shrieks and waterfall of tears opposed such a notion.

The bedroom door suddenly flew open. Amanda and Missy howled as the arching barrier shoved them into the branch wielding ghoul.

"What the hell is going on in here?" Mr. Horton yelled from where he stood in the doorway.

The girls ran into their father, nearly knocking him over. They hugged him tight while wiping their disgustingly wet faces into his apron. "Momma's here!" Missy screeched. She pulled away from her father to spare her bedroom a glance. Of course, the specter was gone. "She was here. And she whooped us!"

"What?"

Amanda pulled at her shirt so Mr. Horton could see the many rips. "Momma did this!"

"All right. I'm gonna need y'all to calm down so you can tell me what's going on."

Obviously, Mr. Horton doubted their story. He probably thought they had been fighting like a pair of alley cats and were trying to explain it away, but the girls had no time to convince him. Mrs. Horton was not gone. Quite the opposite. The undead woman was a lioness prowling in the high grass, waiting for just the right moment to attack.

"We gotta get out of here!" Missy yelled as she pushed her father aside and raced down the hallway. Amanda agreed with her sister wholeheartedly. She showed her concurrence by chasing after Missy.

Mr. Horton was left yelling at their backsides. "Where the hell are y'all going?"

Missy reached the second-floor landing. Amanda was right on her heels. The two of them descended the carpeted steps two (sometimes three) at a time. Without warning, the lights flickered. A gust of wind – one that carried the stench of death – swept through the stairwell. "Here she comes!" Missy screamed.

The spirit of Mrs. Horton did manifest. This time, however, she appeared in the form of picture frames pulling away from the walls. For a moment, they hovered without the aid of nails or invisible strings. Then the pictures shifted horizontally and flew at the girls' heads like thrown Frisbees. Missy's elementary graduation picture (the one where she was missing two of her front teeth) hovered for a moment before slicing toward Amanda's head. She ducked. The picture crashed into the opposing wall. Family portrait. Slice, slice, slice, slice! *Crash!* Mr. and Mrs. Horton's faded wedding photo. Slice, slice, slice, slice! *Crash!*

"Move it!" Amanda cried as she ran bent over, hoping to avoid a concussion.

"I'm going as fast as I can!"

The two of them reached the first-floor landing, relatively unscathed – although shards of broken glass had nicked them both – then Missy and Amanda sprinted through the dining room. The front door was their goal. Before they could cross half the dining room's width, a large curio cabinet (once known as Mrs. Horton's pride and joy) fell across their path with a tremendous, house-shaking smash. Glass cracked. Fine china shattered.

Missy skidded to a halt, her hands up in a gesture of surrender. Amanda collided with her sister's backside. "Kitchen door!" Missy yelled. Amanda spun around and led the way this time.

While the girls hurriedly carried out plan B, a fantastic thing occurred. The fallen curio cabinet was lifted by unseen hands and returned to its original position. Cups, plates and knick-knacks (those that were not smashed to smithereens) rose from the floor and shelved themselves. A broom and dustpan materialized from nowhere. The cleaning utensils swept up the broken china on its own. The sight was like a scene from Disney's *Beauty and the Beast*. Mrs. Horton might have been a vindictive spirit, but that house located in the Mountain Brook area of Birmingham was still hers, and she would not see it in disarray. The broom and dustpan – the latter loaded with broken bits of dishes – floated after the girls. It arrived in the kitchen just as Amanda and Missy discovered the backdoor was supernaturally barred.

Missy tapped her sister on the shoulder. "Look," she whispered. Her wide eyes indicated the floating household cleaning supplies.

The pair watched as the cleaning tools made their way over to the trashcan. The lid on the small receptacle rose, the broken china was tossed inside, then the top clapped close. The dustpan clattered to the floor. The broom was propped against the wall.

Who is this? Amanda wondered amidst her frightened thoughts. *Jasper the helpful, but not so friendly ghost?*

And then entered Jasper's angry uncle – Slim. "What the hell is wrong with y'all?" Mr. Horton yelled as he stormed into the kitchen. "Have you two lost your minds? Broken pictures are on the stairs! You knocked over the...." He looked into the living room where the curio cabinet stood, with no sign of broken china. "...Sounded like you knocked over the curio cabinet, I could've sworn I heard—"

The girls ran to him a second time, both clinging to the man like frightened toddlers.

Mr. Horton sighed. He wanted to be upset, but he was more confused than anything. "Y'all gotta tell me what's going on."

Amanda and Missy attempted to explain the situation simultaneously. "Missy bought a Ouija board.... Wasn't just my idea! She put in on it.... We summoned Momma! She asked about Janice. Yeah, only because you mentioned her.... How was I supposed to know she'd care? Then the candle went out...."

"Whoa, whoa! I can't understand you when y'all talking at once. Missy, what's going on?"

In the end, it was Amanda who explained the situation. She repeatedly hit her father's arm until she got his attention, and, once garnered, pointed behind him. Mr. Horton turned around to find his late wife standing at the kitchen's entryway.

"Oh, shit!"

Mrs. Horton's face was aimed downward, but she lifted her eyes to fix everyone with a wicked glare. A gust of wind manifested for the third time, a foul-smelling current that whipped sheets of paper around the room. The swirling debris was chiefly made up of Amanda's school materials: class notes and paper used to work out math equations. Some of the paper storm – like the sheet that slapped Mr. Horton in the face – materialized out of thin air. Mr. Horton removed the item from his brow, gave it a quick glance as he prepared to throw it aside, then did a double take.

A foreclosure notice....

And then he understood what his late wife was trying to tell him. "Let... let me... Sarah, let me explain...," he stammered.

Mrs. Horton snapped her attention to the kitchen wall. Letters appeared on the large, eggshell colored surface like some invisible finger dipped in blood was doing the scrawling. The alphabets were arranged so that they eventually spelled out, "Insurance Policy?"

"Well... we, uh... we took a trip to get over our grief of losing you—"

"You and Janice took a trip," Amanda muttered.

"Amanda!"

She shrugged off her sister's rebuke. "I'm just saying."

"Bills! I caught up our bills, bought Missy a car – she doesn't get to drive it much right now, but when she turns sixteen and gets her license, she'll have it."

"Insurance Policy?" disappeared and was replaced with another bloody scrawl. "Where's the rest of the money?"

Mr. Horton stammered.

"Janice is living really good nowadays."

Missy groaned. "Thanks, Amanda. We're gonna die."

Mrs. Horton staggered forward. The flame on the tip of her burnt switch blazed brighter as she advanced. *Squeak, squeak, squeak!* went the IV pole.

"Run!" Mr. Horton told his girls.

Without explaining the rest of his plan, Mr. Horton charged the ghost of his wife like a defensive lineman going for the quarterback. He went in low, arms outstretched and face fixed into a grimace. Before he could knock the ghost flat, however, Mrs. Horton brought her switch across his face – *whip!*

"Goodness!" Mr. Horton cried out as he fell aside and dropped to the floor. He brought his hands up to comfort the left side of his stinging face.

Missy hurdled her writhing father and attempted to circumvent her mother. The woman lashed out with her switch a second time, just as quick as a serpent. She struck Missy's ankle, causing a bloody welt to rise on her flesh. "Ow!" Missy cried out like Mr. Horton had before her and she, too, collapsed to the floor.

Mrs. Horton positioned herself so she towered over her downed husband and daughter. The squeaking IV pole was held in her left hand. She held the charred switch with the burning tip in her other. When her cold shadow fell over Mr. Horton, he removed one hand from his face and saw her standing there like the Grim Reaper. "Please don't hurt us!" he begged while holding his free hand up in supplication.

The ghastly woman raised her switch holding hand like that of the axe-wielding executioner, then brought it down with her final judgement. "Shit!" Mr. Horton cried out. But Mrs. Horton did not stop there. Her arm rose and fell repeatedly, alternating between her husband and daughter. A few lashes were doled out to Mr. Horton: two on his back and one on his butt. The man wiggled across the floor like a snake. Then she motioned to her right side, and whipped Missy.

"Whoop their ass, Momma!" Amanda called, hoping to earn the lady's favor.

Mrs. Horton's response came in the form of an Algebra One textbook floating up from the kitchen table and soaring across the room. The makeshift projectile clocked Amanda upside her head. "Ouch!" The five-subject notebook was also thrown at her, along with a couple of pencils. "Yes ma'am," a teary-eyed Amanda said, rubbing her aching forehead. She got the message loud and clear.

Amanda plopped down where her homework materials landed. *I gotta get out of here,* she thought while fumbling with her textbook. Amanda listened to her sister and father, a fully-grown man and a young woman who thought of herself as an adult, both howling like babies. Then again, Mrs. Horton did have that effect on people. And if she did not get her homework done, Amanda knew she would find herself on the business end of that switch.

"Momma, can I have my phone?"

The mobile device levitated a few inches off the kitchen table, then flew to the other side of the room where it crashed into the wall and broke apart.

"Yes ma'am," Amanda whined. She sniffed in an attempt to recall the snot dripping from her nose, then went back to work. "$3x^2 - 2xy + c$. Solve for 'x'."

Bennie L. Newsome is a writer and graphic designer from Birmingham, Alabama. He is the author of *The Last Days*—a middle grade vampire novel scheduled for publication in July 2017. Bennie has also been published in many other anthologies, the most notable being Hallmark's *Thanks, Mom*. When Bennie is not at his day job as a mail carrier or spending time with his family that consists of a wife and three kids, he can be found on Facebook and Instagram at Newsome Designs 27.

Tentacles

By Jason Purdy

1.

Everybody knows about Werewolves. Everybody knows about vampires. Heck, you've probably even heard of a few Weregoats or Weresheep in your time. If you believe the rumors, you're probably familiar with the idea of a Werewerewolf. That's what you become if you get bitten by a Werewolf when you're already a Werewolf. There's not much difference from being a regular Lycanthrope, except that you have two heads.

I didn't believe that sort of nonsense until I met Steve at the gathering. Steve was bitten at the age of eighteen by an errant Werewolf while backpacking through Canada. He was then bitten again by another Werewolf at a Miley Cyrus concert, though if you ask him, it was a Metallica gig.

He told me that being a Werewerewolf was just like being a Werewolf except that there was an extra set of teeth to brush. It was unnerving to watch one mouth tell me that while the other sipped a Mojito through a bendy straw. The wolf man had someone managed to modify a Hawaiian shirt to fit two wolf heads, and the tent-like billowing of its fabric in the air con of the bar told me all I need to know about the kind of man he was when he wasn't wolfed out.

Though I'm hardly one to pass comment, after all, I'm a goddamn Weresquid. Hawaiian shirt or not, at least he doesn't need to be wheeled around in a giant glass tank.

I can see from that look on your face that you're wondering how a man can become a Weresquid. Let me break it down for you with some simple logic. Have a look at my chalkboard here. Human being plus Werewolf bite equals another Werewolf, right? So how does someone become a Weresquid? That's right children; he gets bitten by a Weresquid. Gold stars all around. I was out for my usual night swim when it happened. I liked night swimming ever since I heard that REM song, which does seem to be about its title, for once. I like when music does that. Save the metaphors and the flowery words, and give me something simple that I can shake my tentacles to.

The full moon cast a particularly beautiful hue across the surface of the ocean, making it look like a kindergarten painting pinned to an old refrigerator. I was naked and freezing, but I felt so alive. Being a marketing executive was great, sure: it meant money, drinks, a nice office, and fancy suits, but it didn't matter how many times I yelled at the interns or bragged to the receptionist about how much money I made... nothing matched this feeling of freedom.

That was, until the appendage wrapped around my leg. There was a curious moment of the world stopping entirely. I could hear the tide crashing on the shore. I could hear the distant howl of a Were-something-or-other. I tried to tug myself free from what I assumed was a reed of seaweed. I realized my error when I felt the great suction cups pull my skin with them, and then reattach on fresh flesh with a little more purchase. The pain was immediate and brilliant, like a hot poker up the ass. I opened my mouth to scream and was pulled under the tide, my howl turning into a gurgle as I was pulled into the abyss.

I woke up on the beach, entirely naked. I wasn't wounded, except for my pride, though there was a very real chance I might die of frost bite too. I retrieved my clothes from the space I'd stashed them under a rock, and walked home in a daze, feeling my shriveled testicles rub against the inside of my now damp and icy cold jeans. I had my towel thrown over my head and shoulders, as if trying to protect my wounded ego with an old Finding Nemo towel. I swear it didn't belong to me.

I called in sick to the office and lay in my king-size bed for one, shivering as if in the grip of a terrible fever. I had hellish visions of the depths of the ocean, of monstrous angler fish and goblin sharks gobbling slightly smaller monsters along the way. I also developed a bizarre animosity for whales. I had to toss all my Blue Planet DVD's in the bin a week later.

Everyone who has been bitten will know that Were transformation feels something like coming off heroin by taking three kilos of coke a day instead. I have some degree of first-hand experience in this matter, so trust me when I tell you that it was terribly uncomfortable. Things got worse the following night, because it was still the full moon, and I was about to experience my first night as a giant squid out of water. Quite literally.

I was sitting in the living room watching some garbage on the TV, wrapped in a blanket, while sweating profusely, trying to keep myself hot and cold at the same time and trying to keep those three sips of chicken soup in my stomach from rising and spewing all over the already puke colored carpet. Plus, I was fighting off a crazy hankering for whale flesh. There is little in the world that makes you feel more insane than craving something that you've never even had before. Unless it's sex.

Anyway, just like that, I went from five foot nine inches Paul Cena, who barely weighed 150 pounds when wet, to a twelve-foot-long squid weighing in at a little over half a ton weight. My eyes were the size of dinner plates, and I'd retained enough semblance of humanity to see my flat mate Jeff crushed beneath my bulk, my tentacles slowly sliding him towards my abyssal maw. Also, I'd crushed the TV and spilled a beer. My security deposit was gone, and I was about to suck Jeff's face off—and not in the way that I'd done at our New Year's party when only guys showed up.

I managed to control myself and curl my tentacles in, meaning that I was now a giant squid with neatly dangled tentacles perched on a sofa that was collapsing under my weight. Jeff looked at me with abstract horror, like I was some sort of Lovecraftian nightmare. I suppose I was, minus the little wings.

The stunned silence was broken by the click clacking of my beak as I tried to speak English to him. It probably sounded like a squid trying his tentacle at rudimental Klingon. As I said before, were creatures were common knowledge, and it'd be a while before I learned to control my concentration and learn English in this form. Jeff and I had a sort of mutual understanding that only two grown men living together have. It dispelled the awkwardness of constantly catching each other masturbating.

"A Weresquid," he said quietly. I kept clacking like I was the slow kid at band practice given a set of conkers.

Then he started to laugh. Great, big whooping belly laughs. I thought he might die, I did. Especially when I picked him up and starting squeezing him like a stress ball until his face turned purple. I realized that he wasn't the only one who was suddenly struggling to breathe. I set him down.

He grasped at his throat, gasping.

"I'm sorry," he wheezed. "Oh Christ, I'm sorry."

I made a splish-splash motion with my tentacles. Water, please.

Comprehension dawned on his face as the color returned to it at the same time.

"Gotcha."

He went to the kitchen and threw a glass of tap water at me.

2.

It had become something of an epidemic by this point. Sort of like a zombie apocalypse, only zombies aren't real. We've got everything but zombies, even folks who've managed to be bitten by ghosts. I'm just as baffled as you are.

There was a government-funded agency set up to help were folk of all shapes and sizes. They offered support from disability allowance, to specialist facilities to help you during your transformation. There was also counseling available, and a degree of training on how to speak English and maintain full human cognitive function when you were transformed. For some lucky folk, they could also teach you how to suppress it completely, but the results varied.

I had been standing in line for five hours, trying to get a grant to buy me a tank for my transformation periods. It was like social security, but for Werefolk. They were creatively named Social Security for Werefolk. Or SSW, for short. You had to cross a picket line of Bible bashers to get in. Apparently, I'm going to hell and I chose to be attacked by a giant squid.

I had to fill out a slew of forms in a humid, stinking room, at which point I returned three weeks later for an interview to assess my condition. Then on top of that, they'd have to keep me under observation for the next full moon to make sure that I wasn't faking it. I feel like the sucker scars on poor Jeff are proof enough, but evidently not. They didn't seem to believe me that I was bitten by a squid, so I nearly suffocated to death in a bare-walled concrete room that smelled like piss and man sweat while a terrified bureaucrat was nearly ground into dust by my colossal beak.

After that, I got my money. It was an extra one hundred dollars a month. I also got the use of an empty tank at SeaWorld. They were getting rid of the whales after that heart-breaking documentary and moving the Were people in, instead. I feel like there's some sort of clever commentary on the relationship between man and beast here, but I'm not going to dwell on it. Just give me my tank and my social security check and don't bother me.

I carried on working at my same old job, and tried to keep it a secret from my co-workers. They found out when I told my boss that I needed a couple of days off at the end of each month. Under new legislation, were people got certain workplace allowances, including days off for the full moon on top of their other paid holidays, sick days, and whatever other health benefits or cycle to work bullshit they might be privy to.

My boss had to give me the days off, and he was supposed to keep my disability secret, but he didn't. Within two days, everyone was leaving calamari on my desk. Not even the kind you could eat. Just little, dead squids. It brought me to tears every time. I now had a deep, emotional connection to one of the shittiest creatures in the world. Why couldn't a shark have bitten me? I contemplated hiding in the office during the next full moon and covering the office in ink. Maybe I'd eat my boss too. Take that, Mr. Benson. You'd taste like eating a lamb doner kebab out of an ash tray.

It was mandatory to attend WFA meetings – that's Were Folk Anonymous. This was part of receiving your benefits. It was kind of the equivalent of being forced to attend an AA meeting because you'd been punched in the face by a stranger during a full moon. It was a weird thing to meet fortnightly in the basement of a dingy church downtown, with an eclectic bunch of relatively average people. You had everyone here: there was a university lecturer, a male porn star, the CEO of a major bank, a single mother, a failed novelist, and a guy in a trench coat that kind of smelled like the inside of an old R.V. He sat away from the group with his hands thrust far too deeply into his pockets.

It was here that I met Sarah. She had a kid, but I didn't let that put me off. Her fundamentalist husband had left her when she got bitten by a Werespidermonkey on the way home from church one night. She later admitted to me that she wasn't at church; she was out at a bar. He seemed to think it was her fault that some dick in monkey skin had opted to bite her instead of staying in and controlling himself.

Sarah was beautiful, kind, easy going, and had a great taste in music. In effect, she was everything that I wasn't, and I was in love with her from the moment she offered me a cup of lukewarm shitty coffee and spilled it on my shirt. She had big brown eyes, lips the shade of an albino dolphin, and when she laughed, she barked like a seal. She was the founder of a start-up company which pursued research into finding out a little bit more about our conditions, and chased funding to find a cure.

It was her idea to move the meeting to the bars afterwards, meaning that the AA meeting that used the room after us was often greeted by us talking excitedly about doing shots and drinking our own body weights in booze as we left. I hate to think that we made things difficult for them, but they all gave us this self-righteous look as we left.

You know, because drinking two bottles of wine every night is just bad luck, while getting bitten by a squid when out for a healthy midnight swim is something that you inflict on yourself.

Jerks.

3.

"You've got lovely color," she says, running a furry hand over my enormous, piebald side. I'm a weird mix of a flaming California sunset at the high of summer, and dried mud. My flesh is patchy and mismatched, and I have a Mickey Mouse shaped cluster of colors beneath my truck tire sized left eye.

"Thanks," I mutter nervously, my beak clacking. "You've got lovely fur. Do you condition?"

I don't know if monkeys can blush, but she tries.

"Y-yes, thanks for noticing. It's coconut."

"What is?"

"My conditioner."

"Oh, right."

We sit in silence for a while. The water laps against the side of my tank, and the moonlight reflects off the water. In the darkness, I can see her crystal clear. Her tiny furry face somehow looks just like her. I'd swear I can see her in those beady eyes. There's no way she sees anything but a monster in my massive, monstrous irises.

It took a while to learn to talk around this ungainly beak, but I'm there. I feel entirely human in this body, except for the fact that I long for the deep sea. Sometimes I dive to the bottom of my tank and bury myself entirely in the sand, pretending that the slight weight of it resting on my body is the crushing pressure of the ocean depths.

Sarah flicks her tail in the water. I hold it in one of my tentacles, gently swaying with her movements. I keep my face away from her. This is more intimate than sex. Even the weird stuff that we tried after she stumbled across all those videos on the hidden folder on my laptop. To have your lover see you in your were-form is a terrifying prospect, especially when you're both afflicted. After a year, we'd finally bitten the bullet. If she can love me as a squid, then I'm going to propose. After the moon, of course. I can't afford a ring the size of one of these tentacles.

"Look at me," she says. Her tiny black lips are like two black jelly beans. I don't want to think about kissing a monkey but I can't help it. I reluctantly sidle around the tank to face her head on. I must be monstrous. I'm fifty times the size of her. I could swallow her whole. I've got suckers the size of her entire torso. Her tiny tail in my hand is like holding a strand of overcooked spaghetti.

I want to bury myself in the sand. Her long black toes fidget nervously on the edge of the tank. The moonlight makes her dark fur shine like an oil slick.

"Your eyes are like supernovas," she says, with awe. She stares into my soul. "I could stare at them all night."

My beak drops open, ever so slightly.

"It's like watching the birth of the universe," she mutters. I want hold her tight, but in this shape, I'd pop her like a balloon. I try to stroke her face but I knock her flying into the water.

"Sorry."

It had only taken two years, but I'd learned to control my size and appearance when I transformed. Not only did it allow me to give myself a lovely, even all over red color to my skin, but it also meant I could keep myself to about the size of a cat when I needed to. That meant I could stop spending a few nights a month at SeaWorld, and it meant that Sarah and I could have something of a normal life when the moon was full. She introduced me to her kid and he thought it was rad that I could transform into a squid. He was twelve years old, so he was getting into that age where my standoffish, sarcastic and aloof brand of social interaction went down quite well. His name was Tyler or something. His mom said it was from Fight Club. I changed the subject. We're not supposed to talk about that.

Plus, I had loads of video games that I let him play whenever he came over. I also let him borrow my high-tech Turtle Beach gaming headset. It blocked out all the sounds of the outside world, allowing you to focus completely on the fact that some guy from Delaware was claiming to be banging your mom, and not pay attention to the guy who could shape shift into a giant squid that was banging your mom less than twenty feet away.

Life was good. At the gatherings, Sarah pushed my little tank on wheels around with her monkey strength, and now that I had full grasp of my body and of my language skills, I could order a shot of tequila for myself, and I'd swim to the surface to let Sarah pour it down my throat. I didn't think squids would be able to get drunk, but luckily, they can, and they can't vomit, either. If you've ever seen a giant squid do a keg stand you might feel like the universe is unravelling at the seams. Sometimes I inadvertently squirted ink when I was drunk, but that wasn't so bad. People thought it was cute.

This is where I met the Werewerewolf I told you about before. A two headed Wolfman, and I thought I'd seen it all. Steve was a strange sort of guy. Do you ever meet someone and get the feeling they're only talking to you because your girlfriend / boyfriend / wife / husband / sister / brother is good looking and they want to get in on that action?

I kind of felt like Steve was only talking to the pair of us because he wanted to get closer to Sarah. Which seemed strange to me, as we'd all only see each other in animal form. You may be a two headed Wolfman, bro, but you're still human on the inside, and you're hitting on a monkey. We can all talk about being attracted to what's on the inside, but sometimes when Sarah and I are fooling about, her monkey face pops into my head and I go limper than one of my tentacles.

It turned out Steve was more interested in me. He wanted to have me over for dinner.

4.

Just to be clear, I mean that he literally wanted me over for dinner. As in, this weird, two headed Wolfman wanted to cook me and eat me. We'd all heard about this happening before, it was something we were supposed to be vigilant about. Like that story of the two best buddies over in New Hampshire.

They went out for a few drinks and a few turned into a few too many. They staggered out into the night, decided to take a shortcut through the forest, and both got bitten by Were creatures. A Werepig, and a Werebear, specifically. They carried on being best of friends until their first transformation where the bear man ate the pig man in his own home while watching *America's Got Talent*.

I'd rather be eaten than watch that tripe, but that's neither here nor there. The courts weren't sure how to handle it. Is a Were transformation a mental illness? A disease? Can you plead insanity, or diminished responsibility? It's a murky area that lawyers love. If I commit a crime, they'd scramble to represent me, not only because of the media circus that would surround it.

Either way, bear man ended up having to attend a WFA meeting every week for the rest of his life, and surrender himself to the police well in advance of every full moon. That's essentially what I'm doing now, so it seems that you can use your transformation as a sort of get out of jail free card. That doesn't fly so easily now following the research showing that you can learn to control your transformation and keep control of your mental state. Still, if Steve did manage to eat me, as long as he could prove it wasn't premeditated, he'd probably manage to wriggle out of it.

Proving it wasn't premeditated? That's easy. Just wash the dishes.

He told me that he was having a sort of boy's night in. No girlfriends, no wives, no fiancées, either. Sarah and I had just got engaged. I got her two rings, one big one with a gorgeous diamond set right in the middle of it, and a smaller band made of gold for her long, monkey fingers. All Werefolk are allergic to silver, strangely. We've never been able to explain why, and it's only when you've transformed too. There's always something new to learn about the world.

To be honest, I was being the perfect husband to be. I didn't want a boy's night. I didn't want to do anything but watch terrible TV with Sarah on our sofa and play Xbox with Tyler. I wanted to order Chinese food and eat it out of those little boxes with my faux new family. Being a squid had mellowed me out somewhat. I'd become as malleable as my body on a full moon. I'd managed to fit myself inside a teacup last week. It was a great prank.

Turns out I was the only man at this boy's night. As in, everyone else cancelled, or at least that's what I was told. We'd scheduled it for a full moon weekend and they were all supposed to be Werefolk too. It was going to be a night for us all to let it all hang out and be ourselves. I was secure enough in my own masculinity to know that I'd rather paint Sarah's toenails than sit in a room with middle aged men drinking warm beer and pretending they didn't miss the shit out of their partners.

The taxi driver was gracious enough to carry me to Steve's door. I was in my tank of course, so I couldn't do it myself. The driver tried to pretend he didn't have anything against Werefolk but when you start a story with *I'm not Wereist, but...* then your whole argument loses water quickly.

Steve answered the door with two heads and one awful shirt. He hugged my tank, and told me it was great to see me. It was weird the way he's start a sentence with one head and finish it with the other. He slobbered into my tank but I let it slide. I had a few pressing questions I wanted to ask him, and they'd feel a little less awkward after a few Charles Brewkowskis.

"The rest of the guys will be here soon," he reassures me, angling a straw towards my beak so I can enjoy a Budweiser the way it was meant to be enjoyed – through a flamingo pink bendy straw.

I was a little on edge already. Steve seemed nervous, but I put it down to a first-time hosting. I never understood why anyone ever wanted to have a dinner party or have quests over. It was a fucking nightmare. Steve's house was very much a bachelor pad, despite him being the only two headed wolf on the planet. It might have something to do with his curiosity sticky anime girl figurines adorning every shelf in the house. It could be the squishy breasts mouse mat, or it could just be the fact that he only owns Hawaiian shirts and khaki pants. Cast your votes, folks.

Nobody else showed up all night. I ate beakful after beakful of Doritos, hot wings, mini pizzas, and M&Ms. It's not a suitable diet for a squid, but Steve didn't have any blubber nuggets. I didn't notice he was only pretending to drink alcohol when I was so plastered that my tank was nearly black with ink, and Steve was calmly skipping through J-Pop on his iTunes to find something that might not make me want to find out how squids hear so I could prevent it from happening ever again.

I take the opportunity to ask those niggling questions.

"What's it like to think with two heads?" I blurt, while blurting another jet of ink into my tank. I angle myself out of the tank, propping my beak on the edge and holding on tight with tentacles that can't seem to find any purchase.

Steve looks up, as if in a daze. I'm about to tell him that he doesn't have to answer, but sure he does. I'm the guest.

"It's weird," he says slowly. It's comes from one head. Weird from the other. "I kind of have to piece a sentence together before I speak, or the wires get crossed and it comes out as gibberish."

"Are you smarter now?" I say.

"I don't think so. It just feels like I have to think in two places." He looks at the ceiling.

"Like, imagine if every time you had to park a car, you were controlling another car at the same time, and they both moved together. It's not hard if you can find the space. It just takes a little more effort."

I nod as if that makes any sense whatsoever.

"Do the two heads ever fight?" I ask, again tactlessly. He looks a little annoyed this time. I scoop up another tentacle of peanut M&M's and crunch them with a loud *clack clack clack* of my beak.

"No, they're both me," he says.

"We all have internal conflict though," I say. "I mean, Captain Crunch or Froot Loops, how do you choose?"

"I generally agree with myself." Both heads nod, following this.

"What if one of you hogs the food?"

"We have the same stomach."

"Sure, but you know when someone swipes your last bite of food and it feels like you didn't eat the meal at all?"

"No."

"Well when that happens, don't you get pissed off at yourself?"

"No. Want another beer?"

I don't remember much after that. It was soon 3am I was long overdue to get a taxi home, but I was too drunk to swim. Not that I was swimming home or anything, but it was a pretty good metric as to whether I was capable of navigating a taxi journey without someone ending up in a pot at a Japanese restaurant.

"I think I should head home," I say.

"Nonsense, stay a while longer," he grins at me. "Stay all night, even."

"I should really get home to Sarah..." I slur.

"One more beer, go on."

He moves into the kitchen before I can object. I hear him fill rattle about, turning on the tap, filling a pot. I didn't think much of it until he lifted my tank, threw me into the pot, and then closed the lid over me.

"Hey!" I say, "This is fresh water!" I start to suffocate, but that's okay because the water is growing uncomfortably hot. "Let me out!"

"Sorry buddy," the Werewerewolf says. "I'm hungry."

It takes me that long to realize that he's planning on eating me.

"Oh no," I say, flailing against the sides of the pot. I push all my tentacles to the lid and manage to lift it slightly, but he slams it back down on me.

"Quit messing around!" I shout. My voice reverberates off the steel walls and bubbles in the slowly boiling water. It starts to hurt. I become aware that I might die in here. I start to slam the lid with my tentacles, but the wolfman is holding it down, and he's stronger than me when I'm this size.

This size.

I struggle to concentrate and remember all those classes where they taught us how to control ourselves and our size when we transform by anchoring ourselves to our human sides: by remembering our loved ones, our jobs, remembering stupid little things like driving a car or waiting in line for an overpriced cup of crappy coffee.

I just let that all go and think about hunting whales in the depths. I think about sleeping in caves where the pressure would turn a human inside out. I think about the horrors on the ocean floor, and how I can count myself amongst their number.

The pot splits open, sending scalding water flying into the wolfman's face. He looks comically affronted.

"Hey! My pot!" he howls, charging at me, but I'm nearly the size of the kitchen now, and I pick him up in one of my great tentacles, wrapping it tightly around his waist. I pull off fresh and fur with my suckers.

"You tried to cook me," I say, "You dick. You're a terrible host."

"There's so much of you," he says. "I could freeze you and eat you for months." He seems to be a thousand miles away. Both of his mouths ooze drool onto the kitchen floor.

"You're nuts," I say.

"I could have squid tacos until Christmas. I'd save so much money."

I wrap a second tentacle around his upper half, silencing his babble as I cover both his mouths, knocking the heads together. He starts to lick my tentacles, making *mmmm* sounds.

"Oh sweet weeping Jesus," I say, very much sober now. I don't want to eat him. It'd feel poetic, but I'd be coughing up hairballs for weeks. I should just leave him alone, hop in my tank and head home, but who's to say he would just try to kill me and fry me this time? Or just eat me whole? I'm not safe with this man, and I've let it out; I lust for metallic tang of blood.

He seems to see me come to the decision at the same time I do. He starts to shake his head, whimpering like a wounded puppy. I twist my two tentacles in opposite directions, tearing him in half and ruining his curtains in the process.

I get the bus home, and an old lady beats me with her handbag for dripping on her coat.

By day, Jason Purdy is a digital marketer, but by night, he writes nonsense short stories, novels, poetry, and pieces about pop culture.

He's from Northern Ireland, but don't hold that against him. In his free time, he enjoys writing, reading, listening to music, watching films and going to the gym. He enjoys video games more than a grown man should.

His debut novel, *Cigarette*, was released in April 2013 with Rowanvale books. He has also written for a number of short story anthologies, including *All Hallows' Evil*, *Undead of Winter*, and *10 Deadly Tales*. He featured in Curiosity Quills' *The Actuator Anthology* with his short story "Anna and Lena". He has had poetry appear in several collections, including the 2015 *Making Memories Anthology*—where he was nominated for the Seamus Heaney Award for New Writing. Most recently and indecently, he contributed an erotic poem to the *Rollercoasters and Bedsheets* collection, an erotic short story to *The Erogenous Scripts* collection, and a horror story to the *Screech Anthology*.

Josiah Luck, Plumber (of Oddities)

By Brandon Ketchum

Man, you wouldn't believe the last job I had. The shower wouldn't stop, so the bathroom flooded. The husband sounded weird on the phone, babbling on about how he didn't dare walk in and inspect the damage. *Dare*, that's the word he used. Or so Janet, the switchboard operator at the United Association of Plumbers and Pipefitters, said when she called me in.

Oh, where're my manners? Name's Josiah Luck, Plumber (of Oddities). At least, that's what my card says. Didn't think a little person like me could get on as a plumber, eh? Have you ever tried to crawl through the labyrinth of pipes inside a wall? Let me tell you, being my size is handy then.

Anyway, my town's plumbers started seeing too much bizarre stuff to sleep well at night. It turns out this city connects to an extra-planar dimension or fifty. Like when you open the taps, you might open a portal to the elemental plane of chaos--or someplace nasty. That's the best way I can describe it. I don't know; I just deal with the crap that leaks through. So, when a plumber gets a call that sounds too weird, they call the UA, and the UA calls me. How'd I get the job? That's a story for another time.

Well, I sauntered into the house, and after I got over the whole aren't-you-a-little-small-to-be-a-plumber crap, the husband let me in. The missus stood beside him, clutching a little girl in her arms. She and her husband had a dazed look in their eyes, half denial, half fear, which didn't surprise me. Nobody wants to believe they've fallen into the middle of a horror story. After some small talk, the husband bucked up his courage enough to direct me to the upstairs bathroom. I prepared myself for the worst.

I wasn't prepared enough.

No way was I in a house, 'cause the hole in the floor could have swallowed Godzilla. It gaped at me, I swear, as menacing as the Grand Canyon's muddy edge in a downpour. The bathroom floor didn't just end in a jagged hole--the hole was *eating* it, inch by inch. It was black as a moonless night, and it wasn't just growing. Nah, that wouldn't be sinister enough. It was belching. Every few moments there'd be a rumble from the depths of wherever that Hellmouth led to, an overpowering sulfuric stench would arise, and a ghost would slip silently from the hole to hover along the ceiling with its buddies.

By ghosts, I mean incorporeal entities without discernible limbs or eyes--but they did have mouths. Oh yeah, big greedy mouths, full of something that looked like solid teeth. A normal person would say an incorporeal ghost can't have solid fangs. Well, I doubted these monsters followed all those clichéd Hollywood rules. They looked like ghosts with choppers, so they *were* ghosts with choppers.

I'd have bet you dollars to donuts they were forming a pack before swooping down from the ceiling to wreak bloody havoc on the world at large. Starting with me, moving on to the house, then to all points beyond. To anyone else that might have been troubling, but to me this was just another Monday at the office. It may sound flip, but I had to treat it like any regular job. The time I start thinking about how crazy it all is will be the time I end up dead.

I set down my tool box, which weighed almost as much as I did, and got to work. My first selection was a baggie of seemingly ordinary marbles that packed a punch. More on those later. Next came a medieval-style torch and a lighter. I wanted to light the torch before I pulled out any more of my toys—er, tools. I wasn't to have a chance, though. Bastards never do give you a chance.

About twenty ghosts had congregated there on the ceiling, writhing around each other. I guess they had reached the magic number, because I suddenly felt like a two-buck soup and salad buffet in a senior community as they all came floating at me. I would have laughed if I hadn't been in deep kimchi. Those ghosts looked ridiculous, like props from an under-funded '70s horror flick, bobbing like apples. Except, unlike in the movies, they had teeth, which factored into my plan.

Enter the marbles. I grabbed the baggie's corners and whipped it around so the marbles shot right at the advancing ghosts. I was betting these were similar to the Ghouliewinks I had run into before. (Ghouliewink is the name I gave to some flying beasties I had vanquished a few years back). In fact, I was staking my life on it.

When those marbles started popping, the holy water stored inside splashed all over the place. They gnawed on the marbles for a while, and even fought each other over them. Unfortunately, the holy water didn't have any effect, and they had almost finished the marbles. They'd be on me in a moment.

Torches or lanterns are good bets in my line of work, because so much of what a plumber like me must face is repulsed by bright lights. I prefer pitch-soaked torches because they put out more light than other mediums, and they also radiate plenty of heat, another useful bugaboo to some of the things I deal with. When all else fails, they make a handy weapon, or can burn down a building, if that's what it takes. I'm paranoid too, checking my lighters every damn day.

The torch took to light just in time, because some ghosties were already darting my way. The light gave them pause, however; that or the heat. Didn't matter much to me, if it held them off. It wouldn't work forever, though. Even if these ghosties weren't all that smart, they'd figure out how to circle around behind me soon enough. I needed something that wouldn't just hold them off; something to destroy them.

The problem was, I had no idea what might accomplish that most desirable of outcomes.

Hell, I didn't have much time, and even less of a clue, so I decided to roll the dice again and grab what I hoped would be something decisive from my tool box. If *this* didn't work, my goose would be cooked. I wouldn't have time to pull out any other tricks.

Now, I figured since holy water hadn't worked, these ghosties weren't undead or demonic entities. If they weren't, I had a shot with one of my other manufactured concoctions.

I set my torch in the sink, to keep the ghosties away and to avoid accidental arson, and searched through my box of goodies. I came up with an old-fashioned spray can sewn into a backpack, jury-rigged with a tube leading to a pump nozzle. I'm real proud of the juice inside the can because I engineered it myself. I may not have the degree, but I put most chemists to shame. This creation was a brew of different compounds that, deprived of oxygen, remained in a liquid state. Once it traveled through the hose and hit the air, it would solidify in a matter of moments. And brother, when it solidified, forget about it. Super glue might as well have been lipstick compared to this stuff. Their choppers didn't stand a chance.

Up to that point, I had focused on keeping my ass alive so I could save the family, and maybe the world. I finally felt like I had a handle on the situation, though, and even if I didn't, I wouldn't have enough time to realize it. I puffed in a deep breath, stared down the oncoming ghosties, and shouted, "Drink it in, baby!"

And they drank the glue, like a man lost in the desert. Those big, gaping maws stayed big and gaping, sure. My glue trick just filled up all that space, and it dropped 'em to the floor. So I pumped and sprayed, and laughed and mocked, and would have done so all the livelong day, if fate hadn't kicked me in the shins.

"Silly ghosts," a voice said from the doorway behind me.

I risked a swift glance over my shoulder, and wouldn't you know it, the sawed-off little munchkin from earlier stood there giggling at the monsters. The kid couldn't have been more than two feet high, making her over half my height, but she didn't have a care in the world. She thought they were *funny*.

"Kiddo, I need you to run back downstairs to your mommy and daddy," I said in a stage whisper, trying to keep the ghosties' attention with the glue gun. "Now."

"But they're funny," she said, laughing even louder.

"Weren't you taught to listen to grown-ups?" I said, desperate to get rid of her. "Scram!"

She probably didn't recognize me as a grown up, and she didn't do as I told her.

"Why?" she asked.

The curiosity of children will get me killed one day, I swear. The question, and the attention I had to give to the girl, turned out to be the last straws.

The ghosties finally took notice. Damn it, doesn't my luck just beat all? I had no choice, of course. I had to shift focus to the monsters making a beeline for the kid, and they sensed an opportunity. Three of them floated in my direction.

I pumped faster than a pervert in a video booth, and I sprayed my goo all over the ghosties. As focused as I was on defending her, I made damn sure not a single monster laid a tooth on that child.

Me, I wasn't so lucky. I elbowed the first one in the teeth, knocking it out of the way to deal with later, and I shifted focus to the second one in time to gum up his works with my glue mix. The third ghostie, though, well, he took a chunk from my left thigh. Not a big one, not more than a baby's mouthful, but I'd be lying if I said it didn't hurt like hell. Yeah, I nailed him next, along with the first one, but not before he took part of my mortal flesh with him.

Gaping wound or no, I had done good work. The little girl had left, I had dropped all the ghosties, and their brethren weren't keen on coming out to play. I pulled a field dressing from my tool box and bandaged my leg, then picked each ghostie up by its teeth and dumped it into the hole. A shiver ran up my spine each time my arm passed through a ghostly body, giving me goose flesh.

There remained a ginormous problem, though. That Hellmouth was still open and still growing. I calculated maybe ten minutes before it ate through the bathroom completely.

I had to figure out how to close the hole. A portal can sometimes be closed from our side by destroying its trigger without crossing over. The trigger's usually something obvious, an object that stands out, which powers the connection between dimensions. I couldn't see anything through the darkness, though, and didn't have a prayer of finding the trigger from our world. I sighed and grumbled. Knowing I had to go down the hole didn't mean I had to be happy with the idea.

The nice thing about being a little squirt is I weigh hardly anything. I didn't have to worry about finding the most secure hard point to anchor my rappelling rope. The pipe running from the sink to the floor worked just fine as an anchor point. The downside to rappelling into that bitch, besides the obvious, was I had to go face first, walking down the wall, Australian-style. I needed to see where I was going and fight if I had to, which would be difficult in a sitting position.

Another big disadvantage was I had my spray can, a miner's light strapped to my head, and a few goodies I stuck in my belt and stuffed in my pocket. I had to leave the tool kit behind. I mean, I might have super-hero arms from lugging the thing around, but it opened from the top. If I tied it to the rope, it'd be tied shut. I determined to get a different kind of tool box if I made it out of there.

I didn't have time to stall, so as soon as I had readied myself, I marched right down that hole of death to God knows where.

Even though the hole looked huge and daunting from the outside, and even though I couldn't see below me very far, my light illuminated its entire circumference. Ghosties no longer poured up out of the hole. Still, the stench of sulfur blasted away, stronger than ever, and I heard all kinds of commotion from beneath me, so I knew this pit remained active. Looking around, I didn't spot a pile of ritual stones, a bloody altar, or any other obvious targets to destroy, just unbroken walls. The Hellmouth didn't have the same kind of physical outlay as the other portals I'd closed, which had all been horizontal, so I had to keep going. Foreboding welled up inside my chest. This one was a doozy, or I was a giant.

Down and down I went, ten feet, twenty, more. It smelled like bathing in rotten scrambled eggs. Felt like it too, what with the heat. I sweated like a whore in church. The heat blasting up from below, along with the smell, kept getting worse, and I swear I could cut the malevolence with a knife.

That's when I heard it, a familiar whooshing sound. It had surrounded me in the bathroom earlier, the sound the departed ghosties had made when they tried to turn me into a smorgasbord.

I swiveled my head down and to the right, the direction the whooshing came from, and lo and behold, there were more of them. It must have messed with their minds something fierce, watching their friends fall down the hole. They just circled there, about ten feet below, and they did not want a piece of me. Or any *more* pieces of me. I noticed where they were coming from, too. A crack stood out in the wall, a big gaping fissure guarded by the hovering creatures.

Well, the time had come to throw down all over again, so I pumped and sprayed, gluing their mouths closed. They might have feared me but, like any right-thinking monsters, they went down fighting. The ghosties charged. Heh, no sweat. I had their number by now. Within moments, not even one had a single ghostly tooth free of the hardened goo as they fell to the depths of the Hellmouth.

Then I got a sickly feeling down there in the bottom of my stomach, and it wasn't the rotten egg smell. Shaking my backpack, I realized I only had a few pumps left before I was weaponless against those ghostly cockroaches. I had dealt with the ones circling below me, but there were more in the cave. I heard 'em clamoring around in there, getting ready to form up for what I guessed would be a final charge. And there I hung, like Custer without his Gatling guns.

There was nothing else for it. I huffed, and I puffed, and I drenched the fissure with every drop of my wonder glue. Those monsters knew what I was about, too, because they howled towards the entrance to their abode the minute glue hit air.

I feared for a second one might get through, but the stuff hardened right as his head peeked out from the cave. He stuck there, hanging just in the entrance to that plugged up corner of hell they called home, mouth glued in place, unable to wriggle free. I shouted my victory down the shaft. Yeah, bad call.

My hooting and hollering did not go unnoticed. Over my ecstatic yells, I heard quite a few different things, none of them encouraging. Several different spirits screamed in affronted rage, their wrath bouncing off the walls of the pit as it rose to my ears. A demon jester cackled madly somewhere above me. A giant pot of hellish chili began a rolling boil far below me, and the stink of sulfur got worse with each pop of a bubble.

Oh, Lordy Lord, what had I done? This was it. My ass was toast. I might be able to save the world, though. *My* world. No one would mourn my heroic sacrifice, because no one would know they had been in any danger. But that's what I signed up for when I became the first and only plumber of oddities, right?

What the hell. Time to gamble on a little something else I had brought along with me. I pulled a small bubble-wrapped package from my pocket and opened it, dropping the wrapping down the hole. In my hand sat a marble, a shooter, bigger than my holy water marbles. It contained a gel explosive I had created from-- well, let's just say the pinch of enriched uranium was the most difficult ingredient to obtain. It would create a thermonuclear detonation, which had a high likelihood of destroying whatever I needed to destroy to close the portal. I hoped it would swallow the radiation as it closed, because if it didn't, the bomb would fry a couple hundred square miles of civilization along with it--and I wasn't even sure it would close the portal.

But what choice did I have? It might have been a huge risk, but I didn't have much firepower left, and the Hellmouth still had many nasty surprises in store, judging by the sounds reverberating through it. I had to take the chance. Unfortunately, dangling in the middle of the hole, I would be on the wrong side of the equation either way.

Aw, the hell with it. I pitched that shooter straight down the gaping maw, deliberately trying to miss the pit's rocky sides. Hey, I knew I couldn't make it out in time, but that was no reason not to at least *try*.

I flipped around, took hold of my line, and started hightailing it out of those smelly depths. As fast as I could go, anyway, which proved little more than a slow crawl. I muttered an Our Father, threw in a couple Hosannas, and even slipped in not a few four-letter words that didn't count as prayers. The marble bomb would—

My lights went out then, mid-thought. A half-second later I woke briefly to blurred vision and concussed pain, then slammed face first into the ceiling of the bathroom and conked out a second time. Good night, Irene.

A while later I blinked heavily, forcing my eyes open with a groan. For a few moments, the remainder of my drained strength was spent just maintaining that puny mumble of pain. Eons later I lifted my head and opened my eyes far enough to take in the carnage of the second-floor bathroom, now a wet and burned-out shell. The blast's force must have thrown me up and out of the Hellmouth. The bomb had closed the portal without loosing its nuclear fury on our world too, because the house remained intact, and I wasn't glowing green. Portal closure one, nuclear physics zero.

My subsequent groan wasn't one of pain, although I still had that in spades. It was an acknowledgment of the hassle I was going to get from the man downstairs when he discovered his bathroom had become a charred and soaked disaster area.

I propped myself up on my hands, rested there for a couple of decades, and finally levered myself to my feet, slowly, painfully. I bent down and tried to touch my toes, spine popping like bubble wrap, and did my best to stretch all the kinks out of my muscles. My leg throbbed something fierce, and I was going to bear a bucket of aches and bruises for weeks. And yeah, the homeowner would give me a new headache in a few minutes, to go with my fresh concussion.

Screw it. I'd slip out as fast as possible, get hold of Janet over at the UA, and let *them* deal with the cleanup.

What the hell. I had done the job, killed the baddies, closed the portal, and saved the world. Just a typical night on the job for me, Josiah Luck, Plumber (of Oddities).

Brandon Ketchum is a speculative fiction writer working out of Pittsburgh, PA. He has attended the Cascade Writers Workshop and the In Your Write Mind Workshop, and his work has appeared in a variety of publications. His most recent story, "Halloween Nosh," has been published in *MASHED: The Culinary Delights of Twisted Erotic Horror*. The anthology can be found here: https://www.amazon.com/dp/B01N38T1OU/

Are You There, Azathoth? It's Me, Margaret.
H.P. Lovecraft's "The Thing on the Doorstep" as written by Judy Blume

as told to Kevin Wetmore

Are you there, Azathoth? It's me, Margaret. We're moving today. I am so scared, Azathoth. I've never lived anywhere but Innsmouth. Next week I start sixth grade. Suppose I hate my new school? Suppose everyone there hates me? Please, Azathoth, blind idiot god, Daemon Sultan at the center of the cosmos who gnaws hungrily in inconceivable, unlighted chambers beyond time and space, don't let Arkham be too horrible. Let me find a friend. And don't let sixth grade suck.

Seven months later...

I know you think me mad, Mr. Wingate. It is true that I have pushed my best friend down three flights of stairs during passing. It is true that this resulted in her death. And yet I hope to show before my parents get here that I am not her murderer. You can suspend me. You can expel me. You can send me to talk to the special counselor out in the trailer to find out why I did this. But I assure you I am not mad. Even now, here you sit, my guidance counselor, asking how I could be driven to push the only girl who befriended me since I moved to Arkham down those many flights, to then be trampled by eighth graders. But even now you also know, Mr. Wingate, that others have strange things to say about Asenath Waite, and so I say I have not killed Asenath. Rather, I have avenged her, and in doing so have purged Arkham Junior High of a horror whose survival might have loosed untold terrors on all the kids, even the ninth graders.

It began that day in Mr. Derby's English class, the first day of school here at AJH. My family had just moved here from Innsmouth and I was very alone. The other kids in Mr. Derby's class were ignoring me. We were reading poems from Justin Geoffrey's *The*

People of the Monolith and we were supposed to write our own Baudelairean nightmare lyric about our sinister, witch-cursed, legend-haunted town. I had just thought of a way to include a unicorn in my poem when I felt rather than saw someone at my side, looking at my work.

"Hi. I'm Asenath Waite. I know you're Margaret and we're both in sixth grade. I also know your family just moved into the old Crowninshield place." She looked down at my poem. "There are no unicorns in Arkham, but there is a family of ghouls out in the old burial ground. Do you like Siouxsie and the Banshees?"

The girl was dark, taller than me with bouncy, dusky hair and was very good looking except for over-protuberant eyes and a nose that was turned up so much I could look right into her nostrils. I would learn later she was eight months my junior, but so precocious that she could pass for thirteen, though only eleven and a half. She wore a black dress with a white lace collar and written on the front of the dress in purple script were the words "Dark Princess." She was smiling, but under it was a look of genuine sadness.

"Uh..." I responded. "I guess?" I looked down at my poem, which now seemed stupid. "I just moved here from Innsmouth."

"I know," she said, spinning in a circle. "My family is originally from Innsmouth, too, but we moved here years ago when my mother, who always went about veiled, mysteriously passed away."

"Oh," I responded. It seemed like the best response. But then I thought about what my mom would tell me to do and said, "I'm sorry."

"It's okay. My dad just died this summer. So now I'm an orphan and a ward of the guidance counselor."

"Oh," I said again. "I'm sorry." Now I sounded really stupid. I felt my face growing red.

"It's okay. My dad was mean and practiced the dark arts. I have my own room now. Want to come over after school?"

"Oh," for the third time. "Okay."

Her smile widened and some of the sadness left her. "Great! We can practice kissing, talk about boys, and do each other's hair." And she skipped off to finish her poem before the end of English.

I was overjoyed. I had a friend. I was less alone. I tore up my stupid poem about the unicorn drinking from the Miskatonic River and wrote one about the bones of mastodons coming to life and destroying the huddled, sagging gambrel roof and crumbling

Georgian balustrade of our next door neighbors, the Peasleys. Their dog was mean. I thought maybe it would get an A from Mr. Derby and my mom would hang it on the refrigerator.

The school day seemed to linger like a miasma from some foetid swamp, dismal and unending, when the final bell rang at three. I met Asenath in front of the school after classes ended and we walked to her house. We climbed the decrepit steps which groaned like they were giving up the spirit. The door slammed loudly behind us as I found myself in a foyer, dark and warm yet somehow conveying a chill. "Asenath? That you, dear girl?" came an eldritch voice from the back of the house.

"Yes, Mrs. Wingate. I'm here with a friend."

We walked to the back room and, ensconced on a small settee with her legs covered by a tartan blanket, an elderly woman reading a large-print edition of the *Book of Eibon* looked up as we entered. One eye was bloodshot, the other had a milky white haze over it. She stared at me, then she smiled. It was not a welcoming smile, but a sinister one, like snakes in cartoons have.

"Mrs. Wingate, this is Margaret Upton, my friend. She just moved into the Crowninshield place with her family. We were going to play in my room."

The hideous bloodshot eye moved off of Asenath's face and focused on mine. Mrs. Wingate looked me up and down and said, "Welcome to Arkham, Margaret. Your house has ancient mysteries and secrets that still live under its roof. Ia! Ia! Praise the Black Goat of the Woods with a Thousand Young!"

"Uh...Ia! to you, too, ma'am" I said awkwardly and stared at the floor for what seemed like an eternity. I don't always know how to talk to grown-ups.

"What brings you from legend-shrouded Innsmouth to witch-cursed Arkham? Most Innsmouth folks never leave the decaying seaport, and those that do often return before long." Her voice was like wire in my ears and around my heart.

"Uh...my dad got a new job at the university?" I said, although I made it sound like a question.

With that, her eye with the milky haze seemed to glow with excitement and delight. "And what, pray child, does your father do at Miskatonic? Is he a librarian, a guardian of many a quaint and curious tome of forgotten lore? Or a professor, perhaps? Yes, a professor of history, delving into the dark past of these witch-haunted lands, or perhaps of science, gazing at the far, cold reaches of the universe and knowing the bleak, unkind emptiness of existence, or perhaps anthropology, studying the dark brutes of Africa or the sinister peoples of the Orient, who remember things civilized men have forgotten."

"I think he's an admissions counselor," I said. "He talks to the kids who want to go there."

"Oh," she said, her mouth collapsing as if she had suddenly found a slice of lemon in it. "How...interesting." She returned her focus to the book on her lap, and it was as if I had never even been in the room with her.

"Come on!" yelled Asenath and dragged me down the hall and up the stairs to her room.

We exploded into her room and she slammed the door behind us. Her walls were covered with an ancient wallpaper, the colors of ochre and brown intertwining. Her bed was an elaborate, old thing like the kind you see in old movies about knights and princesses or that one about the Scrooge guy. She had also put up a number of posters, including one of David Bowie, a few boy bands I never heard of, and one of a warrior woman fighting an octopus. It looked kind of Japanese. In the corner opposite the bed was a white desk with gold and pink highlights and a tall bookcase filled with books. I glanced to see if there were any books I had read, but they were mostly educational, school-type books and a well-worn copy of something called *My First Unasuprechlichen Kulten*.

"Cool room," I said.

"Thanks," she said, flouncing down on the bed. "You're from Innsmouth. Have you ever kissed a boy?"

"You mean really kiss? Like on the lips?

"Yeah. Did you?

"Not really. Boys from Innsmouth aren't really that kissable, you know? A lot of them have, like really big mouths and they drool a lot. Many don't have lips."

"Me neither. I mean I do have lips—I haven't kissed any boys. I practice a lot though."

"How?"

"Like this," and she picked up a pillow and embraced it, pushing her lips into it and making moaning, kissy noises. Then she stopped and wiped her mouth. "Wanna try?"

"Uh...okay," I said and took the pillow from her. I flipped it and pressed my face into the other side. It was kind of like falling asleep on your tummy—I just had my face pressed into the pillow, but she seemed to think it was cool.

"I'm really getting good at kissing. I think I'm going to be a really good kisser when some boy finally kisses me."

She was staring at one of the boy band posters. I noticed it was autographed. It said, "To our #1 fan Asenath, kisses, Erich Zann."

"How old were you when your mom died?" I asked. I am certain if my mom were here she would have been mortified, but we had just been kissing her pillow together.

She looked sad again and took a deep breath before answering. "Nine years ago. It was weird because she was a lot younger than my dad. I am the child of his old age with a mysterious, veiled wife. I have little memory of her. I was raised by my father, who had a wolfish, saturnine face with a tangle of iron-grey beard. We moved here so he could consult forbidden tomes in the college library. He also owned a video store for a while, but it went out of business. He died under queer circumstances last year."

"Oh," I responded. "My dad is weird, too."

"The Wingates allowed me to bury him in the cellar here when I became their ward. Until then I had been his morbidly avid pupil, but now I think there might have been something wrong with him."

"At least he let you go to concerts," I said, pointing at the autographed poster.

"Yeah, but I don't think he was super interested in me other than my staying healthy and unharmed. It's less interesting with the Wingates, but more normal, you know?"

I looked in the direction of the bedroom, door. "I think Mrs. Wingate is a racist."

"Yeah. And she smells funny, but her and Mr. Wingate took me in, so I suppose I'm grateful."

Suddenly she shifted on the bed and looked uncomfortable. "Excuse me," she said," I have to go to the bathroom."

She abruptly walked out of the bedroom and I heard a door creak open then slam shut down the hall. I looked around the room. It seemed like a perfectly normal bedroom. Still, something felt off about it. I couldn't tell what.

Suddenly, a scream erupted from down the hall, followed by laughter.

"Keep it down, girls," Mrs. Wingate's voice slithered up the stairs. "I am reading and need peace in which to do so."

Asenath bounded back into the room and threw something into the hamper next to the closet.

"Margaret, are you ready for amazing news?" She positively glowed.

"Sure?" I asked, again making it a question.

"I am a woman!" she whispered triumphantly.

"Uh...OK." I responded. "We both are, though, right? I mean you already knew that, right?"

"No. Just now, in the bathroom. I looked down at my underpants and I could not believe it. There was blood on them."

"Oh my God! Are you OK?" I started to jump up, ready to get an adult, even Mrs. Wingate. That's what my mom always told me to do in an emergency.

"No. Yes. My period. I've got my period! I am growing for sure! Now I am a woman!"

She picked up the *My First Unasuprechlichen Kulten* and began flipping through it, savagely, as I sank back onto her bed.

Suddenly she stood shock upright and started at the poster of Erich Zann. She stayed like that, unmoving, for over thirty seconds.

"Asenath...are you all right?" I asked tentatively.

She said, "Sure, sure, sure," but I don't know if she was talking to me.

"Do you want me to get help?" I began to rise again.

Suddenly, she turned sharply and looked at me. Her expression made it seem like she did not recognize me. She stared at me for another thirty seconds and then said, "Little girl, it is time you returned to your home."

"'Little girl'? I'm eight months older than you! If you didn't want me here, why did you invite me?"

"I am sure she was looking for companionship. Now you must excuse me." She turned from me and gave all her focus to the book.

I was so confused. "Who's 'she'?"

She looked up at me, befuddled before comprehension washed over her face. "I meant me. I wanted your companionship. But now it is time for schoolwork. I must study. Please, little girl, see yourself out."

I was so stunned, confused and hurt I could only gather my backpack and head down the stairs. Mrs. Wingate also ignored me on the way out.

I cried on the way home. It was unfair. Just because Asenath got her period didn't mean that she could treat me that way. As soon as I get mine I'm not going to be like that.

I saw her again the next day at school.

She came over to my desk during first period. "What happened to you yesterday?"

"What are you talking about?"

"We were hanging out in my room, I got my period and was looking something up in a book and when I looked up again you were gone and it was an hour later. I hope I didn't make you jealous."

By now I was very confused. "Asenath, don't you remember calling me a little girl and telling me to leave?"

"OMG, what are you talking about? I did no such thing. You just left quietly."

"I *did not*!" and everybody looked at me because I was yelling. I strained to calm myself. "I did not. You told me you got your first period, then you ordered me out."

"And why would I call you little girl? I'm eight months your junior!"

"I know, right? So what's going on, Asenath?"

"Maybe it has something to do with my getting my period. They told us in health class that all sorts of changes happen, both physically and emotionally, and my father said you become fecund and draw the attention of dark gods and deep ones. He dreaded having to buy tampons. I suppose that is one of the good things about him dying before I hit puberty. He never had to purchase tampons."

"Still, that was a real stinky way to treat a friend, Asenath."

"It was, forgive me?"

And I did, Mr. Wingate. I did. For the next six months we were inseparable. We studied together, talked about boys together, watched movies together. She loved Bela Lugosi, but I had a thing for Christopher Lee. But every once in a while, she'd get weird.

Like that one sleepover just before Thanksgiving. I was in a sleeping bag on the floor and she was in her bed and we had been talking about how much we hated Lavinia Whately because on Monday she wore a tight sweater and all the boys were staring at her. We both agreed she was a total tramp and a disquieting slut and we would never get boys to pay attention to us like that.

Then Asenath sat up in bed and said, "Things that come from outside."

"What comes from outside? You mean like a cat or something?" I asked.

"Things that follow no conceivable geometry. Things from outside. Margaret—for God's sake! The pit of the shoggoths! The boys' locker room! I would never go with him there, but then I found myself there."

"You were in the boys' locker room? OMG, when?" I was amazed.

She held her arms up in a supplicating gesture. "The shape that rose up from the altar! The Hooded Thing bleating, 'Kamog! Kamog!' That was daddy's name in the coven. I was there where he had gone with my body. I saw a shoggoth—it changed shape...I can't stand it...I won't stand it! I will kill that entity with my own hands."

Her arms then dropped. "Goodnight!" she said cheerfully and flipped over, her back to me.

Weirdest sleepover ever.

The next morning over breakfast she said, "I hope you'll ignore my attack last night, Upton. I was practicing for a play. The Hall School is performing 'The King in Yellow' this spring and I am auditioning with that piece."

"Yeah...sure...uh, why are you calling me by my last name, Asenath?"

"I thought that's what you kids do when you're friends."

"'You kids?' Listen to you, old lady."

"What? Oh, yes. Sorry, Margaret. Let us meet later for play and the discussion of boys."

"Sure..." She was getting weirder and weirder.

I mean, I know things change in junior high, Mr. Wingate, but Asenath was like two different people. I saw less and less of Asenath. Finally, one day, she stopped talking to me altogether. I'd see her with the very kids we used to make fun of. She and Lavinia Whately became thick as thieves. They sped past me once in a car with some high school boys.

Finally, I saw her hanging out just outside the school fence before class one day with Lavinia and some boys from the high school down the street. She was wearing a tight sweater and a miniskirt and she was smoking.

I could not control myself. "What happened to you, Asenath?"

"What's that baby's problem?" one of the high school boys snarked.

"Don't worry about her," said Asenath. "She's still a child. She hasn't even gotten her period yet."

"Why are you treating me like this?" I asked, trying not to cry and, to my shame, failing, "You were my best friend."

She blew a smoke ring in my face, dropped the cigarette and stubbed it out with her toe. "Gotta grow up sometime, Margaret. Can't love unicorns and be a kid forever. Call me when you need a tampon."

They all laughed at me and I realized the true horror of being an outsider who had lost her only friend. At least I thought that moment I had lost my only friend. I soon learned I had lost her long before then.

One night, two weeks later, the phone rang. My mom told me it was Asenath. I almost didn't pick up the phone but I wanted to give her a piece of my mind.

"Margaret?" She sounded panicked and did not even wait for me to respond. "You need to help me. He cannot get me now. I have to save myself. He'd have gotten me for good by Beltane. My body would be his for good!"

"My God, Asenath, have you slept with a boy?" I couldn't believe we had practiced kissing pillows only a few months before.

"No! Listen to me, Margaret. You must have known that girl with Lavinia and those boys wasn't me. It was that predatory wolf in my body. I must get out of that accursed house as soon as I can."

"Look, Asenath. I understand you're going through puberty and something strange, but you can't treat your friend the way you treated me. It's like you're two different people. I miss the girl who used to practice kissing her pillow. I don't know who you are. Goodbye."

As I hung up the phone, I heard her say, "No! He has almost fully taken..."

I now know what she was talking about and believe everything Asenath Waite told me.

The next day, Asenath was missing from class. But after lunch, as I was walking to my locker, I saw a strange figure next to it. As I approached, an insufferably foetid wind almost flung me prostrate, like even worse than the boys' locker room. A dwarfed, humped figure was putting a note in my locker. It was wearing Asenath's overcoats—its bottom almost touching the ground, and its sleeves rolled back yet still covering the hands. On its head a slouch hat was pulled low and a black silk scarf covered the face.

"Asenath?" I called. It looked in my direction and fled down the arts hallway. In my locker was a note in Asenath's handwriting. It said:

Margaret-

When you see it at school, kill it. Exterminate it. It is not your best friend any more. He got me. My father is in my body. The tugging in my brain was not the onset of puberty but him seizing my body even as he put my soul in his buried in the cellar, changing bodies with me.

From the moment I got my period, he has been trying to switch bodies with me.

Kill the fiend in my body and see it is cremated. If you don't, it will live on, wearing too much makeup and going on dates with boys like Allen Halsey and Warren Rice. It will be popular in high school through black magic and promiscuity. And what happens when it goes to college? My mind, trapped in this corpse, will go mad thinking about all those hookups. No, Margaret, that is a horror that cannot be. Goodbye. You've been a great friend and I'm damnable sorry to drag you into this. But kill my body. And, if you have time and a magic marker, write something nasty about Lavinia Whately on the second floor girls' room bathroom wall. She's been really mean to me, too. And kill that thing—kill it!

And there was a drawing of a heart shape and a flying unicorn and under that she had written "B.F.F. Yours—Asn".

Later that afternoon, I went to your house, Mr. Wingate. In the basement I found a mass collapsed over what I assume was Mr. Waite's grave. The dirt had been pushed up from below. The bundle on top was Asenath's oddly assorted clothes, liquescent horror and bones and a crushed in skull. She had come to my locker in her dead father's body! That night, I finally got my period. The next day, I went to school with a purpose.

So now you see, Mr. Wingate, how I had to push her down those stairs into the crowd of eighth graders. Now you see why I say I did not kill my best friend who was months dead before I pushed her, why I say I only avenged her death. And now you see why I wrote those things about Lavinia Whately on the bathroom wall. Asenath was right—she is a mean bitch and I should have pushed her down the stairs, too. I can hear my parents coming out of the principal's office now. I know they are coming for me. Goodbye, Mr. Wingate. I don't think I'll be in school tomorrow.

Are you still there Azathoth? It's me, Margaret. I know you're there, Azathoth. I know you are an amorphous blight of nethermost confusion which blasphemes and bubbles at the center of infinity, dancing to the maddening beating of vile drums and the thin monotonous whine of accursed flutes. Watch over me in your gibbering vacuousness as I begin my time in reform school with the other girls who have killed. Don't let it suck, Azathoth. Amen.

Kevin Wetmore is an award-winning short story and non-fiction writer whose fiction can be found in such anthologies as *History and Horror, Oh My!, Strangely Funny III, Midian Unmade, Enter at Your Own Risk: The End is the Beginning,* and *Whispers from the Abyss 2* and such magazines as *Cemetery Dance* and *Mothership Zeta.* He is also the author of *Post-9/11 Horror in American Cinema,* among others, and works as an actor, director and professor in Los Angeles.

Microbrew

By David Bernard

Senior year at Gray Haven High just isn't going to be the same without Max. Max was my best friend and had been since we were both freshmen, where survival meant having someone to watch your back. He had his flaws; most infamous of which was that Max was a horny bastard. He was, on a good day, only average looking, a lousy student, and couldn't make a varsity squad even if the current team got wiped out by a meteor. But, being a horndog, he got crafty. He was always looking for an angle to score. Most of the time it ended up with Max getting slapped silly, beat up, or put in detention—sometimes all three.

The odds finally went in his favor and he started dating Patsy: kind of pretty, but not very bright, even for a sophomore. She adored him to the point where she'd do anything for him (or to him). Now that he was getting some regularly, Max had decided it was time to get me laid.

He came up to me at lunch, with a triumphant look on his face. This concerned me. The last time I saw that look, it was 15 minutes before an irate cheerleader had her linebacker boyfriend try to throw him off the roof.

"We're double dating tonight. Patsy and me, you and Celene. We're just going to hang out at my house." He wandered off to find Patsy and a deserted stairwell before I could ask him exactly who the hell Celene was.

I spent the rest of my lunch trying to figure out exactly who I apparently had a date with before I placed the name. Celene was the new girl in school. She was "out of my league" gorgeous, but really laid back. Nothing bothered her, and half the time, she gave off this "been there, done that" vibe. The rumor was the family just relocated from Chesuncook rather quickly after the cops found her one morning, wandering around Baxter State Forest naked.

I'd known Max long enough to know how he thought. In Max's world "naked in the woods" meant she was easy. I was more of a realist. She could have been drugged, drunk, a Wiccan, or just plain old crazy. With my dating track record, my money was on last one...

I arrived that night, right before the girls. Max's father was a manager at the pulp mill and his parents were in Portland at some sort of trade convention. Max was about as thrilled about going to a hotel full of middle managers and accountants as his parents were at being trapped in a hotel with Max. So they all agreed that as long as Max avoided having any parties while they were gone, he could stay home. Contrary to the opinion in the girls' locker room, Max wasn't an idiot. He had made the mistake of having a party in the house once before, and he was still paying for the repairs to the drywall. Now, his social events were conducted out in the sunroom: screening is faster and cheaper to replace.

It was a new moon, and the stars were shining brightly through the screen roof. It was actually kind of romantic. Of course, Max then ruined it and turned on the strings of tiki lights that hung from the ceiling. Sadly, turning romantic into tacky was one of Max's trademark moves.

Patsy was standing near Celene on the side of the Ping-Pong table. They were a study in opposites. Patsy was short and skinny, with mousy brown hair. Celene was tall and blonde, and with an air about of her that made her seem older than a high schooler. No one seemed to know much about her other than the sudden move from Chesuncook, but she seemed unfazed by the attention and mildly amused by attempts to rattle her.

Celene and I chatted. We didn't hate each other, which was always a good start. Patsy kept looking at Max, who would slightly shake his head.

I looked at Celene. "Ever get the feeling you're being set up?"

She looked over at Max. "He really is about as subtle as a kick in the teeth."

I smiled. "Max has been kicked in the teeth more than once. That's why he's not allowed to attend any more ballet recitals."

Celene looked at him again, with a look that was equal parts pity and disgust. "So, we're sacrificial lambs being led to the slaughter?"

I nodded, "We'll be leaving here as a couple or as fleeing escapees."

Celine was about to say something when Max wandered over and coughed loudly. Patsy was carefully examining a Ping-Pong paddle. He coughed again. She looked up at him questioningly. He nodded.

Patsy paused for a moment and carefully recited her lines "Say, I know. Let's play beer pong? That is always fun." Apparently, Max wasn't much of a dialogue coach either. A ventriloquist dummy would have been more believable and probably less wooden.

Max agreed, of course. I look at Celene, she just shrugged. Max smiled that smile that never ended well, and told Patsy to take the net off the table.

He grabbed a couple of cans of beer from the mini-fridge in the corner and some plastic cups. He carefully filled the cups and had Patsy arrange them.

"Boys versus girls," he gleefully announced. "Put the ball in the cup and someone on the other team drinks the beer."

Celene and Patsy went over to the far side of the table. Max pulled me aside.

"Our cups are filled with that light beer shit my mother drinks" he whispered.

I didn't have the heart to tell him that the light beer was also my mother's brand. It was reduced calories, not reduced alcohol. He'd find out soon enough.

I looked over at Celene and she smirked. Somehow I knew she had spotted the scam and already figured out Max was only fooling himself. Max thought he was crafty, but he never was particularly good at it.

Celene had either played this game a lot or had the physics of bouncing Ping-Pong balls figured out. She rarely missed the cup. Max, not knowing better, volunteered to drink most of the cups. After guzzling the contents of two, he was already looking a little off his game. I took over and tried to get Max to alternate, but he hadn't figured out his competitive edge was all in his head (or in his liver by that point). Even with less beer, I could feel it. We were juniors—neither of us had really done much drinking. Of course, Patsy was a real lightweight and was already a giggling mess after the first cup. Celene was drinking most of the cups on the girls' side and seemed unaffected. Of course, Max and I were doing most of the drinking overall, so that didn't surprise me. We lost. Max had guzzled 4 of the cups to my two, and the way I felt, I was impressed he was still standing.

I sat down to clear my head. Celene sat beside me and patted my shoulder. "You are going to be so very sick in the morning."

Giggling erupted on the other side of the room. We looked over. Max was copping a feel and Patsy thought it was hilarious. I'm sure Max was thrilled that his drunken groping of Patsy's various girly bits was causing laughter, not passion.

Celene wrinkled her nose in distaste. "Why don't we leave and see if we can't sober you up?"

I shook my head. "Max will never let me out here until he's sure we're hooking up. He's stubborn when he sober, and I don't think he's any better like this."

Celene looked at me and leaned into a long kiss. "Then we'll have to convince him. He doesn't look so good. How about when he starts puking his guts out, we bail?"

I nodded and she stood up. "Hey Max," she called, "how about a rematch?"

He looked up as Patsy tried to straighten out her clothes. He leered at Celene, "Let's make it interesting. How about Strip Beer Pong? Ball in the cup and one downs the beer and the other loses some clothes."

She looked at him in disgust. "All right. Go get more beer. I can see you're up to it."

Max looked down and blushed. I liked her already. Max was shameless. Getting him to blush was a momentous occasion.

The mini-fridge was empty, so he headed out into the kitchen and came back with some bottles. He refilled the cups with a less than a steady hand.

It didn't take long for Celene to get us down to pants and boxers. She and Patsy were fully dressed. Through sheer dumb luck, I hit a cup. Celene downed the cup and Patsy managed to pull off her sneakers without falling over. Then, Celene missed. She was shaking her head like she was trying to clear it. It looked like the beer was finally getting to her. Patsy was still useless from the first game but insisted on drinking her share.

I was still sober enough to get the ball in the cup occasionally. Patsy was not happy about dropping her tee shirt and complained louder when she dropped her pants while Celene was down to her bra and pants.

Max and I were both down to boxers when I managed to hit the cup again. Celene downed the beer and looked at Patsy. Patsy rolled her eyes, pulled off her bra and flung it across the table at Max, who was so drunk he was swaying. He looked down at the bra, then across the table at his topless girlfriend. He smiled a stupid drunken smile and yelled "Boooooobies!" and slumped to the floor.

I looked at Celene wistfully and at her bra even more wistfully. The game was over. While Patsy tried to wake Max up, Celene stood there. I pulled my pants back on and walked over, awkwardly trying figure out a way to reposition a boner so it wasn't so obvious. Celene didn't notice; she did not look well.

She looked at me and smiled weakly. "Alcohol doesn't usually bother me."

She suddenly grabbed her stomach and doubled over. Covered in sweat, she asked, "What the hell was in that beer?"

I went over to the empties and grabbed one. I walked over to her, reading the label as I went. She had dropped to her knees and looked flushed.

Concerned, I dropped down to face her. "According to the label, it's just beer. In fact, it's one of Max's father's fancy microbrews called "Full Moon.""

Her eyes popped open wide and she stared at me. "What?"

"Don't worry," I said, trying to sound reassuring, "this is high-end stuff. It's a specialty beer he has shipped from Japan." I read the label. "They only brew it during the full moon 'to imbue the beverage with the spirit of the moon' – it's right on the label."

She looked at me and I noticed her eyes looked strange; her blue eyes were turning yellow.

"Listen," she growled at me. "Get out of here. Run and keep running. Don't look back and — and —"

She doubled over again and I saw her bra strap snap as her back stretched and widened. Hair began sprouting along her spine. By the time her pants burst open to make room for the tail, I had backed out of the sunroom.

I ran.

I was almost out of the house when I heard the howl. I could hear Patsy's screams halfway down the sidewalk. I never heard a peep from Max. I hope that means he never knew what hit him...

The police made a few inquiries when Max's parents came home a couple days later to an empty house. But it was pretty obvious to the cops that Max and Patsy had either eloped, run away, or something similarly stupid that teenagers do. Knowing Max, his parents had to agree. The police thought they'd be back soon enough, once living in the real world bit them in the ass.

I was interviewed and I saw no reason to mention anything to change their minds. I figured if I suggested a werewolf killed them and then disposed of the bodies, I'd be the crazy one. And I've watched enough TV to know that if they asked Augusta to send one of the State Police CSIs to look around, there'd be enough blood trace on the floor that Mr. "I think a werewolf killed my buddy" would suddenly be the prime suspect. So, I grieve alone and quietly.

I hear Celene's family has moved out of town.

David Bernard is a native New Englander who now lives (albeit under protest) in South Florida, a paradoxical place where, when temperatures drops below 60°, locals break out parkas to wear over their plaid shorts and sandals. His previous works include short stories in anthologies such as *Snowbound with Zombies* (Post Mortem Press), *Legacy of the Reanimator* (Chaosium), and *Twice Upon an Apocalypse* (Crystal Lake Publishing).

Incense

By Trent Kollodge

LeafBoy420: Dude, I'm so sorry. I think someone broke into your house.

Adeptus333: That's not possible. My spells are sound. Nothing gets in or out without my permission.

LeafBoy420: Srsly dude, the place is trashed. I don't know what happened. I must have forgotten to lock the door or something. Sorry.

Adeptus333: Did you burn the incense? You have to burn the incense every day. I'm sure I stressed this.

LeafBoy420: Every day. Hell yeah man! That was some proper stuff. Thanks.

Adeptus333: What do you mean?

LeafBoy420: Like you said, I "burned the incense." Course I did, bro.

Adeptus333: Wait a minute, did you smoke it?

LeafBoy420: That's what it's for right? You got to burn the herb.

Adeptus333: Idiot. That was for the tulkafu. The whole point of you watching my house was for you to maintain the sedation until I got back. How long has it been?

LeafBoy420: What's a tulkafu?

Adeptus333: It's like a violent poltergeist. When was the last time?

LeafBoy420: A polterwhat?

Adeptus333: A really evil ghost! When was the last time?

LeafBoy420: Last time what?

Adeptus333: When was the last time you burned the incense in my house?

LeafBoy420: Ooh, right. Um. Thursday.

Adeptus333: Four days ago! What the hell have you been doing? I told you, you have to be there every day!

LeafBoy420: Relax dude, I'll clean it up. Doesn't look like much is actually broken, things are just sort of tossed around everywhere. Probably just some kids. You should thank me. If I'd locked the door, they might have busted some windows getting in. Besides, I told you, schedules are for suckers.

Adeptus333: Listen very carefully. Stop what you're doing, and light the incense now.

Adeptus333: Did you light the incense?

Adeptus333: Chris! You still there? Answer your phone.

LeafBoy420: My phone's busted dude, I can txt but no calls.

LeafBoy420: Hey, do you have a cat or something you didn't tell me about?

Adeptus333: There's no cat. You must light the incense now.

LeafBoy420: Srsly, something just bit me. I think it's under the couch now, but I'm not messing with no wild animals man.

LeafBoy420: Do you have any band-aids? I'm really bleeding here.

Adeptus333: There's no Shit. It shouldn't be able to draw blood yet. Are you sure you burned the incense on Thursday?

LeafBoy420: Wednesday. Thursday. Who cares man? There's something in your house. It better not have rabies goddamnit.

Adeptus333: Chris. I want you to listen very carefully. Leave. The. House. Now. Don't worry about the mess, don't shut the door. Just leave.

LeafBoy420: No can do, mon frere. Couch is between me and the door.

Adeptus333: It moved the couch?

LeafBoy420: Nah, man, it's not that big. I'm just not getting within ten feet of that couch. F-ing thing is watching me. I can feel it.

Adeptus333: Use the back door, idiot. Through the kitchen.

LeafBoy420: Oh. Right.

Adeptus333: Okay, once you're clear of the house, gather what's left of the incense, and contact me. Even if it's been since Wednesday, we should be able to get it back under control. Just don't screw up again. If you wait too long it could break through the charms on the house.

LeafBoy420: It moved the vouch.

Adeptus333: What?

LeafBoy420: It moved the goddamned couch, man! This shit ain't funny anymore.

Adeptus333: Where are you?

LeafBoy420: I tried to leave through the kitchen like you said, but the lock was stuck tight so I decided to just make a run for it.

I wasn't halfway across the living room when your couch jumped in front of the door like a goddamned linebacker.

Adeptus333: Yes, but where are you now?

LeafBoy420: Upstairs bathroom trying to chill the fuck out. You sure you didn't lace that herb with something?

Adeptus333: What herb?

LeafBoy420: The "incense" you left me, man. I've blazed my share, but I've never seen shit like this before.

Adeptus333: The incense should not cause hallucinations. If you have any left you should burn it, not smoke it, just burn it, now.

LeafBoy420: Cuz that shit ain't right. Nothing's lower than poisoning a man's herb. That's his soul you're messing with, man. It's just not done.

Adeptus333: One: that incense was not meant to be smoked, and you have no one to blame for that but yourself. And Two: like I said, there is nothing hallucinogenic in it. The tulkafu is a real, and dangerous, entity. Fortunately

LeafBoy420: Fuck you dude! You can't scare me with this shit. You can't terrorize me like this. I'll call the fucking cops.

Adeptus333: Your negligence has created this situation, not me. And even if your phone is not broken like you said, the spells on the house would prevent the authorities from taking you seriously.

LeafBoy420: Fuck dude fuck. I don't deserve this. I didn't set out to bang your girlfriend man, she came to me. Call this tulkawhatever off me, man.

Adeptus333: You slept with Erica?

LeafBoy420: Shit dude. I thought that was why you were doing this. I didn't mean to spill nothing man. And I didn't mean to sleep with her, it just sort of happened.

LeafBoy420: Sorry.

LeafBoy420: Won't happen again.

LeafBoy420: Srsly dude, you've got to help me. Your polterthing ripped the bathroom door off its hinges and now it's giggling and tearing things up in the hallway.

LeafBoy420: Please, man, I promise, I'll never even look at her again.

Adeptus333: You're an asshole, Chris.

LeafBoy420: Yes, I'm an asshole. But seriously, it won't happen again. Ever.

LeafBoy420: That thing's getting closer man, you've got to help me.

Adeptus333: Unfortunately for me, the last thing I need is your corpse in my house and a motive in the phone records. Fortunately for you, you picked the safest room in the house to hide in.

LeafBoy420: What are you talking about? I'm trapped in here, man. And that thing is right fucking there. I can't see it, but it's right fucking there in the hallway. It ate my shoe.

Adeptus333: No, there isn't a way out, but the tulkafu shouldn't be able to get in.

LeafBoy420: Shouldn't?

Adeptus333: I put some very serious spells on that room. Didn't want to be fighting demons while sitting on the throne, if you know what I mean. Now, do you have any of the incense with you?

LeafBoy420: No, man. I told you, we smoked all that.

Adeptus333: We?

LeafBoy420: Yeah, I had some friends over to share.

Adeptus333: At my house?

LeafBoy420: Nah bro, I took that shit over to my place.

Adeptus333: I'm not your bro, Chris. You're the asshole who seriously fucked up my house with your stoner bullshit, slept with my girlfriend, and set loose a dangerous entity I've worked for months to capture and contain.

LeafBoy420: Right. Sorry. No incense.

Adeptus333: Do you have any drugs on you?

LeafBoy420: Just some cheap Mexican.

Adeptus333: Mexican?

LeafBoy420: M.J. man, from Mexico. Do I need to spell it out for you? Oh, and I've also got rolling papers.

Adeptus333: It's not perfect, but it may be enough to get you out of the house safely. From there, I can give you a list for the herbalist at Min's Witchery Shoppe, and you can make some more incense.

LeafBoy420: Hey man, you get me out of here, and I'm gone. You don't need to ever see me again. I think that would be best for both of us.

Adeptus333: That would be best, I agree. Unfortunately, your ineptitude has given the tulkafu a taste of your blood, and without proper sedation, it will likely break the charms on the house before I return to town. Then, if the legends are to be believed, it will pursue and devour you.

LeafBoy420: WTF dude. That's the kind of shit you need to mention beforehand. No way I'd risk this for $50 and some herb.

Adeptus333: There was never any "herb," it was incense, and if you'd followed the simple instructions I left, there wouldn't be any risk. Now, do you want my help or not?

LeafBoy420: Fine, I'll go to your Witchy Shop. How do I get out of here?

Adeptus333: Roll what you have into a long thin stick. This needs to be at least six inches long. Use as many papers as you need.

LeafBoy420: That's my expertise, man. Just a sec.

LeafBoy420: Done. This sucker's at least eight inches dude, and still smokable.

Adeptus333: Don't

Adeptus333: smoke it!

Adeptus333: I repeat: DO NOT SMOKE

LeafBoy420: Chill out, dude. I'm the one with the biting ghost snapping at me. What now?

Adeptus333: Okay. Now you're going to perform what's called a minor banishing ritual. It won't actually banish the tulkafu, but it should give you a moment or two to make a run for the door. You're probably better off moving the couch and going out the front door, since it seems to have jammed the back one.

LeafBoy420: Banishing ritual. Right. You sure you know what you're doing?

Adeptus333: You want my help? This is it. Take it or leave it. I'll be back in three and half days if you want to hole up in my bathroom, although I can't guarantee the spells will hold the tulkafu that long on their own.

LeafBoy420: Okay, okay. This thing is just nasty, that's all. It took the shoe I threw at it and made a little doll that looked like me. Then it sort of twittered while it slowly ripped the dolls face off.

Adeptus333: Just do what I say, asshole.

LeafBoy420: Hey man, no problem. You're the boss.

Adeptus333: After you light the Mexican stick you've made, use it like a wand to draw a five-pointed star in the air in front of you. Start with the star's left foot, draw to the head, then the right foot, then left hand, then right hand, then back to the left foot. The order and direction is important. If you feel the tulkafu back off at that point, run for it, and text me again once you're outside. If it doesn't back off, let me know and we'll try something else.

LeafBoy420: Okay dude. Wish me luck.

Adeptus333: Chris?

Adeptus333: Chris, are you still there?

LeafBoy420: Dude. I found your secret lair.

Adeptus333: Where are you?

LeafBoy420: I had a little toke before trying your smoky star thing, you know, for courage. It worked fine, but then I got turned around and ran the wrong way. Ended up in the bedroom when the polkafu caught up with me and slammed me right through the bookcase into your little black hex room here.

Adeptus333: You shouldn't be in there. It's very dangerous for you to be in that room.

LeafBoy420: Dangerous for me or you, bro? You must have some pretty good spells on here too. Ghosty can't get in at all. You've got some weird shit, man. What is all this stuff?

Adeptus333: Leave now!

LeafBoy420: "On using the tulkafu to enslave a woman's heart." Srsly dude?

Adeptus333: Put that book down and don't touch anything! Your life could depend on it.

LeafBoy420: And your little shrine to Erica—gross. You can't chain a free spirit like hers, man. Can't be done. Don't you know the number one rule about girls like that? You can bone 'em, but you can't own 'em. And that's the truth.

Adeptus333: Let's just work on getting you out of there. Do you still have the Mexican stick?

LeafBoy420: Nah, man, I dropped that when I got slammed through your bookcase. You're kind of a messed up dude, man. You know that?

Adeptus333: Okay. I'm going to let you borrow one of my talismans. It's like a necklace that will protect you. Do you see the shelf on the south wall, the one with the red triangle painted on it?

LeafBoy420: Holy shit dude, I think your polkafu is getting high. It's out there building little towers out of your books, and balancing them on their corners and shit.

LeafBoy420: Tulkafu's gonna toke a few. Lol.

Adeptus333: Now's your chance! Quick, while it's distracted, run for it!

LeafBoy420: Nah, bro. Says in your book here that the tulkafu will pursue the last person whose blood it tasted. And that's me.

Also says they're only dangerous if they're held against their will. But I'm guessing you know that already.

Adeptus333: Chris, listen to me. You have no experience with that sort of magick. Those books are very technical, and can't be taken at face value, it's very important that you don't meddle in things you don't understand.

LeafBoy420: Dude, I'm high, not stupid. I can fucking read. Nice "binding square" by the way. I'm guessing you're the "magician" in whose "blood it must be written?"

Adeptus333: Don't you fucking touch that Chris! The tulkafu will kill you!

LeafBoy420: Did you know that if you take the "binding square" out of the "protective circle of the ritual chamber" the tulkafu can suck that blood right out of it?

Adeptus333: You didn't. Tell me you fucking didn't.

LeafBoy420: The blood pulled right off the page like disappearing ink, and now my tulkafriend doesn't seem to care about me at all.

Adeptus333: Fuck you Chris.

LeafBoy420: I'll be leaving the door open like you said. Maybe when ghosty is done with the little book towers, it'll come find you on your trip. If it can get through your house spells. If not, I'm sure it'll be happy to see you when you get home.

Adeptus333: You'll pay for this. I'll make you pay.

LeafBoy420: You can't chain a free spirit man. Can't be done.

Adeptus333: Fuck you.

Trent Kollodge is the author of the novel *Two-bit Angel*, and has a story in the Lovecraftian anthology *Autumn Cthulhu*. He is a professional animator by day, a family man full time, and a writer in the wee hours when the house is quiet. He currently lives in Austin, Texas.

Slow Day

By Kristal Stittle

The day was dreary, dull, boring, and mundane. Outside, a light drizzle was soaking the streets, the cars, the pedestrians, and the glass-sided buildings. The grey clouds hung low and uniform, thick enough to block out the sky but not dark enough to be spooky or interesting.

I was sitting and staring at my screen, doing absolutely nothing. Recently, the company had hit an important milestone with our project, but then we came to a grinding halt. All the heads were busy, in meetings, planning the next phase, but grunts like me had nothing to do. We were just waiting on orders. There were only so many times I could play solitaire before it drove me insane.

I turned and looked into the cubicle across from mine. Paul worked there, although he was currently asleep at his desk. I knew he would get in shit if he were caught. Although we all had nothing to do, we had to at least pretend we did. We were supposed to be revising our code, checking for any missed bugs, but there were only so many times you could look at the same thing. I had been looking at my section for the past three months. If I could kill it, I would have. Instead, I ripped a page out of a nearby notebook, wadded it up, and threw it at Paul's head. The man, who was ten years older than me and had remarkably less hair, awoke with a start. He snorted and grumbled as he sat upright, rubbing his eyes.

"Wha was tha for, Jacob?" he mumbled, turning in his seat to look at me.

"You were asleep," I informed him. "If Mike came by, he'd tear you a new one."

"Mike's in a meeting until four. So's pretty much everyone else that would throw a hissy fit. You couldn't let me sleep until then?"

"You never know, someone might come down here to get something. Also, Fred would totally rat you out."

"Fair 'nough." Paul turned back to his computer, tapping the mouse with his hand to get rid of the screensaver. Both he and the screen would probably be asleep again in ten minutes.

I turned back around to my own computer knowing that Paul wasn't going to entertain me. It was only 1 PM, but I had already exhausted all my usual battery of websites. There were other sites I would like to visit, but the company blocked them on my computer. At least they hadn't yet discovered the one I was using for solitaire. I hated the company. I didn't like writing the boring software code, the cubicles, the off-white walls, the blocked websites, or the dress code. I didn't even like the other people. They were boring, unimaginative, uninteresting, and many were decades older than I was. At twenty-five, I was the youngest person on the floor by far, creating a wide generation gap. What I wanted to do was make video games. I had designed and programmed a few simple things, but nothing I could make any money from. Currently, I was working on something that I should be able to sell; I just needed more time to work on it. If only the company hadn't blocked me from connecting with my home computer, I could be doing it now.

I pulled my notebook to me and began doodling with a pen. I'm not a very good artist. The mini-games I had made had all their art done by my roommate. My roommate went to art school and also wanted to make games, but currently he was stuck working for his cousin's exterior house painting company. I doodled out some ideas to show him later.

As I sat there, sketching out a level design for the platformer game I was making, my stomach began rumbling. I wasn't hungry—I had eaten my lunch that day—it was my food's outward descent that caused the rumbling.

So, I got up from my chair and left the cubicle, obeying nature's call. As I suspected, Paul was asleep again, drooling on his own arm. I could have woken him up as I went past, but decided against it. Maybe on the way back I would. Although I didn't particularly like Paul, if Paul got chewed out, he'd complain to me about it. Paul complained about nearly everything.

As I walked toward the bathroom, I glanced into other people's cubicles to see what they were up to. Fred was the only one I spotted actually working. Nicole was drawing a monster in a sketchbook that looked disturbingly real; far better than my scribbles. Andrew was chatting with someone through email. Danny had a word doc open and was typing furiously, probably writing another story. Trevor was putting together a model airplane to join the other five he already had decorating his desk. Everyone in the office had their quirks and hobbies, I wasn't an exception.

I left the cubicle area and stepped out into reception. Betina, the receptionist for our floor, was chewing bubble gum and typing away at her own computer. She probably had actual work to do.

The door to the bathroom was a pale blue color. Pushing through that led me to a small antechamber with another pale blue door to push through. The bathroom itself was painted white and the stalls matched the doors. The sinks were steel and set into a black, speckled, marble counter. The ceiling in the bathroom was interesting. It was high up, allowing pipes and duct work to be exposed.

I walked to the stall at the far end to do my business. It was my favorite stall, although I had no idea why. Maybe I just liked being far away from the entrance. Once the door was safely latched behind me, I pulled down my pants and sat on the toilet. Because it sometimes took me awhile to get going, I usually played games on my cell phone. When I took the device out of my pocket, however, it was dead. Considering I had charged it last night, I wasn't at all happy about this. I never had much luck with phones.

The ducts above hummed and rumbled, forcing AC air down on my head.

As I sat, waiting for my bowels to move, the door to the bathroom burst open with a mighty slam. I jumped where I sat, nearly spilling myself off the seat, due to the sudden crash. Considering the door was on a pneumatic hinge, it probably shouldn't have been able to open so quickly. Whoever had just come in probably broke the door in the process.

And did the air just get a degree warmer? Probably a warm draft from the hall.

A sound not dissimilar to a woman's clicking heels travelled across the floor. Had a woman just come into the men's bathroom? The sound travelled right up to my stall and stopped before it, but I couldn't see their feet. The owner of the footsteps politely knocked upon my door.

"Occupied," I informed whoever it was. The other stalls were clearly empty; I don't know why he, or perhaps she, didn't just go into one of them.

Whoever it was knocked again, louder this time. The stall door shuddered from the force.

"Occupied!" I called louder, my voice wavering. This whole thing was very odd and I admit to being a little scared. Having my pants around my ankles didn't help.

The air got warmer.

"I have come for your soul," a deep and certainly male voice grumbled from the other side of the door.

I grinned. It must be someone playing a practical joke. "Very funny, guys."

The temperature flared higher. Whoever it was outside my door slammed their fist loudly into it, the latch barely hanging on. I jumped again with fright, an uncomfortably high pitch "eek" escaping my mouth before I could clamp my hands over it.

Who would possibly play such a joke on me? Surely not Paul. I couldn't think of anyone. Danny maybe? Was Steve in on it? Maybe if I could make out their footwear...

Slowly, I leaned forward on my seat and looked beneath the door. They weren't the kind of shoes I was expecting. In fact, they weren't shoes at all. A pair of large, cloven hooves stood before my stall, attached to a pair of ankles covered in a coarse, dark brown fur. As I watched, the weight shifted from one foot to the other, causing a subtle movement to the feet that made me think they were real and not just custom boots. But how could they be real? A tail, or what I assume was a tail, swung down near the feet. Before it lifted back up out of sight, I noted it was covered in a finer fur of the same color as the feet and ended in a spade shape.

I tried to swallow, but my mouth and throat had dried up worse than a block of wood in the desert. Surely my bored mind was just overreacting and I was seeing things that weren't true.

"Open the door," the heavy voice grumbled.

"Still occupied." Why I said that, I have no idea. Why my voice squeaked was a little more understandable.

"I'll break it down if you make me. And you don't want to make me." A heavy fist slammed into the door three more times, rattling the bolt lock.

"Who is it?" When I get scared, I resort to jokes. It's a quirk of mine.

"I have many names."

"Tell me one." Perhaps if I stall him long enough, someone else would walk into the bathroom, and they could call 911.

"Lucifer."

I shuddered at the sound, which managed to be both a growl and a hiss; like it was spoken by more than one voice.

"Ah, Lucifer, I've heard of you." My mouth was running on autopilot, for better or worse.

"I'm glad."

"So, what can I do for you, here in the public bathroom?"

"I've come for your soul."

"My soul?" I squeaked. I coughed once to clear my throat, although there wasn't anything in it that needed clearing. "What could you possibly want with my soul?"

"To bring it to hell with me, of course."

"Of course. Why *my* soul?"

"You sold it to me."

"What? No I didn't." I think I would have remembered selling my soul to Lucifer.

The heat in my bathroom stall jumped into the Sahara Desert range. I also heard billions of distant voices, crying out through the ductwork and pipes in the ceiling. I clearly had just upset him.

"I don't remember selling my soul," I told him earnestly. Perhaps I had been a small boy, who was goofing off when it happened. How was I to know then that the devil was real?

"Here is the contract," the voice grumbled as the temperature dropped to more survivable levels.

The hooves stepped forward to where I could see them without having to lean down. The spade at the end of his tail swept in under the door and then out again, as quick as a snake tongue scenting the air. I instinctively tucked my feet farther back from the door. A thick, powerful-looking hand reached under the door, its nails pointed and shiny black like obsidian. Clutched in the hand was a scroll of paper wrapped in an ink black ribbon with a broken, blood red seal. I pinched the edge of the scroll carefully between two fingers, trying my hardest not to touch the hand. As soon as I had a grip, the hand released the scroll and disappeared from my stall.

The paper was unlike any I had ever felt before. It looked old, slightly yellowed, but was very tough and coarse. It had been woven out of a material I couldn't identify. Slowly, I unrolled the scroll, revealing the black ink upon it. The ink was like holes that had been cut into oblivion, not like something that had been merely scrawled upon the paper. I didn't dare run my fingers over the text, for fear that my eyes would be proved right and that I'd be sucked through them. The text it formed was unreadable, at least to me. I had always been terrible at reading other people's handwriting, and this was such an overly elaborate text that I could only make out a handful of letters. My eyes ran down the page, to where I expected a signature in blood. There was a signature, but it was in a basic, regular blue pen, nothing strange about it at all. It wasn't my signature though.

"Umm, this isn't me," I told Lucifer. *Lucifer!* And I was telling him he made a mistake? Let's just say that it was a damn good thing I was sitting on the toilet.

Silence was my response, but I could feel the heat starting to rise.

"No really!" I bent over and pushed the paper under the stall door. "I can't read the signature, but I know for a fact that it's not mine."

"It isn't?" He actually sounded like he believed me.

"No. Whose is it? And what did he ask for?"

"Steven Evans. He wanted a regular bowel."

"Well that makes sense." Relief washed over me as I realized he had the wrong guy. "Steve is in the stall at the other end."

"I fucking hate you, Jacob," Steve finally spoke up from where he had been doing his own business in silence the whole time.

"Steve!" Lucifer boomed, turning toward his stall, his hooves clicking along the floor. "I have come for your soul!"

"No wait, please!" Steve begged.

I listened as the stall door was ripped from its hinges and tossed to the ground.

"Noooooo!" Steve screamed.

A sound like tearing came from the ceiling above. I looked up, but couldn't see anything near me. A strange, red light was coming from over toward Steve however. Again I heard the sounds of billions of distance voices. They were crying out in pain and ecstasy. From closer, over by Steve, there was a horrible crunching and slurping. A bizarre suction sound and then a loud snap. After a strange zipper sound, the red light faded and all other sounds silenced. I sat with bated breath, wondering what was going to happen next.

Lucifer was still here. I listened as he walked on his hooves to where the door had fallen. It scraped along the ground as he picked it up and slammed it back into place. The devil seemed to be cleaning up after himself. The hooves then walked back over to my stall.

"What's your name?" he grumbled.

"Jacob." I was squeaking again. Perhaps he was going to get rid of the witness?

"Is there anything I can do for you, Jacob?"

"What?"

"Is there anything you want? I can give you anything."

"Umm, no thanks."

"Are you sure?"

"I'd rather not go to hell."

"How do you know you're not already?"

He had a point. I had no idea. I mean, I wasn't a saint or anything. Based on what I knew of religion, I was definitely on the hell list.

"I can make sure that game you're working on is a best-seller. And that woman you see on the bus a lot; I can make it so that you hit it off well. Maybe baldness runs in the family, or... smallness."

"What if I asked to live forever?"

"I'd still collect your soul. That's how zombies are made you know."

"What did Steve get?" I was amazed at myself for even thinking about it.

"He made the deal when he was five years old. Poor kid had crapped his pants just one too many times at school. I gave him fifty years of the healthiest bowel you can imagine."

Steve had always been regular, everyone knew. You could set your watch by him.

"Yeah, you know what? I really think I'm good."

"You're not that good." Lucifer's tail whipped under the door again with its snake-like quickness.

"Good enough."

"Suit yourself." The heavy hooves retreated from the bathroom.

I was finally able to take the shit I had gone to the bathroom to take. Although, the entire time, I expected Lucifer to come barging back in. After pulling up my pants and flushing, I exited the toilet stall. The rest of the bathroom looked just the same as it had when I first entered, as if nothing had happened there. I washed my hands in the sink and turned to Steve's stall. The hinges were a little bent out of shape. I walked up to the door.

"Steve?" Why I expected an answer, I have no idea. I pushed on the door, which wasn't locked anymore.

There was Steve, pants around his ankles, slumped over sideways with his head on the toilet paper roll, dead as a doorknob. He looked sad and pathetic.

"I hope it was worth it," I told his corpse. I then left the bathroom and went back to my own desk. Paul was still sleeping across the way. I could've called someone about Steve, but decided against it; let the next guy find him like that.

I did, however, pull my notebook over to me and write down the date and time. Underneath, I wrote and underlined the words "In case of emergency, call Lucifer."

Kristal Stittle was born and raised in Toronto, Canada, where she still lives with her cat. She's always working on several writing projects at a time, from novels and short stories to scripts. Trained in 3D animation, she continues to paint and illustrate regularly while dabbling in photography.

Dead Man Dancing

By Jonathan Shipley

Marianna smiled as they waited for the herb-roasted chicken to arrive from the kitchens of the Stable Cafe. "Seriously amazing. Of course, I knew that George had collected 23,000 books over his lifetime, but I never realized he had a hand-written manuscript of Shakespeare's Macbeth in the collect—"

"No one did," her brother Justin interrupted. The two siblings, experts in rare books and antiques respectively, were independent consultants often called in by the staff of the huge estate. "Someone on the maintenance discovered the hidden panel in the library that neither the family nor the curatorial staff had any inkling of. And given the importance of the manuscript, staff wanted an opinion of authenticity immediately."

"Do we know where George found a Shakespeare manuscript?"

Justin gave a shrug and a sigh. "Wherever. Since he collected constantly, it could any place where he was purchasing furniture or decorative items for the house."

The house in question was Biltmore with its four acres of rooms behind a chateau-esque facade, and George was George Washington Vanderbilt II, the Gilded Age millionaire who built it in 1889. And the unique expertise that Marianna and Justin brought to the situation was their heightened awareness of old—often dark—objects. This evening's discovery was a happy exception to their usual consultations.

The waiter appeared with two platters of chicken. "Compliments of the chef . . . of Herb, who roasted the chicken. Sorry, he told me to say that."

Justin rolled his eyes at the old joke—Herb never missed an opportunity to inject himself into the herb-roasted chicken. "Thank you—message received," he said with a nod. As the waiter retreated, his phone rang.

Marianna promptly tuned out the conversation to concentrate on dinner. The estate's Stable Café was literally in the old stables next to the mansion proper, but there was nothing horsy about its cuisine. It prided itself on its BBQ, but—

"Mack, calm down," Justin urged. "Calm down and please repeat that."

The agitation in his voice drew Marianna's attention because her brother was usually so unflappable. With his perfectly groomed salt-and-pepper hair and urbane manners, he always came across as cool and suave. All he needed was a British accent to complete the image. But not today.

"— say that one more time, Mack," Justin insisted into his phone. "I want no chance that I've misheard you." A lengthy pause. "Yes, that's what I thought you said. Marianna and I will be right over."

"What in the world was that?" Marianna demanded as soon as he disconnected. "And who is Mack?"

"New dealer in town with a booth in the College Street Antique Mall. I only know him through the Facebook antiquarian group, but he knows my reputation, apparently. He has a situation he can't begin to handle."

"Hmm." She took another bite. "If it's that sort of situation, I insist we finish dinner first. Who knows when we'll have another chance?" They rushed through the meal in record time and headed out to the car.

"So?" she prompted as they buckled in and started the drive from the Biltmore estate on the south side of town to College Street in downtown Asheville.

"It's a case of an unusual corpse," Justin said.

"So why is he calling you instead of the police?"

"An antique corpse. Apparently part of Mack's inventory in his antiques booth."

"Wait—what? He keeps a corpse in his booth?"

"He's young and inexperienced," Justin offered with a shrug. "Beyond that I'm just guessing."

"Confusing dead bodies with antiques is more than inexperience," she retorted, then her eyes narrowed. "Who exactly is this Mack person?"

"Not what you're thinking," Justin said quickly. "I've heard absolutely nothing dark about him. He was so rattled on the phone, we can safely assume that corpses are not his usual merchandise. He truly doesn't know what to do."

Marianna gave a nod. "No surprise. How antique is this antique corpse?"

"It's fully taxidermied from the early 1900's."

"I don't recall pickling your relatives being a social trend in the early 1900's," she observed dryly. "What's the back story?"

He shook his head. "No idea. Mack was babbling more than talking. But you can ask him yourself. We're almost there."

Sure enough, they were nearing the intersection of Biltmore Avenue and College Street. A right turn took them toward the Pack Square Cultural District with the antique mall on its outskirts. The mall stayed open late to lure in the evening crowd coming from performances in the district, and from the lines of parked cars, it looked like something was going on tonight. Marianna glanced at the Eventology app on her phone and saw that the Asheville Lyric Opera was giving a special children's performance of Humperdinck's Hansel and Gretel.

"Somewhere on the second level," Justin said as they entered the mall and headed for the staircase. "I don't know the exact booth location, but Mack should be—"

A wild-eyed young man approached them at the top of the stairs. "Ah, good. You're just in time."

"Yes, I'm Justin Tyme—"

"I just said that," he interrupted impatiently.

"I mean," Justin persisted, "that I'm Justin Tyme—T-Y-M-E—and this is my sister, Marianna Trench."

"Glad you're here," the young man nodded. "Sorry about the mix-up. Guess with those names . . ."

"It happens," Justin supplied. "You're Mack?"

"Yup, Mack Donald.

"Old MacDonald?" Marianna felt compelled to ask.

"Nope, that's my granddad. This way." He seemed to be a jeans and t-shirt sort of guy, with shaggy brown hair and a nervous twitch. The twitch might be the immediate situation, but the rest was a younger, sloppier look than most of Justin's dealer friends. Antique dealers, she amended mentally. The other sounded downright druggy.

"I hear you're new to Asheville," she said as they walked.

"Why is this happening?" he groaned in response, or not in response, actually. She wasn't sure he'd even heard her. His accent sounded more Deep South than Appalachian.

She was about to try again with the obvious "why the hell was a corpse in your booth" question when Justin gave her a subtle shake of the head.

"So, Mack," he said smoothly. "Is the item in question new inventory or old?"

"Brand new. He was inside that chest that came in yesterday." Mack pointed to a big blanket chest standing empty in the corner with its lid raised. "Never even knew he was in there until I was unpacking. It was a shock, but what could I do?"

Call the police, idiot, Marianna supplied silently. And curious that Mack used "he" not "it." She probably wouldn't use that personal a pronoun for a strange body she had no connection with.

"So I left him in the blanket chest. Then it got strange."

Oh, then it got strange. Marianna raised an eyebrow at Justin. He ignored her. "How so?" he asked Mack.

"Well, things started moving around. I came back from dinner, and he was sitting posed in a chair, staring out the window with his glass eyes. That's when I called you."

"Someone's idea of a prank?" Justin asked carefully.

Mack shook his head. "Thought that at first, but then he stood up and walked out of the mall."

"Ahh." Marianna and Justin in unison. This seemed to have just advanced from strange but mundane into their realm of the supernatural.

"So this is about a missing walking corpse?" Marianna asked.

Mack frowned. "Except he's not really missing." He pointed out the window across the street to Pack Square. "I saw him walk into the theater."

Marianna blinked, surprised yet again. "Into the Wortham Theatre's *Hansel and Gretel*?" A corpse among children. Never a good mix.

Mack nodded vigorously. "He might come back after the last act, but then he might not. Should I go over and try to wrestle him back across the street against his will? If not, someone might recognize he's dead when the lights come up and start a riot. I really don't know what to do. But y'all know, right? You being a witch and all."

Justin threw him a sharp look. "I'm an antiquarian, not a witch. Despite opinions to the contrary, there is a difference. We don't know what to do yet. But we shall. Marianna and I need to strategize. And you need to calm down."

"I need more coffee," Mack muttered.

"Anything but. I'm sending you across the street to keep an eye on the situation. Do nothing and we'll be there soon." With a quick nod, Justin hurried from the booth with Marianna only a step behind. "How long before *Hansel and Gretel* ends?" he asked as they headed for the stairs and out to the car.

She checked her phone again. "It runs just under two hours and it started at 7:00. So almost an hour and a half until the curtain comes down. "What are you thinking?"

"Back to Biltmore," he said as they buckled in and pulled into traffic. "A revenant is out of our usual scope. But if we call the police, they'll just hand the situation back to us—like last time with the haunted cottage."

She nodded. Their area of expertise might be tainted books and antiques, but the local law enforcement expected them to deal with anything supernatural. "So back to Biltmore for . . . ah, the grimoires," she concluded with a grimace.

George Vanderbilt had collected other old manuscripts besides Shakespeare, four of them dark or semi-dark grimoires. Three of them were sixteenth century copies of medieval editions, and the fourth one—the one written in Sanskrit—was definitely much older. "You know I hate touching those pages," she added. The three grimoires were stored in a silver-lined cabinet to keep their darkness from seeping out into the library.

"I see no other choice," Justin shrugged back. "Souls returning from the dead are several steps beyond the usual purification of objects that we practice and well on the way to an exorcism."

"Which we have no experience with," she reminded him. "That's priest territory. Or witch territory," she added pointedly. Justin rolled his eyes, but didn't rise to the bait. She settled back to think this through. One of the essentials of witchcraft versus other forms of occultism was the reliance on spells that could be passed down to a successor in the form of a Book of Shadows, as it was known within the craft. Outside the craft, a grimoire. Biltmore's grimoires were their best chance to put down a zombie.

"I'll call Craig to meet us," she said, pulling out her phone. Craig was the Assistant Curator for Oblique Decorative Arts, who owed them both a laundry list of favors for their unique services. "But Craig would lose his job if we took those grimoires off the property. What sort of work-around do you have in mind for that?"

"Nothing . . . yet."

"Not to mention," she persisted, "the rather awkward logistics of an exorcism in a theater full of people. Mack may have been over the top, but he was right about a corpse causing a riot. Just imagine the people in the seats next to him—it."

Justin gave a non-committal grunt as he passed through the main gate of the estate.

From the service entrance through the service corridors, the walk to the library was not the grand promenade of reception rooms that tourists experienced, but the end destination was still amazing. Even having just been there, Marianna gave her usual sigh of appreciation as she stepped into the huge library with its ten-thousand volumes of gilt Moroccan leather under a three-hundred-year-old painted Venetian ceiling. It was one of George Vanderbilt's favorite rooms and guaranteed to be the absolute favorite room of any book lover.

"What's this about?" Craig asked as he circled the room, clicking on lights. "You said an emergency?"

"One of our special sorts of emergencies with a ticking clock," Justin nodded, heading directly for the special cabinet lined in insulating silver. "We need to access the grimoires."

Craig shook his head. "More strangeness in Asheville. It never seems to stop."

"Thanks for opening up us," Marianna added, giving his arm a pat as she passed. "You're a dear." When she reached Justin, he already had the four oversized grimoires carefully laid out on a reading table. She shuddered as their inherent darkness wafted up like a cloud of smoke. She closed her mind as best she could in order to focus. "Not that one," she said with a nod at the oldest manuscript. "I can't handle Sanskrit under pressure. And I have no idea which of the Latin grimoires would be better. Are we calling this a possession?"

"Possession, overshadowing, haunting," Justin nodded. "Something has attached itself to the corpse, possibly the original soul and possibly a demonic spirit. So we need some form of a purification spell crossed with an exorcism."

"Let me check the index for that," Marianna quipped as she gently turned vellum pages to scan the Latin page headers. "Craig, can you help skim pages?" His Latin was excellent, possibly better than hers. "This will go faster with all three of us."

Craig came over to the table, albeit a little reluctantly. "I heard purification and exorcism. That's what I skim for?"

"Exactly," she nodded and turned another page. "We may need to mix and match spells, but only in the last resort will we mix and match between grimoires. These may not represent compatible magic systems."

He frowned. "Isn't all magic the same? Or is that secret witch information?"

"Craig," Justin growled warningly.

Marianna suppressed a grin. When Craig had been hired, he'd assumed Oblique Decorative Objects was going to be a normal museum curatorship. Now he was half in, half out of their supernatural adventures and always playing the witch card at Justin's expense.

A few minutes of silence followed. "Here," Craig abruptly exclaimed. "A cleansing ritual—'for all dark beasties, both greater and lesser,' it says."

She pushed closer to him. "Sounds possible." She gave the page a glance, then bent over to decipher the Latin in earnest. "It seems to be an all-purpose cleansing spell—which is good for us. And I found an exorcism spell in my book. That's two possibilities on short notice." She straightened up. "Anything from you, Justin?"

From the other side of the table, her brother shook his head. "Just love potions." He came around the table. "Here's how I think we should proceed. To have magical effect, the spell must be performed by a magical person or be intoned from a magical source. And since we do not have a convenient witch in our company"— pointed look at Craig—"and the grimoires aren't mobile, we'll have to create a sympathetic link. Craig, you'll keep the spells at ready here in the library, and Marianna will intone them in the theater over FaceTime."

"We're going to FaceTime a spell," Marianna repeated dubiously. "Have you ever tried this before, Justin?"

"No, actually. But the theory has been discussed in the Carolingian Theosophical Society—you should consider joining, by the way."

"I have a life, thank you, and don't need a group of would-be occultists."

"We're researchers, not occultists. And you would—"

"I thought the clock was ticking," Craig interjected.

"Right," Justin nodded with a sigh. "And the last thing needed for this link is a metaphysical connection. I think the Trench ring should suffice."

Craig blinked. "The what?"

"This." Marianna stretched out her hand to display the ornate silver ring she always wore. "The engagement ring from my marriage."

"Ah." Craig shifted his weight awkwardly. "You never mention Mr. Trench. Was the marriage such an abyss?"

"Not now," Justin interjected. "The important point is that the ring is solid silver, which is the most mystical of metals. And something in constant physical contact, such as a ring, should be a good connector."

Marianna handed the heavy ring to Craig. "And we need to go. We have less than an hour." She and Justin turned and hurried down the corridor. "Thanks again, Craig," she called over her shoulder. A minute later, the Audi was barreling down Biltmore Avenue toward downtown.

"You know," she commented as they closed on the cultural district, "we don't have a plan for the inanimate corpse—assuming we successfully exorcise the spirit."

"True," Justin acknowledged. "But the problem of an inconvenient corpse on the floor is insignificant compared with one walking around. If we get that far, I'll be content to improvise."

She didn't disagree. It was the difference between grotesque and terrifying.

They parked at the antique mall and hurried the half block to the Wortham Theatre. Mack was waiting in the lobby. "Where is it?" Justin demanded. "Has there been an incident yet?"

Mack grimaced. "Not yet. You'd think a strange costume and pasty white complexion would send up an alarm, but in a theater, that blends right in." He nodded at the inner doors. "Take a look."

Marianna scooted across the lobby to stick her head through the door. She pulled back with a frown. "Well. Apparently—despite all odds—a well-taxidermied body with glass eyes can pass as alive."

Justin frowned back. "What are you not telling me?"

"Our target is on stage with the cast."

Justin blinked. "Singing opera?"

"No, dancing at the back of the stage."

Justin gave her a strange look, then beckoned to them both. "Stage entrance."

A moment later, they were standing in the wings of the stage, watching the spectacle of an obviously dead body cavorting among the actors. But apparently "obviously" was in the eye of the beholder. The other actors merely looked irritated, especially the Gingerbread Witch, who was just climbing out of the wheelbarrow fronted with the semblance of a burning oven. "That idiot ruined my death scene," the witch muttered as she dropped her cape and hat in the wheelbarrow and headed toward the dressing rooms.

Chuck Waggoner, the director, wasn't a close friend, but familiar enough that he didn't react to them appearing uninvited in the wings. Of course, his attention was on the dancing corpse. "Who is that, who is that?" he kept muttering to himself in a stage whisper. "That's not part of this scene."

Justin gave Marianna a nudge and nodded at the oven-wheelbarrow. "You intone the spell. When the corpse drops, I'll be in position to wheel it offstage." He stepped over and draped himself in the black cape and hat.

It was a far too public plan, but the alternative was letting the corpse dance. That would lead to disaster. She nodded, pulled out her phone, and tapped the app. Craig's anxious face appeared next to a vellum page. "We're ready," she told him.

He turned slightly, picked up the Trench ring, and pressed into against the grimoire as Marianna read the spell. She could feel the power of the words as the Latin syllables rolled off her tongue. She finished the last words and added the *ultima verba* before shifting her glance to the stage. Justin was wheeling the wheelbarrow across the stage, even though the oven scene was over and the witch supposedly dead. But their target, the corpse, was still hopping around.

She turned back to her phone. "Other spell, Craig."

On screen, she saw Craig jump up from his chair and rush to the other side of the table where the second grimoire lay waiting. Pushing it carefully with the insulated gloves, he positioned it in good view of the phone and carefully opened it to the bookmark. "Ready."

Marianna took a breath and started again. As before, she felt the words as she spoke each one. This spell was shorter, less about revenants than expelling demonic influences. As she finished, she glanced toward the stage as Justin crossed again with the oven. But the corpse still hopped.

"Those are powerful grimoires," she murmured to Justin as he joined her in the wings again. "Either spell should have worked—but neither one did. What are we doing wrong?"

"And you're sure about the delivery?"

She nodded. "I'm no witch, but I can intone a spell with the best of them. And both spells felt like they were activating." Her eye went back to the dancing figure. "Justin," she said slowly. "Since when do zombies dance?"

Her brother gave a start. "They don't—they shuffle. Good lord, we're completely wrong. That can't be a revenant in the usual sense—"

"Oh, is there a usual sense for things that come back from the dead?" she muttered under her breath.

"—but an odd possession," he continued.

"But—"

"No, listen. It's a stuffed scarecrow that happens to look like a revenant because the bag is made of human skin. It's exactly like the cursed objects we've encountered that shift around on their own. I suspect the blanket chest. Perhaps some energy rubbed off from chest to corpse. Tell Craig to look for a spell to de-animate a magically animated object."

"I heard," Craig said over the phone. "And I'm looking."

"The last minutes of the last scene of the last act," Marianna whispered to Justin. "As soon as the opera stops and the lights come up, the other actors will figure it out pretty quickly."

Suddenly Craig was back. "I overheard the part about the chest and found a reference to a *continens magicae* that fits. It animates its contents as long as the chest remains open. To stop it, you simply—"

"Close the lid," Marianna and Justin finished together.

Justin whirled and caught Mack by the shoulder. "Mack, go to the blanket chest and close the lid. Run!"

He rushed off, leaving the two of them to wait. It took a long minute. Then the corpse wavered in its frenetic dance and seemed to glow. No, it was glowing like a cloud of fireflies swarming around it. As Marianna kept staring, she saw it was the stuffing coming out of the corpse in tiny bits and pieces and hovering around it. None of this was according to Hoyle, but it was beautiful. And everyone in the theater seemed totally entranced. Even the other actors had stopped acting to watch.

Justin shook his head. "A whole hall of people witnessing the unexplainable."

"No, it's OK," she murmured back. "We're in a theater— people expect special effects. The light show is too pretty to be scary. Look at all those smiling children. This can't be dark energy, Justin. We're still wrong in our assumptions."

He was silent a moment. "Be that as it may, we still have cleaning up to do." He grabbed the portable oven again and wheeled it onstage toward the glowing corpse. As the light effects faded and the form wavered, Justin was in just the right place to scoop it up in the oven and shift it off to the wings. A wave of cheers and applause followed him.

"I don't think widespread panic is a problem anymore," he said as he kept going.

Marianna nodded and followed. To her eye, the much deflated corpse still seemed to collapsing on itself. Evaporating in little spurts of light.

The director was all over Justin a second later. "OK, I admit it—that lightshow was fantastic—completely off-script but fantastic. And how were you manipulating the puppet? Remote drone control?"

"Of course," Justin answered with a perfectly straight face.

"What did you do with the puppet, by the way?"

Both siblings glanced at the wheelbarrow that contained only an empty old suit. "We'll talk later, Chuck," Justin said abruptly. "Got to dash at the moment." And he set off at top speed with Marianna right behind him.

"So, what's happening?" a voice in her hand demanded.

"Oh, Craig," she said. "Sorry, forgot about you. You were right—closing the chest lid de-animated the corpse, and it basically came apart in a burst of light. Not enough left to even identify as a body. Now we're heading across the street to the blanket chest. So thank you. Situation contained, and you are now free again."

She disconnected just as they reached the antiques mall. "We have to commandeer the chest, you know," she told Justin as they climbed the staircase.

"Absolutely," he snorted. "Can you imagine the succession of animated blankets on the loose if we don't? Ah, Mack," he transitioned as they reached the booth. "Corpse taken care of, and we're here to contain the chest."

Mack gave a shudder. "Cursed—don't have to tell me twice."

Justin was all over the blanket chest like an Antiques Roadshow expert. "Large proportions, bracket feet, walnut primary wood, poplar secondary, hand-cut dovetails—definitely an 18th century Pennsylvania piece. So the chest has only a random connection with the corpse."

"Hold," Marianna send suddenly as her brother upended the chest to check the underside. "I see a chalk inscription on the bottom." She leaned down to read the flowery cursive letters. "Latin—that fits," she said. "And look at this—*magicae continens ludibriae*. Magical toy chest. And this—*ut delectet filios*. To delight the children. This chest is sounding less dark by the moment."

"Agreed," Justin nodded. "Certainly magical, but not cursed."

"Something a sorcerer-carpenter might make for his own children, perhaps?" Marianna suggested. "Certainly the dancing corpse did delight the children—in fact, it sought out children to delight."

"We'll need to take the chest, you realize," Justin told Mack.

"Please do," Mack said with another shudder. "It scares me."

Justin's phone played a little Mozart. "Justin Tyme," he said, most of his attention still on the chest's inscription. "Oh, what's up, Chuck? Has something else happened at the theater?"

Concerned, Marianna reached over and turned on his speakerphone.

"—and we've decided to rewrite the last act of the opera to match tonight's performance," Chuck gushed. "And you, Justin, are key to replicating the same success tomorrow."

"I'm no actor," he protested.

"But we need you," Chuck persisted. "Quite frankly, you make a great witch."

"I'm not a—" he began, then caught Marianna's smirk.

He gave a long sigh of resignation. "Thank you, Chuck, but no. This witch is not available."

Jonathan Shipley, a member of Science Fiction Writers of America, writes short stories and novels in the genres of fantasy, science fiction, and horror. In the writing profession, there are two huge challenges. One is the writing itself, and the second is getting the works published. In terms of output, he has written nine novels and over a hundred short stories. On the publication front, he has had over seventy short stories published since 1992, and one of the novels, a World War II occult thriller, is currently shortlisted by New York publisher Baen Books. Several more stories are sold and due out this year in anthologies and magazines. A listing of his short stories can be found at www.amazon.com/author/shipley or www.shipleyscifi.com.

When not writing, Shipley teaches high school where his classes include—not unexpectedly—creative writing. And when not writing or teaching, he works on the restoration of his 1914 historic home and collects antiques to go in the home. And when you add up all those things together, it always seems to come out to more than twenty-four hours in the day.

An Unclean Spirit

By Lance Shoeman

The irony of this situation is killing me. Or rather, it would be, if I weren't already dead.

Goddamn, I could use a fix.

"God damn the affliction of addiction to Hell! In the name of our Lord and Savior Jesus Christ I cast thee out, foul demon!"

The asshole—sorry, God's *anointed* asshole—in the cheap linen suit is Pastor Wayne Switzer, and he's currently trying to accomplish what two stints in rehab couldn't... twice that many if you count reasons which aren't immediately apparent to those in attendance. Speaking of whom, Dad's squeezing my right hand like he's trying to save someone from falling off the edge of a cliff (which, to be fair, isn't an entirely inapt analogy), and Mom's salon-fake nails aren't doing my left hand any favors, either.

The only other witnesses to this... I can't decide whether to call it a "spectacle" or "debacle." I think I'll err on the side of "bullshit." At any rate, the only others present—aside from, obviously, Tommy "Pickles" Nichols (nickname courtesy '90s Nickelodeon cartoons)—are three caged guinea pigs, and God only knows what's up with that. God, and the good reverend.

"Behold! I have given you authority to trample on snakes and scorpions and to overcome all the power of the enemy, Luke 10:19... for those who believe will drive out the impure, just as Jesus did when he came upon the Gadarenes demoniac!"

And now he's going on about liminal areas, ruins and tombs, his rubicund complexion gone full-blown scarlet, sweat droplets forming at the tip of a bulbous nose covered in a spider's web of visible but not quite broken capillaries. Seriously, the guy looks like he's about a half a chapter and verse shy of needing the kind of salvation only 9-1-1 can provide.

The thing is, I've heard it all before. A couple of months ago I skipped out on exactly this sermon, dry-mouthed and jonesing, headed for the modern-day ruins of the rundown tenement where Pickles and I were squatting with Arden, our roommate-slash-supplier. Now I don't know if it was the rainwater trickling down the stairwell, or the general disrepair of the steps themselves, but I lost my footing just shy of the third floor landing. Upended, flying backward through too much space, I called out in alarm and surprise... I don't remember what famous last words I might've been trying to say, but doubt I'll ever forget what I actually managed to say, especially since it sounded like shorthand for a hemorrhoidal blood fart.

"Blart!"

And that, as they say, was that. I stood there, confused, staring down at my lifeless body with its pulped head and shattered neck. It wasn't long before Pickles—who almost took a header himself, but was spared a similar fate courtesy the splintered remains of what passed for a bannister—and Arden joined me, the horror of what had happened slowly sinking in for all three of us.

"Fuck, he's dead!" Arden said. "He's dead, isn't he?"

Two things happened then to confirm that, yes, I had indeed shuffled off my mortal coil. The first was that my opioid-induced constipation resolved itself in a rather spectacular manner (surely you've seen those laxative commercials on late-night television aimed at users with legit oxy scripts). The second was that a tunnel of bright white light opened up at the top of the stairs. The latter was seen only by the recently deceased; the former smelled only by junkies and horse-traders. Seems a sense of smell isn't required to navigate the afterlife.

"Man, he stinks!" Arden said.

"I... I can't deal, dude." Pickles turned away from my corpse and toward Arden, who was comically pinching his nose shut. "I need a bump, *muy pronto.*"

"Yeah... Yeah. Definitely."

They started back up the stairs to our condemned apartment, and I followed. But my objective wasn't the Tunnel of God's Eternal Love. No sir, in proper ghostly fashion I had unresolved business to attend to, that being feeding an addiction that was every bit as much psychological as it was physiological. As one might expect, my life had flashed before my eyes, and the final image—that of the detoxorcism I'd ditched out on—had given me one hell of an idea. If evil spirits can in fact be cast *out* of people, well... they've got to get in there in the first place somehow, right?

As it turns out, getting in's a cinch for the non-corporeal. The trick is to do it without passing *through*, a trick I accomplished by using Pickles' own impacted bowels as an anchor. By the time we reached where I'd taken my final, fatal step I had enough control over Pickles' nervous system to not only bypass the light entirely but to flip it the bird. It disappeared with a flash, and mere moments later Pickles tapped a vein and granted me the kind of peaceful repose I'd imagine even Heaven itself can't offer.

The next several weeks were a blur of whores and heroin as Pickles and Arden tried their level best to assuage their guilt over my passing. Arden, in particular, was convinced that I might have lived had they immediately called an ambulance... in retrospect I probably should've made my presence known and assured him that it wouldn't have made a difference, but I was enjoying the pity-party way too much. As time passed, though, Pickles' grief gradually turned toward a desire to get his act together and turn his life around, a determination exacerbated by my folks' influence. The three of them had reconnected at my funeral (a ceremony presided over by the same imminent heart attack overseeing today's proceedings), and tentatively started down a path of good Christian fellowship that ultimately led Pickles full circle... unbeknownst to him, of course.

So here we sit; Dad on Pickles' right, Mom on Pickles' left, and me center stage and fighting like a son of a bitch against the urge to crack wise about finding myself in quite the pickle. Tempted to say something, though—especially in regard to the drizzle of sweat and spittle running down Switzer's paper-white moustache and blowing into my face—but I've elected to ride the entire affair out best I can. Figure it's the least I can do.

"Fuck you, fatass!"

Wait, what?

"I wipe my ass with pages from your Gospels!"

Pickles is talking, but... that's not Pickles talking. And it sure as hell isn't me, so what the fuck?

"The demon reveals itself!" Switzer bellows, triumphant. "Identify yourself, spawn of Satan!"

I have a sudden sinking feeling in Pickles' stomach.

"I am... Bacchus, you putrescent fucking primate," the demon exclaims.

"Holy shit, you're real?!" I say, and Mom blanches.

"Surprise! Ha, ha!"

"My baby," Mom cries out. "That other *other* voice is my baby boy's!"

"He does the slow roast in Hell with me!" Bacchus says, and Mom instantly bursts into tears.

"He's lying!" I try to assure her. "That's what they do, right? Trust me, the only Hell I'm in at the moment is figurative."

"My poor baby..."

"He's okay, dear," Dad says unconvincingly, and then mutters a quick prayer under his breath for his son's soul.

"He's lying about everything! Pickles doesn't wipe his butt with the Bible because we can't even take a dump, and c'mon, '*Bacchus*'? I somehow doubt that we're possessed by the Greek god of debauchery."

"He's got a point," Pickles chimes in.

"I know, right...?"

Our mutual appreciation is interrupted by Switzer sprinkling our face with what can only be—based on Bacchus's violent reaction—holy water. But to me? It's no more painful than the various bodily fluids Switzer's 'stache has been spritzing us with.

"Aauuugh!" Bacchus screams. "You may not be in Hell yet, smartass, but I'm sure as hell going to drag you down there with me, you damned dirty ape!"

"The power of Christ compels you!"

A thought suddenly occurs to me, and not just that Switzer and Bacchus are obliviously engaged in an impromptu movie quote-off.

"Speaking of apes, who's the monkey on whose back, here? I mean, were you already inside Pickles when I possessed him, or did I bring you in with me?"

"Either/or! We are Legion, stupid!"

No. Oh, no... I think I might know where all this is headed.

"Legion, indeed," Switzer says, smug and smiling, his round cheeks more appropriately cherubic than ever, "and just as you begged the Son of God for mercy, so too shall you entreat those of us who act in His name lo these two thousand years hence!"

I turn and look at the guinea pigs, and both Bacchus and I begin to panic.

"I cast thee out," Switzer continues, "and grant you leave—as Yeshua before me—to enter these swine!"

It's over just as quickly as my life was. One second I'm looking at the ruddy butterball that is Pastor Wayne, and the next second I'm watching Bacchus—now inhabiting one of the three guinea pigs—drown himself on the rodents' no-drip water bottle... which is actually kind of impressive, given the mechanics involved and the amount of effort required. I'd follow suit, seeing as how I'm also now looking out at the world through beady black eyes, but to be totally honest I'm just happy that my hands (paws?) are no longer being pulverized by parental concern. That, and that—since I'm taking anatomical inventory—it would appear I at least have the correct genitals (the other surviving guinea pig does not, so I dodged a bit of a bullet, there).

There are hugs and handshakes and congratulations all around, and Pickles asks if he can keep us (minus the dead one, naturally). The as-it-turns-out genuinely holy man obliges, and offers my folks what comfort he can, assuring them that the demon had no power over my disembodied spirit, and that I've gone on to a better place.

I'll try and keep an open mind about that last part, I guess.

So once again life's come full-circle, as I sit amongst the cedar shavings and guinea pig turds, contemplating the various ironies that fit together like puzzle pieces to form my current situation. There wasn't anything remotely like it on the box top of how my life was previously pictured... with one admitted exception.

Goddamn, I need a fix.

Only heroin isn't the dragon I'm chasing these days. Nope, the name of the game this time around is Vitamin A or free sugars or whatever the fuck it is in carrots that my new body chemistry can't seem to get enough of. Think you know the ecstasy of mainlining black tar or China white? I'm here to bear witness that that almost religious experience is as nothing compared to taking a nibble on the one true God of edible taproots. Amen brother, testify.

The only problem is, a month or so ago a clean and sober Pickles read all about the dangers of carrot addiction on some online forum dedicated to guinea pig ownership, so now I'm lucky if I get one small baby carrot a week. Again, you think you know withdrawal? You know nothing. To get me by between all-too-infrequent fixes, Pickles gives me a single grape with my morning food pellets (which taste, incidentally, about the same going in as I imagine they do coming out). Now the grapes aren't entirely unwelcome, it's just that they're a piss-poor, sickly sweet substitute for the bliss of orange-colored vegetables... they're basically the herbivore equivalent of methadone.

On the whole, though, things aren't so bad once you accept your fate as some bizarre variation on a Buddhist theme. Strung out on Thompson Seedless and hoping against hope to score some carotene I may be, but Pickles has decked out the cage with tubes and hidey holes I find surprisingly entertaining, and the female guinea pig, Sadie, lets me fuck her whenever the urge hits (which is often... don't judge me).

And those guinea pig turds I mentioned?

Yeah, well... at least this go-round I'm regular.

Blart.

At the age of sixteen, Lance Shoeman's first published story appeared in the horror magazine *Haunts*. Fast-forward through 25+ years of wife and kids to when an old friend of his (Todd Hanson of *The Onion*) convinced him to get his head back in the game. In the period since then he's had quite a few stories published or accepted and awaiting publication. These include "I'm Not Going to Be That Guy" in the BSA-nominated anthology *Slices of Flesh*, and "All This'll Be Yours" in the upcoming anthology *Strange California*.

The Valhalla Arms

By Robert Allen Lupton

Cassandra helped Pamela dress, lifted her into a wheelchair, and pushed her into the hall. The hallway was lined with photos and framed newspaper clippings of the two of them and their teammates, wearing brightly colored spandex and leather costumes.

Cassie stopped and pointed at a color reproduction of a magazine cover which read, "Victory in Brazil". The twelve masked young women were draped across a disabled army tank that displayed a *Dia de los Muertos* symbol. The women were posed like WW2 pinup girls painted on the nose of a B52 bomber.

Pamela turned toward Cassie and said, "Damn, woman, we sure looked good."

Cassie answered slowly; her stroke and the Parkinson's demanded full concentration in order to pronounce words properly. "We still do. That was fifty years ago. I'd be happy to have the head of hair I had back then. It'd be nice to have real knees again. I'm grateful for the titanium, you understand; they're the only joints that don't hurt."

"At least you can walk," said Pamela. She straightened her glasses and said, "It's hard to believe it's been fifty years, and there are only four of us left. Time was the real villain."

"Yes," said Cassie. She struggled to find the words and pronounce them clearly. "You aged better than any of us; you're still a perfect vision."

"Don't call me Perfect Vision, it embarrasses me. Red hair gone white, coke bottle eyeglasses, and my legs don't work. I'm a long way from the cover girl superhero I used to be. Getting old isn't for sissies."

"Sorry, code names are only for missions. Don't call me Spellbinder, and I won't call you Perfect Vision. Let's have breakfast and give the twins a bridge lesson," said Cassie and she pushed Pamela into the dining nook.

Margaret, the maid, cook, nurse, and building manager took the wheelchair from Cassie and rolled Pamela to the table. "Good morning. I cooked sausage and mushroom quiche. Water's hot for tea, and my homemade crumpets are ready. I haven't seen Wanda and Wilma. I guess they're sleeping in today."

Pamela laughed, "Probably afraid to get their Louisiana clocks cleaned at bridge again. Playing cards against a couple of old Victory Valkyries is a far cry from hustling tourists at three card monte on Bourbon Street. We'll have some tea while the Cajun Cuties finish their beauty sleep. Those girls are barely eighty years old."

Margaret put the tea set on the table and disappeared down the hall. Cassie said, "You're not being fair to the girls. They don't have a good leg between them. They manage their osteoarthritis with pain killers and booze. It's not a good plan, but works for them.

"Being wheelchair bound is hard for everyone, but it's especially difficult for former Olympic champions. Wanda's Alzheimer's is worse, and Wilma's mind has never been right since Blackout mind-zapped her in our final battle against the Jaguar Death Cult. I'm amazed the girls can still play bridge, but they learned to count cards before they were ten years old. It's like muscle memory for them. They still believe I can see through the cards with my x-ray vision."

Cassie raised her teacup to a framed photograph of the twins. Wanda and Wilma, young and beautiful, were dressed in Olympic uniforms. The headline read, 'Cajun Cuties win multi-discipline Olympic medals.' "They were the media darlings that year. They finished first and second in every gymnastic event. They were even better at track and field. Wanda won the high jump, long jump, and pole vault. Wilma won the heptathlon, steeple chase, and one of the dashes. One won a boxing gold, and the other won gold in judo."

"I remember. My body doesn't work, but my mind's fine. That's why we recruited them to join the Victory Valkyries. This tea's a little cold; could you hit it with a warming spell?"

"I'll give it a try." Cassie, the Spellbinder, gestured with her right hand and her fingers trembled uncontrollably. She pointed her index finger at the teacup and said, *"Fervidus aqua"*, the magic phrase for hot water. Her stroke-damaged lips couldn't say the word, aqua. Her magic enforced the one command word she'd spoken, *fervidus*. Everything she pointed toward got hotter. Her Parkinson's-ravaged aim ignited the table cloth, the carpet, the window shades and cabinets.

Flames erupted, following the path of Spellbinder's quaking finger around the room. Pamela pushed back from the blazing table, threw her burning napkin to the floor, and screamed for Margaret. "Fire, Margaret, fire. She's set the kitchen on fire again. Bring the extinguisher."

The right synapses finally fired and Cassie said *"aqua"*. So much time had passed since she'd invoked the *fervidus* command, though, that her powers treated it as a new command and water spewed from her shaking index finger. Cassie grabbed her wrist with her other hand and managed to aim the spray at the fires. Before she could say *"Aqua desista"*, the hard spray shoved Pamela's wheelchair across the room and into Margaret as she charged into the room with a fire extinguisher in her hand.

Margaret tripped over the wheelchair, and the fire extinguisher flew into the air. It discharged as it bounced across the floor and sprayed Cassie and the table with sticky white foam. Cassie cleaned her face with her napkin, looked at the charred sodden mess, laughed, and said, "At least the quiche and crumpets are still in the oven. Let's have breakfast on the patio?"

Margaret helped Pamela change into dry clothes and took her to the patio where Cassie, her hair wrapped in a bath towel, was seated. "I brought the quiche and a couple sodas. We can't cook anything else until the contractor fixes the kitchen. I called the insurance company and they'll send an adjuster this afternoon. This was the third fire this year. I expect they'll cancel our coverage."

Margaret continued, "I forgot to tell you in all the excitement, but Wanda and Wilma are gone. They took their motorized wheelchairs and left early this morning. They left a note. They saw something on television and are convinced the Jaguar Death Cult is back, and plans to attack downtown sometime today. They took their female jester masks, but not their costumes. I notified the police to be on the lookout for two eighty-year-old women in battery powered wheelchairs wearing New Orleans Saints' jerseys and Mardi Gras masks. I told the officer they were probably festooned with purple, green, and gold beads, and he asked if I was reporting missing persons or a parade."

Pamela spit her soda across the table and said, "Cass, let's go after them. If they think they're still fighting the Jaguar Death Cult, they won't recognize the police. When they see men in uniform, they'll fight. Crippled and old as they are, once they get their hands on a policeman or anyone who makes them feel threatened, people will get hurt."

"I know they're tough. They teach wheelchair karate at the senior center. How do you propose we find them? I'm afraid to try a searching spell. Maybe you can see them?"

"If I can find a high enough vantage point. My powers still work. I can use my telescopic and microscopic vision because they won't damage my glasses. I hope we won't need my laser or x-ray vision. The last time I used laser vision, my glasses melted and the burning plastic ignited my blouse and bra. I ripped off my top and brassiere and flashed my old tits at everyone on the street. X-ray vision isn't any better. Once my glasses melt, I can't see crap."

"I'll take you high enough to see the whole city. I'll need the gurney stored in the garage. We'll put the sides up and strap ourselves in. I'll enchant the gurney, and it'll work like Apollo's chariot being pulled through the sky by flying horses. We'll fly around the city until you spot the girls."

"Great plan, a hospital bed and flying horses, what could go wrong?"

Margaret retrieved the gurney from the garage, rolled it down the driveway, and placed it next to the entrance sign, "VAHALLA ARMS – Women's Retirement Center". She set the wheel brakes to keep the gurney from rolling into the street and raised the guardrails on three sides.

Spellbinder and Perfect Vision didn't wear their old spandex costumes; they wore brightly colored exercise pants and windbreakers over an assortment of leg and arm braces. They didn't wear masks, but Perfect Vision wore a strap to hold her glasses.

Margaret pointed to parallel rut marks in the grass front yard. "If they didn't turn around, they're headed toward the river."

Pamela said, "This is a mission. Since we're on a mission, we'll use our code names. Until we're back home, I'm Perfect Vision and you're Spellbinder."

Spellbinder put one hand on the gurney, concentrated, and managed to clearly pronounce "*Apollinis Chariotus*". The gurney shimmered and quivered with excitement. The guardrails rattled as it bounced and vibrated. It wanted to fly.

She focused her attention on a mouse hidden in the marigolds, pointed one shaking finger, and said, "*Transformus Pegasus.*" Unfortunately, she actually said,"*Transformus Pigasus.*" There was a flash of light and a confused-looking winged pink pig walked toward the gurney.

"My God, what have you done? A flying pig? What good is a flying pig?"

While Spellbinder tried to enunciate an answer, her trembling finger continued to spray the spell across the flower bed. Five more pink winged pigs appeared in flashes of light and followed the first pig to the gurney.

"Sorry," said Spellbinder. "How embarrassing, but I'm sure the pigs will be fine. Three on each side are strong enough to carry us. Margaret can help me harness the pigs and we'll be on our way."

The pigs were harnessed, Spellbinder belted herself to the gurney, and Margaret raised the final guardrail until it snapped in place. Spellbinder tapped a rail to get the pigs' attention and raised her arms like a symphony conductor. The pigs took off with the precision of a ballet company and lifted the gurney into the sky.

The noise of the city faded to a dull buzz and the only sound was the metronomic regularity of six sets of pink wings flapping in perfect rhythm. Perfect Vision said, "It's been years since I've been airborne. I didn't realize how much I miss it. Sorry I complained about your pigs; they're doing great. Keep us steady and I'll search the city."

Perfect Vision swept the city street by street with her telescopic vision. She spotted two motorized wheelchairs on Wharf Street. The twins rolled at full speed toward the abandoned warehouses that stood as silent sentinels along the old wharf. She shouted, "I see them. Take us to the warehouse district."

Spellbinder motioned the pigs to descend. The gurney dropped at three hundred feet per minute. One of the pig's harnesses broke and the gurney lurched and tilted. The other five pigs flapped harder to compensate. Perfect Vision panicked. "Pig down! We're a pig down."

"Don't worry. Five pigs are enough. Be quiet, I need to concentrate."

"Can you make the pigs stronger or make us weigh less?"

"Maybe, but I don't want a spell to misfire while we're almost a mile in the air."

Another harness broke, and the gurney tipped dangerously toward the unsupported corner. Perfect Vision slid backwards and pinned Spellbinder against the guardrail. The four remaining pigs flapped their wings like big pink hummingbirds trying to keep the gurney in a controlled descent, but it dropped even faster. As it fell, it began to spin. The rotation was slow at first, but the spin picked up speed the further they fell.

"Do something, even if it's wrong," screamed Perfect Vision.

Spellbinder held the guardrail with one hand, raised the other, and said, "*Pigasus Enormous.*" Only two pigs were affected by her spell. They grew larger until their harnesses broke under the pressure from their expanding girths. The two remaining pigs squealed in terror as the freefalling gurney dragged them spinning and tumbling toward the ground.

Spellbinder shouted to be heard over the screaming pigs, "*Pondum Imperaro.*" The magic phrase meant 'control the weight' and gave her the ability to adjust the weight of gurney. Spellbinder knew everything fell at the same speed, regardless of weight, except things that are lighter than air like balloons or dirigibles. She used her free hand, palm held level, and lowered her hand to lower the weight of the gurney. She stopped the descent, but the gurney didn't hover in the air; it started to go back up.

She moved her hand up and down until she found the buoyancy point where the gurney didn't descend or ascend. She freed the two terrified and exhausted pigs and rebalanced the buoyancy to compensate for the loss of their weight. The pigs gathered in a flock, squealed and flew away.

Perfect Vision said, "Whether I live through this or not, I'm going to kill you when this is over. Maybe not today, but twenty years from now a 105-year-old woman is going to wheel out of an alley some dark night and hit you with a baseball bat. Get me on the ground."

"I want on the ground too. First, I need to level the gurney." She turned her palm slightly and the gurney mimicked the motion. Once the gurney was level, she raised her palm and the gurney started to descend.

"Why does it go down instead of up when you raise your hand?"

"I'm controlling the weight. When I increase the weight, we go down. If I lower my hand and decrease the weight, we'll go back up. It's like backing a car, it doesn't steer the same as it does when you drive forward."

"Spare me the stupid details. I lost sight of the girls when we were spinning like a top. I'll try to find them again."

Spellbinder cautiously brought the gurney closer to the ground. During the descent, the gurney didn't go straight down; it drifted with the wind. They were still higher than the tallest buildings when she noticed the wind was carrying them toward the river.

When Perfect Vision noticed their direction of travel, she said, "You have to get us down before the river. I can't swim. If we land on the other side, we'll have to call a handicap-certified cab to drive us back across. I don't want to use a cab on a rescue mission; riding in this stupid gurney is embarrassing enough. "

"All right, hang tight." Spellbinder raised her hand and tripled their rate of descent. She stopped the gurney about twenty feet above an abandoned warehouse, and hovered while they drifted with the wind toward an overgrown parking area. As soon as they cleared the edge of the building, she raised her hand and the gurney dropped to the pavement, bounced over a pile of rusted pipes and concrete rubble, and came to a stop against a broken light pole.

Spellbinder and Perfect Vision sat on the mattress and waited for the adrenalin rush to pass. "Nice landing, Amelia Earhart. What happens to the pigs? Will they turn back into mice? If they're flying when they change, will they die?"

"I didn't put a time limit on the transformation. It wasn't a Cinderella spell; the pigs don't change back at midnight. Pigs are smart and they can survive almost anywhere. If flying pigs behave like pigeons, I'd hate to park my car under a pig roost."

"The last time I saw the girls, they were less than a mile from here on Wharf Street. I can guide us, but I can't walk and we didn't bring my wheelchair. What are you going to do, make a flying carpet? I hope not, I've had enough flying for today."

"What a wonderful idea. We don't have a carpet, but this mattress will do. I'll use two of those pieces of pipe for controls like on a biplane. You can pilot. One pipe controls direction, forward is down, back is up and left and right are left and right. The other pipe controls speed. Forward is faster."

Spellbinder lowered a guardrail, lifted Perfect Vision from the gurney, and pulled the mattress to the ground. She found two short sections of pipe with sharp ends and jabbed them into the mattress near one end. She helped Perfect Vision into a seated position with the pipes between her knees.

Spellbinder sat behind Perfect Vision and chanted, "*Matteresso volanto*".

"Nothing happened. It didn't work."

"You're the driver, it won't move until you operate the controls. Bring the stick back to raise us off the ground and then move the other stick forward until we move as fast as you want."

"We won't go very fast or very high." Perfect Vision moved one pipe and the mattress quivered and hovered about a foot off the ground. She inched the speed control forward until the mattress flew at a fast walking pace.

"The gate's locked—don't fly into the fence."

"I won't be taking any flying lessons from you. I see the fence," said Perfect Vision, and she elevated the mattress over the razor wire coiled atop the fence and then dropped it back to a foot above the pavement. She increased the speed, drove on the right side of the road, and weaved her way through the maze of old warehouses until they reached Wharf Street. "This corner is the last place I saw the girls. I've used my telescopic vision, but I can't see them anywhere."

"Try microscopic vision instead. Maybe you can track the wheel marks from their motorized chairs."

Perfect Vision scanned the area and didn't see wheel tracks on the crumbling asphalt. Suddenly she smiled and laughed. "Beads, I see Mardi Gras beads. They left a trail for us." She pointed to a spectacularly dilapidated building and drawled, "Partner, they went thataway."

She engaged the mattress controls and flew slowly above the trail of purple, green, and golden beads. The path led to a rusty corrugated metal sliding door. Spellbinder crawled off the mattress and managed to force the door open far enough for the mattress to pass through. They flew inside.

The inside was lit by sunbeams shining through holes in the metal roof. The dust in the air made the beams seem solid, like glowing columns extending from the ceiling to the oil-stained concrete floor. Perfect Vision indicated four parallel tracks through the dust on the floor. The tracks disappeared into the darkness across the warehouse.

"Wheelchair tracks," she said and held one finger in front of her mouth for silence. Spellbinder slashed one finger across her throat to acknowledge the need for quiet and motioned into the warehouse with her other hand.

The two balanced on the mattress and Perfect Vision flew them above the tracks. She whispered, "My telescopic vision isn't any good in here. There's too much dust in the air."

The warehouse was gigantic, almost three hundred yards long, and the women crossed most of it before they saw the stacks of pallets piled from floor to ceiling. The bead trail continued into the darkness of a forklift aisle between two tall rows of pallets. Perfect Vision said, "I can't see in the dark without melting my glasses. Can you make some light?"

In a low voice, Spellbinder said, "I think so. I have a great light spell. I say let there be light." She raised both arms to encompass the entire warehouse and said *"Et Eras Lumen"*. However, what came out of her mouth was *"Et Eras Lignum"* or 'let there be firewood'. The warehouse brightened considerably when the pallets began to burn.

"That's plenty bright, but not what I had in mind," said Perfect Vision in a deadpan voice.

Three men ran from between the pallets. Two other men followed, dragging another man between them. A moment later, Wilma motored out of the stacks. Her carnival mask was askew and she drove her wheelchair with one hand. The other hand held a scarf tightly wrapped around the neck of a man who stumbled at one side of her wheelchair. The five men circled back and surrounded Wilma. The shortest man held one arm limply at his side and said to Wilma, "You better let George go. You let him go, and we'll all leave and go our separate ways. Those pallets are loaded with guns and bullets. When the fire gets to the bullets, this place will be a shooting gallery."

Wilma twisted the scarf tighter and said, "Make me let him go. Come over here and I'll break your other damn arm for you."

The little man said, "We can rush her, there's six of us."

One of the men held his knee and said, "The last time we tried anything, she broke your arm, punched out David, and kicked me in my knee. I think we should leave George and the old lady to work this out."

"Don't be stupid. There's six of us and one of her."

Wanda rolled clear of the burning pallets. A man in a black watch cap and *Dia de los Muertos* shirt walked behind her holding an assault rifle to the back of her head. Wanda said, "That's six to two, little man. Make that seven to two. I can count, even if you can't. This Death Cult soldier doesn't have the guts to shoot me. When he gets close enough for me to grab him, I'll make him eat his rifle."

Wanda rolled to her twin sister. Wilma tightened the scarf and said, "Drop the rifle or I'll break his neck."

"Break his neck and I'll shoot you both."

The men and the twins were so occupied with each other that they hadn't noticed Spellbinder and Perfect Vision sitting on a floating mattress in the brightening firelight. Spellbinder shouted, "That's seven to four and two of you are injured. Drop the rifle."

The little man said, "Seven to four and I don't think any of you can walk. Besides, you're a bunch of old ladies. I'm going to count to five and he's going start shooting." He yelled at the man with the watch cap, "Shoot the one with the scarf before she breaks George's neck. Once George is loose, we'll run for it. Leave these old bitches to burn."

Spellbinder whispered to Perfect Vision. "Blast the gun with your laser vision."

"When I do my glasses will melt and I won't be able to see anything."

"No, I've been thinking about that. Only use one eye for laser vision. Keep the other one closed. You'll only melt one lens. Open the other eye, aim again, and keep zapping them until they've had enough."

"I never thought of that. Good idea. What are you going to do?"

"I'm going to stay behind you and be a backseat driver. I've burned our kitchen, set a stash of guns and ammunition on fire, and created a race of flying pigs. I think that's enough for one day."

"If the melted glass burns my tits, there'll be hell to pay," said Perfect Vision. She closed her left eye and focused the right eye on the assault rifle. A beam of vivid red light burst from her right eye and punched a hole though the assault rifle and the hand holding it. The gunman and Perfect Vision both screamed in pain. He grabbed his hand and dropped to his knees. She brushed molten glass from her breast and slapped at her burning blouse.

Wilma popped a wheelie, spun her wheelchair in a tight circle, and rolled into the kneeling man. She punched him in the throat and he went down. She turned toward the men surrounding her sister and said, "This old lady is going to kick your sorry asses."

She charged and the men broke and ran. Wanda maintained her grip on George and said, 'We'll keep this blood-sacrificing, death-worshiping, gun-smuggling bastard. Wilma, bring that skinny piece of crap on the ground. These two can identify the others and tell us where their temple is hidden. We'll roll through them like grease through a goose.'

Spellbinder shouted, "We have to leave; this place is going to be an inferno any second. When the bullets start exploding, this'll be like a pinball game. We have to go now."

Wilma rolled around her victim and grabbed him by one foot. She made it out the door behind Wanda and her choking captive. Perfect Vision drove the mattress out the door. They didn't stop until they were across the parking lot. Bullets began to explode and it sounded like popcorn when it just gets to temperature, only a few pops now and then. The popping increased and foreshadowed the cacophony to come.

Spellbinder said, "I think I can stop this. I have to try."

"Hell, honey, you started it. Take your best shot," said Perfect Vision.

"*Aqua Columna Erecta*," shouted Spellbinder at the river. A waterspout churned and grew wider and taller. Spellbinder moved her hand toward the building and the top of the waterspout bent and discharged thousands of gallons of water into the flaming warehouse and doused the fire in seconds."

Spellbinder clenched her fist and the waterspout dissolved. Wanda gave George's scarf another twist and said, "That was impressive. Why so dramatic, couldn't you just tell the fire to go out?"

"I couldn't remember the words."

Wilma shook her unconscious victim's foot and said, "We need to make these two Death Cult members tell us where their partners have gone. I'll find their temple and tear it down, stone by bloodstained stone."

Perfect Vision piloted the mattress to Wilma's wheelchair and touched Wilma on the arm. "Wilma, the Jaguar Death Cult is finished. We shut them down years ago. They had a million soldiers in their army, but their army is gone. There aren't any more sacrificial temples, we destroyed them all. This man and his friend aren't cultists, they're criminals, gunrunners. We'll turn them over to the police. They can handle it."

"Don't tell me there's no Jaguar Death Cult. Their emblem is on his shirt. I know the Jaguar leader, Blackout, is responsible for this."

"It's just a shirt," said Spellbinder. "The emblem signifies *Dia de los Muertos*, the Day of the Dead. It's not the symbol of death and blood sacrifice anymore; it stands for the day to honor your ancestors. Blackout's been dead for fifty years. He tried to control your mind and your sister's mind at the same time. He wasn't strong enough, and you threw him into a volcano in Chile."

"I did, didn't I? I don't always remember things."

"Somehow you and Wanda found a gunrunning operation. People across the city have seen the smoke and the waterspout. I imagine there's been a thousand 911 calls. We should be gone before the police get here. Let's tear the mattress sheets into strips and tie up these two for the police to find. The cops will find the other men and the guns. Margaret will be worried, let's go home."

'Lunch?" asked Wilma.

"Lunch, but maybe a shower first."

The girls tied both men to a chain link fence near the smoking warehouse. Wanda hung tricolored sets of Mardi Gras beads around their necks. "A little hint to the police about who to thank."

Wanda and Wilma each held a rear corner of the flying mattress and Perfect Vision towed them to the gurney. Spellbinder did most of the lifting and placed the mattress and Perfect Vision on the gurney. She used the flying pig harnesses to attach the motorized wheelchairs to one end of the gurney.

Wanda and Wilma took the lead and team-towed the gurney to Wharf Street and turned toward home. The four women waved at the parade of police cars and firetrucks. Only one policeman stopped. He asked if they needed help. He said it wasn't every day he encountered two motorized wheelchairs towing a hospital gurney down a city street.

Wanda told him, "Mind your own business, flatfoot. We're out for a walk, except we can't walk. It sounds stupid to say we're out for a roll, but we're out for a roll. You got a problem with that?"

"No, ma'am," said the officer and tipped his hat. "You ladies have a nice roll."

Just before sunset, two enormous pigs flew through a missing skylight atop an abandoned warehouse near the wharf. Four smaller pigs flew behind them. The warehouse was dry and comfortable. There was plenty of water and food along the river. The pigs started building a nest, since this was the perfect place to start a flock. The pigeons abandoned the building three days later.

Margaret had meals delivered until the kitchen was repaired. The girls took their meals and played bridge under the magnolia tree on the patio. They got caught in the rain a few times and twice the flying pigs deposited an unpleasant surprise under the tree, but what's a little rain and pig poop to the women who put the Jaguar Death Cult out of business?

The first morning after the kitchen work was finished, Cassandra helped Pamela dress, lifted her into the wheelchair, and pushed her down the hall.

Cassie stopped and pointed at an enlarged color reproduction of a magazine cover which read, "Victory in Brazil." The women in the picture posed like World War Two pinup girls painted on the nose of a B52 bomber.

Pamela turned her head toward Cassie and said, "Damn, woman, we sure looked good."

Cassie smiled and said, "We sure did. After breakfast, let's go find those damn pigs."

Robert Allen Lupton is retired and lives in New Mexico with his wife, Sally, where they are commercial hot air balloon pilots. Robert runs and writes every day, but not necessarily in that order. Visit www.amazon.com/author/luptonra, his Amazon page, and www.goodreads.com/author/show/15292457.Robert_Allen_Lupton (his Goodreads page) and blog for current information about his stories and books.

Me, My Zombie-Self, and the Blonde Girl

By Patrick Winters

So, yeah, my story...

Okay. Here goes: I was a ghost, for a while. But, I was also a zombie. At the same time.

Yeah, I know—stay with me. Maybe if I try starting from the beginning...

Well, I'm not sure how "in the know" you are with news and goings-on of the mortal world and all, but... things kind of went to shit. Like, *real* shit. Real, solid, coiling-in-the-toilet kind of shit. And it just wouldn't flush. The politicians you always saw yelling on television had started yelling louder, and the ones who used to talk calmly and were all trite ended up joining in on the shit-storm. Fears started to rise. Riots broke out in every major city, in just about every nation. Armies started locking and loading globally while their governments saw to closing borders and holing up behind newly-made walls. Reports of nukes wiping out small but "potential threat" countries were flooding in and scaring everyone all the more.

And that was all before the Outbreak even began.

That's what it became known as, over time. Some kind of disease or something. No scientific name, or explanation. At least none that the public was ever told of. There were theories, of course. None of which were ever corroborated by any sort of official or whatever. It just seemed to start happening, all across the U.S. And the rest of the world, too. People dying, getting bitten, coming back to life, and then repeating the process.

I, uh... I didn't pay a... a whole lot of attention to the Outbreak and everything going on with it. Especially at the beginning. All the politicians and newscasters on TV, the Facebook and Twitter feeds flooding with rants and articles, the protests that started up, people wanting information and answers... It all kinda bummed me out. And, I never really "did politics," you know? Had other things on my mind and matters at heart. Getting a girlfriend. That was a big one. Paying the rent. Bong hits. Lots of bong hits, actually... So, yeah—veering more into my lane now.

I had been born and raised in Sandwich, Massachusetts, and sure enough, that's where I was when things went south for me. Well, further south, I suppose. *Deep* south. I...

Huh? Yeah, there really is a town called Sandwich in Massachusetts. In Barnstable County, right along the Cape Cod Canal and Cape Cod Bay. It was always pretty quaint and quiet, even after the Outbreak started up. The disease and those affected by it hadn't reached that far north. At least, not yet. Get this—the town motto is... was... "after so many shipwrecks, a haven." Sort of ironic, in retrospect, huh? Well, anyways, I'd lived there all my life. I'd been working at the local Dollar General for the last year of my life and had just started living on my own. I was finally starting to 'adult.' Had an apartment all to myself. King of the castle! Me, myself, and I. No one else... at all... ever...

I was never the most sociable of people, no matter how much I wanted to be. Didn't have regular hangouts with buddies, and my phone wasn't exactly blowing up with texts from anybody. And, like I mentioned, I didn't have a girlfriend. Girls... I just never really seemed to be on their radar. And they never seemed to want to be on mine, so...

N—No, I'm *not*! Yeah, I have done that! I'm not *that* pathetic. Why do you wanna... ? What do you care?! Yes, I have! When? Well, this time... in high school, this girl and I, uhm...

Look, that's not the point of the story, okay? Geez! Can I get back to what I'm actually trying to tell you?

Okay. Like I said, I was living alone, and I didn't have a whole lot to do besides work. So, it wasn't surprising that I was home that Thursday night. The night it all happened. I'd just come off of a shift, night had fallen, and I was dead on my feet. Er—I mean, I was tired...

All I wanted was to have some dinner, some peace and quiet, and relax. As soon as I reached my apartment, though, I knew that wasn't gonna happen. My asshole neighbor, Gavin, was having one of his college-kid parties, so peace and quiet was out of the question. People were coming in and out of his place with kegs, laughing and screaming to the music vibrating through the walls. Some were even lounging out in the halls with red Solo cups in hand and their arms around each other. I guess a part of me wished I had been invited over, but I knew Gavin wasn't about to do that. We never liked each other. So, I awkwardly weaved my way through them and reached my apartment, only to find that someone had set a condom over my doorknob—unused, thankfully. I peeled it off, snuck into my apartment, threw it away, and scrubbed my hands for ten minutes, trying to get the lubricant off of them. Better safe than sorry.

I had to listen to some awful dubstep or pop-rock or whatever you call that crap while I ate a microwave dinner at my kitchen table. Country fried steak, burnt. I threw it away when I found myself chewing to the repetitive beats of the music, and neither the food nor the tunes were doing much for the headache that was brewing in my noggin. When I'd tossed it in the trash, I almost gagged; something had gone rank in there. Smelled like a dead fish took a dump on some cottage cheese. Or a hobo took a shower in pee, with a skunk for a loofah. Or... Sorry, you get the picture.

I sealed up the garbage bag and went to toss it into the dumpsters behind the apartments. I took the stairs on my balcony—although I thought about just going out the front and through the halls. Maybe scare off the party people with the smell.

It was probably ten o'clock by then, and it was really dark out. I held my nose as I reached the dumpsters, lifted one's lid, and threw my garbage in. I turned around, taking in some fresher air again. And that's when I saw her.

Some girl was walking my way, groaning and shuffling along as she turned the corner. I couldn't see her very well in the darkness. She was kinda wobbling, though, and I figured right away that she was one of the people from Gavin's party, close to being drunk off her ass. I didn't know what to do. I could barely hold a conversation with a sober person, let alone a tipsy one. I gave her an awkward hello. Her, uh, moaning and all got louder, and she was coming at me pretty quick. I thought she was so out of it that she was gonna try to make out with me. You know, one of those "friendly" drunks. I just stood there, not knowing what to do. She was sticking her face up at mine before I could tell her to cool it.

And then she bit me. Sunk her teeth right into my neck. I screamed and started shoving her off, and she bit down harder. When I finally pushed her off, I felt bits of my skin and muscle tearing off in her mouth. Warm blood poured out onto my shirt; it felt so weird. I fell down screaming and she fell down in front of me. She started crawling right for me. I was kicking frantically at her as I held my neck; one lucky shot hit her square in the face, and she fell back again, smacking her head on one of the dumpsters. Hard, and with a cracking sound. She didn't get back up after that.

I looked at my hands, all covered in my own blood, and I nearly hurled. I was growing dizzy and my skin was already burning hot. I was about to cry out for help when I heard more groaning. When another two shambling people came around the corner, I understood what was going on: the Outbreak had finally reached Sandwich.

I got to my feet and I bolted. I think I called out as I ran, but I'm really not sure. No one came to help—that I am sure of. But from all I'd heard of the Outbreak and its effects, no one could have helped. I'd been bitten. I was done for. But I ran anyway, through my neighborhood, down the streets and in between houses, wanting to get as far away from those things as possible. I wound up in the western part of town, by the woods, and I went on in. I don't know how far I went into the trees before I collapsed. I felt like my skin was on fire, and all of me was soaked with either blood or sweat. Maybe, uh... maybe even a little pee... Don't judge me.

The last thing I remember seeing—while I was still alive, that is—was trees and stars. And then I was gone. I faded.

Then morning came. I opened my eyes and, well, I was just floating above the ground.

Tried rolling over onto my side, and next thing I knew, I was just hovering, face to face with pale dead-me. My corpse, that is. Boy, did I freak out at that one.

I stood up, such as it was, even though I didn't have legs anymore, and I would have been panting like a wuss if I'd had breath to breathe. I looked down at myself and I was... blue. And transparent. And naked. Like baby-blue fog with shape. Just my arms and my torso; everything below that had just disappeared. Don't get me started on that fact...

It didn't take me long to realize that I was a ghost. I'd watched enough movies to put that together, though I sure as hell wasn't happy about it. And looking down at my dead body kind of supported that idea. But, uh... dead-me didn't stay dead for long. I was busy trying to get a handle on floating when my body's eyes opened, it groaned, and it started to get up.

I freaked again. Or just prolonged my already established freak. Er—the point is, it didn't matter that I was already dead; I was scared and tried running away. From myself.

I turned and floated away in a hurry. I made it maybe five feet before I was just stopped. I couldn't go any further. I turned and tried floating/running the other way, and again, didn't get very far. Kept on trying, and nothing. I turned back and faced zombie me, who was just kind of looking around. Didn't even seem to notice me. He, it, whatever—started walking, and as he moved, I moved with it. It was like there was a tether attached to my non-existent ass.

Now, I would eventually realize that I could only go so far from my undead body. I was basically the leashed puppy to my zombie-self's dumb, slow owner. And it. Was. Dumb.

It hadn't even walked a couple of steps until it smacked right into a low-hanging branch. Cut up my—its—forehead pretty good, too. And as if that wasn't enough? Got its collar stuck to the branch. And it could. Not. Get. Off of it.

Seriously, it took it hours to get free. Kept on trying to walk and just couldn't tear the freaking collar. If I weren't dead already, I could have died from embarrassment.

I eventually tried getting it free myself, but my ghost hands weren't good for anything. My fingers just kept sinking through. I couldn't touch, move, or feel anything. So, I hovered around and waited. Got used to—or as used to—my situation as I could. Tried letting reality sink in, as much as it sucked. And it suuuucked.

I was dead. Or undead, or whatever you want to call it. But what was with the whole being a ghost thing, too? Never saw that before in any movies. Couldn't explain it. Why was I like that? Unfinished business? Well, yeah, I obviously had that. I think you could say that just about the whole world did, though; but as it would turn out, I never saw anyone else like me. No Ghosts and Mr. Zombies—no dead people floating around their old selves. But, it was what it was—I was what I was—and... I just couldn't change that...

Just like I couldn't change how dumb my zombie-self was. Damn it, it took him forever to get off that branch! Finally, after noon came and went, he got free and went on his way, dragging my ectoplasmic ass along with him.

He headed right back to town.

It took the apocalypse to make Sandwich an exciting place. By the time Dead-o and I got back, it was in shambles. Main Street and all of its stores and historic buildings were on fire. So were several houses and apartments. Blood and body parts were just about everywhere—lawns, streets, cars, trees, the docks. There was screaming coming from somewhere on the south side of town, but I wasn't seeing many live people, myself. Just hordes of those already turned and in various states of gory. Might have blown chunks seeing them, if my old stomach weren't standing five feet away from me.

I saw Merle the Mailman, looking pretty worse for wear. He was chasing a Rottweiler down the street. Not sure if that's poetic justice or just plain sick.

My zombie-self bumped into Nancy Cartwright's zombie and knocked her down an opened manhole on King Street. I'd had a huge crush on her in junior high, and I tried shouting apologies to her down the hole as zombie-me just kept walking. It turns out that even death can't kill insecurity.

At one point, zombie-me tried getting a bite from an old dead guy lying in his yard. Another zombie was already at him, though, and it kept pushing zombie-me away whenever he got close. I think it was Bradley Murphy, but it was kind of hard tell, what with half of his face being torn off. It'd be fitting if it were him; he always took my tater-tots at lunch when we were in grade school, and now his zombie was doing the equivalent to zombie-me.

I, uh... I didn't ever see my parents around. Alive or dead or undead. Which, in a way, I guess I'm glad for. I'd like to think that maybe they got away. I haven't seen them anywhere around here, at least, so maybe they did...

Well, after Dead-o and I finally finished our extensive tour of the town, it was nighttime. We were heading down the road leading out of Sandwich; I guess zombie-me was ready to look for food elsewhere. So, we went on, just like that, never to return. Here I was, finally leaving that place behind and moving on, and I was too damn dead to appreciate it. Not a time to be jamming Whitesnake, I can tell you that.

So began our road-trip south. I don't know how long we were going for. Maybe a week. Two? Maybe more. Time kind of stops mattering the same moment that your pulse does. Zombie-me being so damn slow didn't help speed things along, that's for sure. All I know is that it sucked the big one and seemed like forever. We were going through parts that had already been hit by the Outbreak, so it was slim pickings when it came to finding food for Dead-o. Hordes and stragglers were heading north while we went the opposite direction, thanks to my direction-challenged, dumbass corpse. He stuck mostly to the highways and the roads, but would occasionally sneak into the woods—I guess if he thought he'd heard something that might taste good.

The experience was a whole lot of awful. And, oddly, a whole lot of boring—at least for the most part. Just walking, and walking, and more walking. But it wasn't without its excitement and its hiccups, I can tell you that.

The day after we'd left Sandwich, a great big crow came swooping out of the sky and started attacking Dead-o's face. It kept pecking at him, and he kept trying to smack it away. After a while, the bird gave it up and flew off, but not until it had left my old face looking like a marinara-speckled block of Swiss cheese. And that wasn't the only animal trouble we had. Maybe a few days later, when he'd wandered off into the edge of the woods, Dead-o went hunting after a coyote pup he had seen scampering by. Chased it to its hidey-hole and stuck his left arm right in after it. But, as it turned out, either daddy or mommy coyote was home, and it bit down hard on zombie-me's arm and started shaking and pulling at it like crazy. Now, by this point, my old body was going bad quicker and quicker, so it didn't take much for the coyote to tear the arm right off, just below the shoulder. Not a pleasant moment for Dead-o or me, for sure. Zombie-me wised up after that; he got up and wandered back towards the road.

I'm not quite sure why, but I tried picking up the arm from the hole and taking it with us. I couldn't, of course; damn ghost hands and all. I guess I just used to be really attached to it.

Get it? "Attached to it?" Never mind...

Back to our odd odyssey. There was another rough point, when we were trying to go up a big hill in the road, that I started singing the theme music from Rocky, more to pass the time than to spur zombie-me on. But he sure needed it, though. He made it about halfway up the hill before he tripped and rolled all the way back down. Twice. And getting back up was a lot tougher to do with only one arm. After that, he walked with a limp in his leg. Yeah, he actually got slower. Ugh...

As sick and twisted as it may sound, in retrospect, I realize that I sort of looked forward to those kinds of moments. Made me worry about him more than myself and my whole tortured, trapped-ghost problems, you know? And you notice how I've taken to calling him "him," right? Not "me," but not "it," either? Because, I mean he was me. Sort of. But I tried not to see it like that. I started looking at him as being somebody else. A friend, for lack of a better word. That kind of goofball buddy you could point and laugh at when they screwed up instead of you. Like those guys on *Jackass*. Made me feel like all this bad shit wasn't just happening to me. Like I wasn't alone, when I was actually more alone than ever before...

I know, weird, but it helped me get by as we kept on going our lonely way. But, we wouldn't exactly be alone for much longer.

We were about to meet *her*. The Blonde Girl.

We'd yet to pass through any towns on our way, until we finally reached a place called Wilburton—which, when people had still been living there, looked like it would've been even smaller and duller than Sandwich. And here I thought that would've been statistically impossible. But there wasn't much to it, or much left, anyways. Just about one big main street made up most of the town, and like in Sandwich, it had been hit hard.

Someone's truck had plowed into the side of the rinky-dink post office. A dog-pile of zombie bodies lay in front of the police department, with what looked to be the sheriff at the bottom, chewed up pretty good and his gun still in hand. Went down fighting, I gotta give him that.

I didn't see many dead people walking about, at first. Started to figure they'd all headed north like most of the rest. But then Dead-o and I made our way to the outskirts of town, towards the countryside, where we reached an abandoned farm with a pretty big group of zombies swarming around an old shed in the back. Maybe twenty or so, all banging on its door and looking intent on getting in and at whatever was inside. Zombie-me was starting to make his way over and invite himself to the party, and I was wondering what all the ruckus was over, when it happened: the shed door flung open, gunshots rang out, and bodies started dropping. And I saw her...

The Blonde Girl came running through the crowd of the undead, dropping them as she fought her way through with only her handgun. I could see how beautiful she was, even with the bits of brains and viscera hitting her angry, scrunched-up face.

Her golden hair was whipping about, her pink lips were turned up in a cute little snarl, and her eyes flashed with brilliant blue. Even enraged, she looked like an angel, like... Xena, Warrior Princess mixed with Miss Universe. And whatever I still had that could pass for a heart ached to see her. I guess it was kinda love at first sight, or at least the closest I'd ever come to it. But she was the sort of girl that wouldn't have spared a glance at me when I was alive; what chance would I have when I was dead? But still, I was head over ghost-heels for her.

The trouble was, zombie-me was becoming just as interested in her, but for very different reasons. While Etta James' "At Last" was playing in my mind, Weird Al's "Eat It" was starting up in his. He gave a hungry groan when he saw her and managed to pick up the pace a tad.

Meanwhile, the Blonde Girl had taken down a few more of the undead and was sprinting away from them. She turned around the shed's corner and ran off towards an old well a few dozen yards off. When she reached it and looked back around, I realized what she was planning.

Before the other zombies could chase after her and catch sight of her again, she put a leg over the well's mouth and leapt in, grabbing hold of the rope hanging down into it. She skedaddled out of sight just as the crowd of undead turned the corner and went looking for her in the trees beyond the well, none the wiser to where she really was.

Good plan. Would have worked, if zombie-me hadn't have seen her.

He brought up the end of the wandering, moaning crowd, and he went right up to the well while the others disappeared into the woods. I floated up to the well before he got there, hollering at the girl to watch out for zombie-me. But there was no way she could've heard me. I looked down, and there she was, hanging by the rope and starting to climb on up, thinking that the danger must have passed.

She looked right up into my eyes without seeing me, and then Dead-o came charging right through me and reaching for her with a growl. That fight in her eyes was replaced by surprise. She gave a quick scream and lifted a hand to swat his away; she lost her grip on the rope and fell straight down. She screamed again as she splashed down—this time in pain.

Dead-o and I looked down at her, me worried, him slobbering.

She was sitting in the shallow water, about ten feet below, and I could see that she was grabbing at her leg. She was really hurting. She sat like that for a while, cursing and glancing up now and again to zombie-me.

When she was good and pissed off, she pulled out her gun and aimed it right at Dead-o's head.

I remember thinking, "This is it. She'll kill Dead-o, and then we'll both be gone. It'll finally all be over."

When she pulled the trigger, nothing happened. She kept on pulling, looking as upset as I felt, but the gun wouldn't fire. It was out of bullets.

After a dozen frantic tries she broke down crying and threw the gun at the stone wall. Then she held her face in her hands and just let it out. I might have joined in, if I could've. Seeing and hearing her like that... it was awful.

Zombie-me stayed by the well the whole time she was down there, hanging over it and reaching down for her with his remaining arm. Couldn't reach her at all, but he wasn't gonna give up on a meal, though.

I started to get pissed at him and I yelled at him. Told him to leave her alone. Tried to fight him off and pull him away. But I couldn't.

So the three of us just stayed like that, waiting.

By the time the Blonde Girl mellowed out, the sun was going down. She got her shit together again, looking like she was ready for a fight. She pulled out a knife from her belt and tried standing up. She could barely do it; her leg buckled when she rose up, and she was obviously still in pain. But she looked up to Dead-o and me and put the knife in her teeth. She grabbed the rope and started climbing up, and I started freaking out.

There was no way she could get out of there without fighting off zombie-me, and as hurt as she was, I didn't think she could do it and win. Even with one arm, he would bite her and tear her up before she could get a chance to use that knife.

While she climbed, I floated around, totally wigging out and wondering what the hell I should do—and what I even could do. When I heard her give a shout, I turned back around.

She was nearly to the top, and zombie-me was slashing out for her. She was barely holding on as she dangled about, hoisting herself up with the rope in one hand while she tried to use the knife on him.

When he nearly clawed her face off, I rushed over and tried grabbing him again. I wanted—needed—to save her. I put my hands around his arms, I pulled back—and it worked! *It finally freaking worked!*

I totally Patrick Swayze-d it and got him back just far enough for the Blonde Girl to get over the mouth of the well. Then she jammed that knife right into Dead-o's forehead.

All of a sudden, I felt like my body, or my essence, or whatever you'd call it, was being pulled. Like I was falling backwards without falling.

My vision went blurry as zombie-me fell down dead—real, done for dead—and the Blonde Girl hopped out of the well. I heard her give a small cheer of accomplishment and then I heard nothing at all. My vision faded completely into blinding white, the Blonde Girl gone for good.

My last thought on earth was thinking that, after all this time, I had finally done something right with my life. Er—you know what I mean. And it felt good, especially knowing that I'd helped the Blonde Girl.

And then...

"... and then I wound up *here*," the young man finished, waving a hand around to the fiery red cavern. The chains clapped about his thin wrists gave a rattle as he did so. The sound of a cracking whip rang out from a nearby chamber, punctuated by an agonized cry.

"In a line full of people in loincloths, walking up to a big red guy who told me that I hadn't gone to church enough, I had watched too much porn in life, and that I was damned to an eternity spent in the glorious flames of Hell."

The young man laughed with a shake of his head. "And here I thought that being a ghost-zombie sucked balls..."

He went silent and looked down as a burly, winged denizen of the depths passed by them on his rounds. It smelled like sulfur and meat gone bad, and it carried a whipping cane in its clawed fist. When it had disappeared, the young man turned back to the old timer chained up beside him, the man who he'd just told his story to. "So, uh... what are you in for?" he asked him.

The old man blinked, still processing the odd tale, and then gave a shrug. "Well, like you said, the whole porn thing. And I sorta maybe killed my business partner. I thought he'd slept with my wife."

"...Did he?" the young man asked.

"No," the old man sighed. "Turns out it was her hairdresser who was doing that." He paused, looking profoundly reflective. "I sure didn't see that one coming..."

The young man wasn't quite sure what to say to that, so he thought it best to say nothing at all. He leaned his back against the jagged wall of rock behind them, reflecting some himself.

He felt a little better having shared his story, all things considered; a little inner peace didn't come often down here. Like, at all. So it was with a lightened heart that he once again turned his thoughts to the Blonde Girl. While a pyre of fire shot up from the floor a few feet away, charring some unfortunate souls chained up beside it, he wondered where she was right now and what life she had made for herself in the new world above. He hoped it was a good one. He hoped...

"Bare your woes and snivel, you dogs!" came a snarling voice from the adjoining cavern. "Set an example for our new arrivals!"

The young man looked over to see a snake-like soldier of Satan come stomping through, a rusted blade in hand and a group of chained souls behind it. Other demons were pulling the new damned additions away and locking them to the walls as the snake-man kept leading the rest along.

"Put that one there!" The reptilian pointed its blade at the bare spot beside the young man. It was shouting at a bumbling little freak who was leading along...

The young man's jaw dropped as he saw that it was the Blonde Girl, her hair reflecting the light of the fires about them and her body covered in unappealing (and yet very appealing) scraps of cloth. While haunted screams rang out through the caverns, Etta James started singing her song in the young man's head once more. And while it pained him to see her here, it also made him happy just to see her at all. He couldn't believe that it was really her.

The Blonde Girl was shoved down next to him, and her captor attached her shackles to the chains across the walls. Then the freaky little demon joined the rest of the souls and their punishers, moving along into the next cavern. The Blonde Girl tested her chains, shaking and pulling them with a grunt, ever the fighter. She gave it up when she realized there was no give to them.

She looked to the young man with a sigh and a slight scowl across her features.

He froze, his mouth opened and his eyes wide. He was having those veritable Vietnam flashbacks to his antisocial life and experiences with girls. But this was his moment and he had to take it.

He had to find just the right words to say, now that he could finally introduce himself to her after all this time. He needed a way to find some common ground before he eventually expressed all that he felt, to explain to her what they had already been through together, as unbelievable as it may all sound to her. He had to share just what she meant to him and in just the perfect fashion.

Instead, what came out was: "So, uh... do you come here often?"

Patrick Winters is a recent graduate of Illinois College in Jacksonville, IL, where he earned a degree in English Literature and Creative Writing. He has been published in the likes of *Sanitarium Magazine, Deadman's Tome, Trysts of Fate*, and other such titles. Winters is an avid listener of all things hard-rock and heavy-metal, a compendium of comic-book knowledge, can (and will) do a perplexing array of voice impersonations, and can bend his thumbs further back than any person should have the right/capability of doing. It is all quite odd. A full list of his previous publications may be found at his author's site, if you are so inclined to know: http://wintersauthor.azurewebsites.net/Pages/Previous%20Publications.

The Garden Troll

By Dan Foley

"Ricky! Ricky! I told you not to put a bridge over that pond!" Sara's voice, caustic and shrill, leapt out at him from the garden where she was bending over her trampled tomato plants.

"Look at my tomatoes. They're ruined, and all because you had to have that damn bridge. I told you it would be trouble. I told you, didn't I?"

Ricky left the edge of the pond where he had been sitting on a large stone tossing food to the goldfish, trying to coax them to the surface.

"Damn," he said when he saw the tomatoes. The ripe ones had been eaten while the plants and unripe ones had been trampled and torn apart. Worse, it smelled like something had pissed on them.

That something was currently peeking out at him from under the bridge. Ricky could see it out of the corner of his eye. He knew it had taken up residence under the bridge about two weeks ago. First the frogs had started to disappear, and then a few of the larger goldfish. As soon as he glanced over at it, it disappeared into the shadows beneath the bridge.

Ricky looked at his pond and wondered how things had gotten this far. He had always wanted a pond. So, one weekend, when Sara was visiting her mother, he had just rented a backhoe and dug one. It wasn't big: ten feet wide, twenty feet long, maybe ten feet deep. Luckily, the ground was mostly clay and held water without a liner. He had filled the pond from the well, added goldfish, and surrounded it with cattails and other plants. The frogs, and the one turtle, had shown up by themselves.

Later, he had added a smaller pond at one end and connected them by a small channel. A small submersible pump in the new pond recycled water back to a little stone waterfall he installed in the larger one. The channel, no more than two feet wide and filled with stones, became a stream and begged to be crossed by a picturesque, curved wooden bridge. But they were expensive. He knew Sara would really pitch a fit if he bought one of those.

Then he had found one to his liking (it was the price he liked best) sitting on the front lawn of an old Victorian mansion on the outskirts of Albany. A hand-written cardboard sign reading "Free" had been nailed to one rail. At the time he couldn't figure out why they wanted to get rid of it—it was in better shape than the house itself—but now he had a pretty good idea.

Stooping as if to examine the ruined tomato plants, Ricky plucked a golf ball-sized stone out of the garden. Then, with surprising speed, he stood, whirled, and threw the stone at the face that had reappeared beneath the bridge. It was a futile gesture. Before the stone could find its mark, the face once again disappeared and the stone splashed harmlessly into the pond. Before the ripples it generated reached the edge of the pool, the face was back, grinning at him. This time the creature that owned it flipped him the bird.

"Bleeping troll," he mumbled as he turned around to face Sara, just in time to see one of her stolen ripe tomatoes splatter on her ample bosom.

"That's it," Sara screamed. "Tomorrow you get rid of that bridge! Do you hear me, Ricky? Tomorrow I want it out of here."

Ricky reluctantly agreed, but he had no intention of getting rid of a free bridge. He'd figure out some way to keep it, even if it meant listening to Sara complain about it.

"Can't you leave those poor humans alone?" Bertha scolded her husband. "This is a great place, and you're going to ruin it like you always do."

Dinky just shrugged. She was right of course, but it was just so much fun tweaking the human's nose. He was big, ugly, slow, and probably stupid. He fed fish, for Grendel's sake. You don't feed fish, you eat them—any intelligent creature knew that. Fish were almost as good as billy goats.

"Did you hear me, Dinky? I want you to leave those humans alone."

"Yeah, sure," he responded, knowing he had no intention of leaving them alone, especially not Ricky. He loved messing with Ricky. Besides, there were good things to eat over there. He had peeked in their windows once and saw a whole herd of cats. They were everywhere—on the furniture, lying on the floor, sitting on the windowsills. Cats were better than fish, but they were harder to catch and they fought like hell. They were worth the effort though, especially if you barbecued them.

"Ricky, wake up. Somebody's trying to break into the garage."

"Wha . . ." he mumbled, and rolled over, still snoring.

"Wake up!" Sara insisted, and elbowed him in the side.

"What?" he demanded irritably, finally awake.

"Somebody's trying to get into the garage. I think it's that troll and he's after Bruiser." Bruiser, the cat from Hell, was an old tom that lived in the garage because he couldn't get along with Ricky or the other dozen or so cats that lived inside the house.

Ricky got out of bed, peeked out the window and, sure enough, there was the troll trying to get into the garage.

I've got you now, Ricky thought, as he snuck out the back door, Sara's rolling pin in his hand. Suddenly the night was filled with light, compliments of the motion sensor on the porch light. The troll reacted immediately; he threw the stone he was going to use to break the garage door window at Ricky, hitting him in the left knee. Then he sprinted for the bridge.

Ricky cursed when the stone hit him, but he didn't fall. He was off the porch in a single bound and hot on the troll's heels. He almost had him before he ducked under the bridge. Ricky dove in after him only to see his feet disappear into the bottom of the bridge's deck—then he heard a thump, as if something heavy had fallen on the bridge. When he looked, though, he didn't see anything.

When Dinky popped through the trap door on his side of the bridge, Bertha was waiting for him. "He almost caught you that time, didn't he?" she scolded. "What would happen to me and Flower if you got caught over there? Who would take care of us then? Who would take care of the farm? Either you stop going over there, or Flower and I are going home to my mother's."

Dinky shook his head in agreement, too winded to speak. Bertha had guessed right. The human had almost caught him. At a hundred and five, he was getting too old to be baiting humans. When he was finally able to talk without wheezing, he promised Bertha he would stay on his own side from then on.

That night Dinky awoke to his daughter Flower's screams. "Daddy . . . Daddy! Help!" he heard her crying in the night. When he burst into her room, she was huddled in her bed, covers pulled up around her neck.

"What's the matter, honey?" he asked. "Did you have a bad dream?"

Sniffling, she nodded her head. "There was a human peeking in my window," she told him, bravely trying to hold back her tears.

"What?" he heard Bertha exclaim from behind him, "a human? Are you sure it was a human?"

"I think so," Flower answered. "He was big and ugly and he needed a shave. He looked right in my window and grinned at me. When I yelled he ran away."

"Dinky, I want to talk to you," Bertha told him as she left the room. "Now!" she added as she walked toward the kitchen.

"Did you hear that? Did you? I told you to stop going over there. Now we have humans. How are we going to get rid of them?"

"Maybe it wasn't a human. Maybe she just imagined it because she heard us talking about them. Let's just wait and see," Dinky said, trying to placate her.

After the troll had disappeared Ricky hunted around until he found the trapdoor hidden in the bottom of the walkway. After he found the door, it took him another hour to locate the secret latch to open it. When he finally managed to trigger it, the door popped open like a lid on a jack-in-the-box.

When nothing jumped out at him, he cautiously poked his head through the opening. Amazingly he found another world, not much different from his own. Intrigued, he climbed the rest of the way through. This side of the bridge was made of stone and it crossed a noisy brook with steep banks. On one side it was bordered by a dark forest, on the other by what appeared to be a small, neat, farm with a stone cottage topped by a thatched roof. It looked like something out of a fairy tale. A split-rail fence surrounding the garden and a scarecrow on a wooden cross completed the picture.

I've got you now, you little bugger, Ricky thought as he climbed onto the bridge. He had managed to peek into several of the cottage's windows before the little girl had screamed. Now he was standing on the bridge, ready to drop through the trapdoor if anyone came out looking for him. When no one did he went back into the yard.

Ricky crept through the garden, being careful not to step on any of the plants. When he reached the scarecrow he donned its clothes and waited for the troll to appear. When he came out, Ricky intended to deal with him once and for all.

After Flower had been frightened by the human, Dinky had decided Bertha was right. He had to stop going through the door in the bridge to bother the human. It was too bad because he hadn't enjoyed pestering anyone so much in years. At the last place the bridge had been, all the humans had been old and feeble. In fact, for the past several years no one had even come into the garden. The stream below the bridge had dried up and there weren't even any frogs to be had.

As Dinky approached the bridge he noticed the trapdoor was open. Dumb, dumb, dumb, he thought. *What's the matter with that idiot? Doesn't he realize what can happen if you leave the door open? Nothing but trouble, that's for sure.* That little girl Alice had fallen through a door in a rabbit hole and she had wreaked havoc before they got rid of her. And what about the griffin—they never had griffins before that eagle had gotten through and now the damn things were multiplying like crazy. They were even driving the phoenixes out of their nesting grounds.

He knew all this, but when he reached the bridge he couldn't resist one last trip over to Ricky's for old time's sake. Ricky was never up this early and maybe he'd get lucky and snag a cat.

Ricky watched the troll drop through the trapdoor, and then close the door behind himself. Unlike the door on his side, this one had a red stone set into it to show where the release mechanism was. As soon as the door was closed, Ricky threw off the scarecrow's rags and made his way to the bridge. He was going to wait for the troll to come back. As soon as his head popped through the hole, wham, he'd brain him with a rock from the garden.

When he got to the door, though, his mouth dropped open in surprise. The red stone looked like a huge cut ruby. And, the closer he examined it, the more he was convinced that that's what it was. All plans of braining the troll fled from his mind as he tried to pry it out the bridge using his pocketknife.

He was bent over the ruby, furiously working to free it, when something thumped him upside the head. The blow stunned him and he dropped his knife and fell on the bridge, his body covering the trapdoor.

"Whack him, Mama! Whack him!" a girl's voice rang out, shattering the stillness of the early morning. He tried to get up but the blows were coming fast and heavy and he was starting to lose consciousness. Then the door started thumping under him and he heard someone yelling "Open the door, open the door!"

When Dinky slipped through the door into Ricky's yard, it was very quiet, just as he knew it would be. He was going to rip out all of Sara's roses to get even with Ricky for scaring Flower, but he got distracted. Bruiser had gotten out of the garage and was sitting on the back porch watching him. The roses could wait; he couldn't pass up a chance like this. He could grab the cat, take it home, and come back later.

When he approached the fiendish feline he learned why it lived in the garage and not in the house—it was nasty. He was bigger than it was, but it was fast and mean. When he reached for it, it yowled loudly and launched itself at his head. Before he could react, it was on his face, clawing, hissing, scratching, and trying to bite off a piece of his ear. Dinky howled in pain and stumbled backward trying to dislodge the beast. That's when Sara burst out of kitchen, rolling pin in hand. Bruiser saw her and ran for the hills. He knew what the rolling pin meant and didn't want any part of it.

With the cat gone, Dinky felt pretty good until the first blow from the rolling pin landed on his back. He rolled to his right to avoid the next attack and managed to get to his feet before Sara caught him with another mighty blow, this one to his shoulder. That was enough for Dinky, he turned tail and ran for the bridge. When he got there he tripped the hidden lever, but nothing happened. Something was holding the door closed!

"Open the door, open the door!" he yelled as Sara advanced on him, murder in her eyes.

"That's my Daddy!" Flower cried. "That's my Daddy! Let him in!"

"Dinky?" Bertha yelled, "Is that you?" She whacked Ricky one more time and said "Move, human, that's my husband."

As soon as Ricky rolled off the trap door, it sprang open and Dinky fled through it like a rabbit being chased by hounds. "Close it!" he yelled. "Close it!"

Before anyone could move, a hand holding a rolling pin emerged from the hole. The rest of Sara soon followed.

A passing griffin looking for trouble flew over the bridge, but decided this was a place even it did not want to be. Ricky and Dinky lay on the cobblestones rubbing their various wounds while Sara and Bertha faced each other, weapons in hand. Flower hid behind her mother's skirt, afraid to go to her father's aid.

"What have you been up to?" Bertha demanded of her battered husband.

"He was trying to catch Bruiser," Sara answered, venom in her voice.

"Who's Bruiser?" Flower asked timidly.

"Bruiser's my baby," Sara answered.

"What!" Bertha responded, and thumped Dinky with her frying pan. "You tried to steal her baby?" Then she thumped him again.

"It was a cat," Dinky said in his own defense.

"He may be a cat, but he's still my baby," Sara said and whacked him with the rolling pin.

Ricky happily watched the troll getting his butt kicked, glad no one was paying attention to him.

"What are you laughing at?" Sara demanded, and whacked him with the rolling pin. "I don't know what's going on here but I'm sure at least half of it's your fault."

Ricky started to proclaim his innocence and she whacked him again.

Bertha watched this exchange with knowing eyes. "Looks like you're married to as big a fool as I am," she finally said. Then she smiled at Sara and added, "My name is Bertha, would you like to come into the cottage for some tea?"

"I'd love to," Sara responded and whacked Ricky one more time for good measure. When Dinky laughed, both women thumped him.

Ricky and Dinky lay on the bridge nursing their wounds and looking at each other distrustfully as the women walked toward the cottage.

"No trouble out of either one of you," Bertha called out as she opened the door for Sara.

Epilogue

"Come in, come in," Bertha exclaimed as the cottage door opened. "Take off your coats, have some cider. Dinky, get Ricky one of those pastries." Dinky shook his head and did as he was told.

"I'm going outside to have a pipe," he said gruffly, after he shoved the pasty at Ricky.

"Me too," Ricky grumbled. He had given up smoking until Dinky had introduced him to the marvelous weed they smoked on this side of the bridge.

"Those two," Sara said after the door had closed behind them. "They won't admit how much they like each other. They're so alike they could be brothers."

"So it's your birthday," Ricky said, after they had their pipes going. "How old are you?"

"One hundred and six," Dinky replied proudly.

"What?" Ricky exclaimed choking on the smoke from his pipe. "A hundred and six, really?"

"Sure, what's so surprising about that?" Dinky asked.

"Eighty is older than most people get on my side, hardly anyone reaches a hundred."

"Huh," Dinky responded. "Then how old are you?" he asked skeptically.

"Thirty-five."

"Flower's thirty-five," Dinky laughed. "No wonder you're such a big baby."

After a minute of stunned silence Ricky recovered by asking what Bertha was giving him for his birthday.

"Nothing, why would she give me something for my birthday?"

"On our side, we give people presents on their birthday," Ricky told him.

"Really?" Dinky said surprised. "I like that idea. Did you get me one?"

"I was going to," Ricky said, "But I didn't know what to get a troll. What would you like?

"A cat would be good," Dinky said wistfully, "but a billy goat would be okay," he added, thinking of Sara's rolling pin. "But make it a small one, I don't like the big ones, they're mean."

Dan Foley is an ex-plumber, ex-Navy Nuke, Ex-Senior Reactor Operator and ex-nuclear operations instructor. He has lived on the East Coast, the West Coast, and places in between. Dan attributes his dark sense of humor on growing up in New Jersey and then serving on nuclear submarines. He currently lives in Connecticut.

You can reach Dan at www.deathscompanion.com, or on Facebook at www.facebook.com/dan.foley.31

Opossum Rex

By DJ Tyrer

"Well, you know what they say, the 'ho gets what the 'ho wants," said Jim-Bob as he scanned the wood for something to shoot.

"Shaddap," mutter Billy-Bob, who firmly believed his ex ought to get what his ex deserved.

"Don't worry, we'll find something for you to blast, then you'll feel better. Believe me," Jim-Bob went on, "killing something is the best way to get over a messy break-up – and, unlike killing her, it's legal, as long as they're in season."

"Shaddap," Billy-Bob repeated.

His cousin decided to change the subject. "You see that shooting star that came down night before last? Nothing on the news, so I'm thinking it weren't no reg'lar meaty-o-thingie. So, I reckon it must be something else."

"Like what?"

"I dunno. Maybe Iran shot a missile at us and Washington shot it down and they're covering it up so's we won't panic."

Billy-Bob laughed.

"Well, there you go," said Jim-Bob with a grin. "Or, maybe it was one of those flying saucer doohickies, like Grandpa saw."

"I can't say I buy into all that alien talk. I mean, why'd they come all this way just to stick a probe up someone's butt?"

"Well, I guess they have to stick 'em somewhere, like a thermometer, or something," he chuckled, still glancing about for prey.

Then, Billy-Bob tapped Jim-Bob's shoulder and he fell silent.

Billy-Bob pointed. "What was that?" He had his rifle up and ready.

Jim-Bob followed his cousin's finger. Something slunk off through the undergrowth. "Mountain lion, I think."

"Let's get it."

They crept forward, trying to discern where the cat was.

Then, Jim Bob spotted it again and pointed.

"I'm not sure that is a mountain lion," Billy-Bob said, slowly. Something about the briefly-glimpsed shape didn't seem right.

"Dang, it's gone," his cousin said.

Suddenly, Billy-Bob screamed as something large launched itself out of the trees at him. He tried to fire, but the bullet hit Jim-Bob in the leg and he fell to the ground screaming. It released his cousin and went for him.

"Doctor Pizer?" asked the man in the uniform of an army colonel who had just rung the doorbell of the New York brownstone.

The doctor nodded, bemused. He didn't normally have visitors without an appointment, and not too many of those. Had the uniform been that if a cop, he would've expected him to ask about the co-ed intern who had objected to his 'hands on' approach to mentoring; but an army colonel?

"Doctor Pizer, I'd like you to come with me," the colonel said, gesturing towards a large black car. It couldn't be her father, could it?

"Um, I think you must have me consumed with someone else, I'm–"

"–a zoologist," the colonel concluded.

Pizer nodded, still confused, and followed the colonel when he repeated the request.

As soon as he was in the car, it started to drive.

"My name is Colonel Mann. I represent a top-secret military organization that requires your assistance."

"Military organization? The CIA? NSA?"

"Not quite. We're the Navy-Army-Air Force Zoological Intervention Service. We don't use the initials, for obvious reasons."

"N-A-A- oh, I see."

"In fact, there is a connection... but, I digress..."

"You said 'Zoological Intervention'?"

"Yes, indeed, I did. Which is why we need you. You see—and, I don't want to put you off—our East Coast advisor was eaten last week, so we have a vacancy."

"Eaten?"

"Yes, eaten. It does happen occasionally, unfortunately. But, not too often."

"I don't understand..."

"Which is why I'll brief you."

Which he did, explaining that the group had been created to intervene whenever some sort of creature threatened the inhabitants of the United States.

"We've handled everything from super-sized alligators and hordes of rabid rats to genetically-engineered killer raccoons and dinosaurs, all without the public at large becoming aware or too many deaths occurring or too much damage being caused. I'll have to get you to sign an NDA."

The colonel produced a contract and Doctor Pizer, skeptical yet intrigued, signed it.

"Where are we going?" he asked, as he handed back the pen.

Colonel Mann pocketed the pen and said, "Virginia. Forty-eight hours ago, NORAD detected an incoming meteor. They tracked it to a landing point somewhere in southwestern Virginia. A scientific team was dispatched to retrieve it."

"And?"

"And, they didn't find it, but they did find the bodies of a couple of hunters; well, parts of bodies, anyway."

"Bears?"

The colonel shook his head. "Something the size of a large mountain lion or small bear, but neither."

"You're not saying they were killed by an alien?" Doctor Pizer asked.

"I'm not saying anything, except that two people have been killed by something large and unknown. It's your job to find and neutralize it."

"Neutralize it?"

"Kill, capture or relocate. You'll make the recommendation and I'll make the final decision."

A couple of hours later, Pizer and Mann were in the converted RV that served as the group's command post.

There was a knock on the door and a trooper stuck his head in and said, "PFC Harris. Sir, you'll want to see this."

They followed the soldier into the woods to an area some distance away where trees had been broken and splintered. There was a large five-toed footprint pressed deep into the ground. The soldiers who had followed the trail of destruction had marked further prints.

"I recognize this," Doctor Pizer muttered as he crouched beside the print, "but the size..." He stood and surveyed the scene. "Whatever it is, it's far larger than whatever killed those men." He shook his head. "Huge."

Colonel Mann snapped his fingers. "Got it—possum."

"You're right," said Pizer. "They look just like opossum spoor. Only, they're nowhere as big as this."

"Opossum Rex?" suggested PFC Harris.

The colonel laughed. "My pappy would've loved to make a pie from this critter!"

Pizer got out a tape measure and his tablet, measuring the length of the prints, their depth and the distance between them. He stood and scratched his head.

"Well?" asked the colonel.

"If my calculations are correct – and they are – then, we're looking for an opossum about thirty feet long and, I don't know, a few tons in weight."

Despite what Colonel Mann had told him on their way to Virginia, Pizer hadn't expected the man to believe him, but he just nodded and said, "Okay."

"At least it won't be too hard to find," said PFC Harris.

Pizer, struggling to believe himself, shook his head and told him, "Don't be so sure. Opossum prefer to hide away in dark places. If it can, it'll go to ground and it may take some work to find it."

The colonel turned to one of his men and said, "Get some helicopters in the air with thermal imaging. It may already be hiding."

A female soldier approached and saluted. "Corporal Jensen. Sir, the location of the meteor strike has been found, but only a few fragments have been discovered."

"Well," said the colonel, "I think that rules out an alien spacecraft dropping off a BEM. I think it also tells us what likely happened."

"Sorry?" Pizer blinked, confused, and pushed his glasses straight.

"He means," PFC Harris said, "that the opossum was probably exposed to the meteorite." He chuckled. "Maybe it ate a chunk. That's why it's grown so large."

"Oh..."

"We had a similar case, just before Thanksgiving last year, when a meteor caused a turkey to grow to an enormous size."

"But, it makes no sense... How could it grow so fast? And, so big? I mean, the square/cube law means it must be far too heavy for its legs to support its weight. How's it managing to walk? It's not possible."

The colonel sniffed. "I'll be sure to tell it that. Maybe the same thing that's supersized it has turned its bones to steel or something. Or, maybe, it's magic! We'll worry about the details later: it's a fact it exists and that's all that matters right now."

"Okay."

"So?"

"So, what?"

"How do we neutralize it?"

"Put it in a pie," laughed PFC Harris.

Pizer ignored him and stroked his chin, then said, "Given its size, speed and ability to climb and escape, it will be hard to capture and cage it. I think we need to kill it."

"Small arms fire won't be very effective," mused the colonel.

"Poison?" suggested Corporal Jensen.

Doctor Pizer shook his head. "The opossum is highly resistant to poison: even ricin is unlikely to affect it, let alone kill it."

"Explosives, then," decided Colonel Mann.

"They would be most effective."

"Okay; break out the LAWs and call in some armor and attack helicopters: we're going to need them."

Night had fallen before they received the news that the beast they were all calling Opossum Rex had been located. The colonel dragged Pizer out of the command post and over to a waiting helicopter. It wasn't an Apache or anything like that, just a small one, but it still had a couple of underslung rocket launchers on either side.

As soon as they were aboard, seated to the rear of the pilot and co-pilot, the colonel gave the order and the helicopter rose into the air.

"It appears," Colonel Mann shouted over the noise of the rotors, "that it's holed up during the day in a storm sewer and is now headed towards a town called, ah Charlesburg. The scout 'copter that located it attempted to engage it with small-arms fire, to no appreciable effect."

Doctor Pizer nodded.

Then, they saw it. Starkly lit by the beam of a searchlight mounted on the scout helicopter, the greyish creature with a reflective-white face was enormous and grotesque seeming, even to those who were used to opossums.

The creature was drawing near to the outskirts of Charlesburg.

"Fire!" the colonel declared.

A pair of rockets whooshed out from the launchers and, a moment later, bright explosions blossomed into life.

They blinked their vision back and saw that the opossum was still running, seemingly unaffected.

"Fire!" the colonel repeated.

Two more whooshes of fire shot towards it.

This time, when they blinked back their sight, they saw that it was lying unmoving on the ground, its haunches splashed with blood.

"Target down," stated the co-pilot.

"Let's watch for a while," said the colonel, and they circled above it for a few minutes to make sure it was dead rather than stunned. As they did so, the colonel called for troops to put a cordon in place to keep back the curious inhabitants of the town from driving over: already they could see the headlights of a pickup truck approaching and, doubtless, more would soon follow.

"I don't want anyone seeing this," he shouted. "I don't know. Tell them it was marsh gas, for all I care!"

Then, they landed.

"It stinks," muttered Colonel Mann as they approached the corpse on foot. He spat, then grinned. "Well, that was certainly easier than some hunts." He took out his radio and put in a call for a flatbed loader to take it away and cancelled the vehicles he had earlier called for.

Pizer took the chance to light up a cigarette and looked at the dead creature. "I still can't quite believe it."

"I'd bet," the colonel said, "when you cut it open, you'll find a bit of that meteorite."

"I have to dissect it?"

"Oh, yeah."

"Then, can I go home?"

"If you really want to. But, you've done quite well for your first day; no screaming, for a start. I'd like you to consider staying on with us."

"Ask me once I've been elbow deep in it..."

The flatbed truck arrived just over half an hour later and a team of engineers hopped down from an accompanying truck and took a good look at it, trying to decide just how to proceed with loading it.

One of them sucked on his teeth and said, "He's a big bastard, alright."

"Yeah, well, just get him loaded," said the colonel, whose patience was thinning.

"Will do, sir."

They approached the giant opossum and began to slip ropes about it. It was then that it woke up. It was still alive.

"It was just playing possum!" Pizer exclaimed as the colonel began to hustle him back towards the helicopter as the creature thrashed and growled and snapped viciously at the engineers attempting to rope it. "It was obvious!"

Men were screaming and there was sporadic gunfire, then the truck was flipped and the opossum was scuttling towards the shelter offered by the town.

Colonel Mann swore as they rose into the air and he realized where it was headed.

Those troops that had stood watch, mainly to keep the curious townsfolk at a distance, fired at it as it passed, but rifle fire seemed to have no effect. Those who had LAWs sent a few shots after it, but their aim was wild, as they dodged out the way or span about in surprise. A few of the civilians, who had been attempting to gawk at the distance disturbance, found a nightmare apparition barreling towards them and opened up with shotguns and hunting rifles, which seemed to be equally ineffective. A couple of pickups got spun aside or flipped as it barged past them.

"Yes, I know I stood them down," Colonel Mann was shouting into his radio as chaos unfolded below, "but I need those choppers and AFVs here immediately – if not sooner!" He followed up with a string of expletives. "No excuses! Now!"

Turning to the pilot, he ordered, "Follow that possum!"

It is said no plan ever survived contact with the enemy, but without a plan, chaos is the only option, and they had chaos in spades. The gigantic opossum had charged into the town with a couple of jeeps and a few trucks full of soldiers right behind it. Their guns seemingly useless against it, their immediate task would be to evacuate the inhabitants of the town and keep the more excitable ones from staging an impromptu possum hunt. After seeing what had come a-visiting, the sheriff proved perfectly amenable to pulling out and letting the army get on with dealing with it.

Colonel Mann was till shouting into the radio in an attempt to get the vehicles he wanted, while Doctor Pizer was trying to keep the beast in sight as it slipped through back streets and slithered into a series of warehouses.

"The truck's here," the co-pilot told them.

"Have them dole out the LAWs to the men," the colonel said. He had a feeling they were going to need plenty of them. "Tell them to shoot on sight," he added.

"Wilco." The co-pilot relayed the order.

Equipped for the hunt, the soldiers began their search of the warehouse district, building by building. Pizer didn't envy them.

PFC Harris, who earlier had been alongside the doctor and colonel, on the other hand, was certainly envious of their position overhead and out of harm's way. Down here, in the darkness, with heavy night-vision goggles jutting out from his eyes and weighing his head down, was where the danger waited.

"Scratch warehouse twenty-three from the list," he relayed to the sergeant at the other end of the radio waves, "Opossum Rex ain't home."

Then, as he and his team neared the exit, there was a sudden scream as one of the men disappeared upward, legs flailing. As his gaze followed the motion, it was too fast for Harris' goggles to adjust the image and all he saw was a wild blur, then the soldier was flying through the air across the warehouse, thrown by what appeared to be an enormous hand. The opossum was up amongst the latticework of steel girders that supported the roof, its tail coiled about a post to steady it as it reached down to scoop up another startled man.

Harris snapped out of his reverie and raised the LAW he carried and fired, just as the tail detached itself from the post and whipped towards him. He avoided it, but his aim went wide, the shot exploding up through the roof of the building even as he was calling for help.

The goggles were blinded for a moment by the flare of the blast; he heard more than saw a second explosion, this too seemingly misaimed as it was followed by the wrench and crash of steel as a girder tore free, narrowly missing them.

Then, vision returned; the beast was gone.

"Cancel that," he said into his radio, tone incredulous; "it's gone again."

Having heard the report of the opossum in Warehouse 23, Corporal Greta Jensen was in a good mood as her team continued the sweep of the mall. Luckily, it was lit up, so the cumbersome goggles worn by other teams were unnecessary.

"I don't know why we're bothering," muttered a private, before spitting out a mess of tobacco-stained spit.

"Procedure."

"How many giant-sized possums do they think are running round this burg?" he replied, spitting again.

"Hey, be grateful we haven't been sent over to help neutralize it, eh?"

Before he could retort, the opossum exploded out of The Gap. The private let out a string of obscenities, further colored by more of his spit.

The opossum spun at the sound and faced them. For a moment, they stood frozen, unable to react. Then, they fumbled to ready their LAWs.

It closed the space with alacrity and bit the tobacco-chewing trooper's head clean off, only to spit it out a moment later, shoving Jensen and the other two soldiers aside with ease. She flew briefly before smashing into the security shutters of a stationery shop. Jensen felt a few ribs pop before she fell, semi-conscious, to the floor.

When she looked up, a moment later, the opossum was gone.

"I don't understand it," complained Colonel Mann." It was located in Warehouse 23, only to vanish, and, then, reappear across town at the mall, where it vanished again."

"Well, it hasn't been using the streets, that's for sure," said Doctor Pizer. "It must be getting about underground, somehow."

The colonel looked at the co-pilot and ordered that "Somebody find out what the hell lies beneath this town!"

The answer came back at about the same time Colonel Mann received the news that an Apache attack helicopter and a couple of Humvees mounting 20mm guns and TOW missiles were almost at Charlesburg.

"Mines?" exclaimed the colonel. "Why am I only learning about these now?"

Nobody had an answer.

"The mines must connect to the individual buildings," Pizer said, "and it's traveling between them."

Colonel Mann sent out the order: the soldiers would have to enter the mines in order to flush it out so the heavier weapons could finally finish it.

"This is worse than the warehouse," muttered PFC Harris. Had he known Corporal Jensen and the rest of her team were in the back of a truck on their way to a makeshift field hospital some distance away, he might have wished he was with her, even if it meant a few broken bones.

"I dunno," said another soldier. "At least down here, it can't just pop up."

"That's true, but keep your eyes skinned, just in case."

The words proved prophetic as, a moment later, a large and distinct heat source appeared at the far end of the mind tunnel. It moved speedily towards them.

This time, the difficulty of focusing on a fast-moving object and the blinding effect of the LAW blasts had no detrimental effect upon their aim, as all they had to do was fired straight down the tunnel at it: they couldn't really miss.

A fusillade of explosions was followed by a pained growl and the sound of supports giving way as the tunnel roof collapsed.

"Get back!" shouted Harris, realizing the danger they were in.

Once he was certain there was no further threat of their being buried in a tunnel collapse, he headed for the surface to radio in the approximate location of their encounter. He doubted they had managed to kill it – they couldn't be that lucky, he felt – but he was certain it was hurt and the cave-in meant it couldn't continue this way.

With a little luck, they might force it to surface...

It did. After two more stinging encounters with LAWs, it burst out of an abandoned church and ran across an empty parking lot, looking for somewhere else to hide. The helicopter carrying Pizer and the colonel fixed a searchlight on it.

Dawn was just nudging its pinkish blush up past the horizon as the two Humvees bore down on the gigantic opossum, popping out a series of 20mm shells that blossomed red on its grey flank.

The beast turned and growled at the vehicles tormenting it.

"I'm sure it's well over thirty feet," said Doctor Pizer. "Unless there are two of them, it's gotten bigger."

The colonel gave a snort. "If it ingested a fragment of that meteorite, whatever is making it grow must still be affecting it."

A shell tore the beast's ear off, and it hissed in pain. Then, it seized the Humvee in its front paws and tossed it over onto its roof. The vehicle sparked across the parking lot.

The other Humvee swerved wildly, desperate to avoid it.

PFC Harris reached the lot and fired his last LAW at the enormous creature. It exploded against its rear paw and the marsupial lifted it with a yelp of pain, blood gushing, and then turned its head to growl at him.

The distraction gave the remaining Humvee the chance to turn and resume fire, striking it several times in its side. The opossum staggered and sagged, the wounds beginning to tell.

Then, the TOW rocket shot towards it, but the creature, still fast despite its size and wounds, managed to scuttle aside and the warhead exploded against a building, causing it to collapse into a pile of bricks.

Colonel Mann swore, then his expression changed and he laughed as they spotted the Apache helicopter swooping in low over rooftops towards the parking lot.

"Now, we've got it," he cried.

Two hellfire missiles *whooshed* from the Apache's launchers and hit the opossum before it had even perceived the threat. A moment later, it was engulfed in flames and one limb went flying, falling a little short of the surviving Humvee.

Soldiers climbed groggily from the wreckage of the upturned vehicle and joined PFC Harris in a whoop of delight at the sight of the opossum collapsing and smoldering.

Remembering killing it once before only to find it had played possum, Colonel Mann spoke into his radio, saying, "Two more missiles. I want to be certain it's dead. In little pieces, dammit!"

It was dead. The fact it was smeared about the cratered parking lot rather indicated as much, but Doctor Pizer jumped down from the hovering helicopter to verify for certain. The colonel was definite on that point.

Amongst the shredded entrails, he spotted a tiny fragment of glowing stone. He compared it to an image of the meteorite fragments on his tablet.

"Just as you suspected," he told the colonel, who had jumped down after him. "Part of the meteorite."

The colonel nodded. "I'll have the men bag it up with the rest of this mess. Once it's back at HQ, you can carry out an examination of the remains. Then, we'll have to talk about your future. I think you would be a perfect addition to the Navy-Army-Air Force Zoological Intervention Service."

"I'll admit I'm tempted. Today's certainly got my adrenaline pumping. But, if I do, I think you really need to rethink the name. Maybe the USZI?"

"I'll think about it," nodded Colonel Mann. Then, he turned to his men and shouted, "Right, you apes, scrape it all up. Opossum Rex has a date with the doctor..."

DJ Tyrer, the person behind Atlantean Publishing, was short-listed for the 2015 Carillon 'Let's Be Absurd' Fiction Competition, and has been widely published in anthologies and magazines around the world, such as *Warlords of the Asteroid Belt* (Rogue Planet Press), *Strangely Funny II* and *III* (both Mystery & Horror LLC), *Destroy All Robots* (Dynatox Ministries), *Steam Chronicles* (Zimbell House) and *Irrational Fears* (FTB Press), as well as issues of Tigershark ezine. He also has a novella available on Kindle, *The Yellow House* (Dunhams Manor).

DJ Tyrer's website is at http://djtyrer.blogspot.co.uk/

The Atlantean Publishing website is at:
http://atlanteanpublishing.blogspot.co.uk/

Death Needs a Job

By M. Kelly Peach

Whiff Migg is muttering to himself as he taps busily at his paper-thin keyboard. The Job Navigator for Magritte Works! The Job Ensemble in Dali County is old, old school and prefers typing rather than voice commands. In fact, he is so old fashioned he has his keyboard set to emulate an antique manual typewriter. Each time the text wraps in his document it sounds like the carriage of an Olympia SG3 sliding to the left and ending in the ring of a tiny bell. This annoys his co-workers in nearby cubicles but he could care less.

A client wearing a deeply hooded, floor length robe of broadcloth blacker than the heart of a lawyer turned politician silently appears at the entrance to Whiff's work space. This is the original hoodie. A one of a kind garment so righteous, even though it is dusty and threadbare, every adolescent on the planet would kill (if only they could) to have it.

The figure, nearly seven feet tall and thin as the long ash handle, worn smooth with use, of the scythe in its skeletal right hand stands patiently. It has much practice in waiting. Its face is hidden in the ebony shadows of its hood. At the proper angle, one seems to see, within its depths, ruby-like glints but that might just be a trick of the observer's eyes.

Under enormous pressure from his boss to obtain job placements for his clients, Whiff is more focused than he has ever been in his long career and does not look up. After tapping rapidly for another minute, he finally tells his new customer, "Yes, come in. Have a seat. I'll be with you shortly."

"Death," intones the client, "never rests."

The case worker, still concentrating on his data entry and with the barest of glances from the corner of his eye for his newest client, comments, "Well then, Death must be pretty damn tired about now, so why don't you park it in the seat? You make me nervous standing there. Also, would you lose the scythe, please?"

Death, accustomed to awe-struck reactions, is taken aback. He sits down and after some hesitation (Where does one place the instrument of execution for billions?), decides to stash the scythe—being careful with the curving, nicked, and rusty blade—behind the seat.

Whiff finishes with his computer work and looks at the eldritch specter sitting in his office. The jaded bureaucrat, after twenty-five years of battle in the employment trenches, has seen it all and decides to play along.

"Mr. Death? Excuse me; I like to see my clients as I work with them. Could you please lower your hood?"

His client displays a skull yellowed with age and black, depthless eye sockets, each containing a scarlet pinpoint of light. Whiff Migg decides this is the most lifelike, frightening, creepy mask he's ever seen and quickly asks him to pull the hood back into place. Whiff, after some shifting in his chair and shuffling of some papers, regains his composure.

He asks his newest addition to an already over-sized case load, "So, what brings you to the Job Ensemble?"

"The same reason as everybody else. I need a job."

"Uh huh. Let me guess. You're out of work these days because of those damned scientists at Duke—"

"—Dr. Quackenbush and his team."

"Right. The ones who developed the drug Immortalium—"

"—D-carbunculous isopropinquitate."

"Right again. Boosts the immune to superhuman levels—"

"—Creating massive leucocytes called suprophils so ferocious they are capable of phagocytosing bb-sized steel shot. That's only a slight exaggeration."

"Do you always interrupt?"

"Of course, that is what I do best."

"Hmmm, actually that makes sense. Anyway, with diseases eradicated—"

"—And the aging process at a virtual standstill."

"These constant interruptions are really annoying."

"I know...I try not to but I just can't seem to stop myself."

"Anyway, you are now out of a—"

"—Job. Correct."

Thoroughly irritated, Migg gives his client his best chastening Leonard Nimoy eyebrow lift as a non-verbal cue to knock off the interruptions.

"Mr. Death, you should have received a CIQ form—that's the Customer Information Questionnaire—as part of your orientation information packet. Do you have it filled out?"

Death reaches under his garment and pulls out the form while explaining, "Of course. Death always finishes appointed tasks. My name, by the way, is just Death—not Mr. Death."

"Hmmm, just one name...kinda like that old-time entertainer. What was her name? Cher? You sure you have enough money for one name? Takes a lot of cash if you're gonna run around with only one name. Most of us poor slobs have to use two names."

"Well, sometimes I'm called the Grim Reaper."

"Excellent! Let's go with that."

Migg makes the correction on the form, then asks, "Listen, Grim, what's the deal with the reddish-brown ink on this form? It's kind of smeared and faded in some spots...not very easy to read."

"I do all my documents in blood."

He drops the form in disgust. "Gross! Can't you use a blue or black ink pen like everybody else? Listen, if you're going to do all your MW! forms in your own blood it will be (a) disgusting, (b) illegal, and (c) fatal before you could even get half of them filled out. That'll give you an idea of how many forms we have."

In sepulchral tones, "I didn't say it was *my* blood...and, think about it, are you sure Death can die?"

He gingerly picks up the form, sets it on his document holder, then replies, "Interesting question; I don't know. I'm just a caseworker, not a philosopher—although one should be a Stoic to work around this place. So, whose blood is this? Wait, never mind, I don't really want to know. Why don't we just do this on the computer, OK?"

"Certainly, if that works better for you."

"It does. So, let's go with last name as 'Reaper' and first name 'Grim.' That's so much more upbeat than 'Death'. Besides, our computer doesn't deal well with single-named clients. Any middle initial? ...I didn't think so. And your address, Mr. Reaper?"

"I am a dweller of the cosmos. I am everywhere and nowhere. I reside in the infant's death wail and in the old man's last gasp. The windows of my house are the vacant eyes of the lamented..."

"Geez, Grim, you don't have to be so melodramatic—a lot of people don't have their own home."

With funereal chagrin, "Sorry."

"That's all right. We'll just put down that you're homeless. Social security number?"

"I don't have one."

"Of course you don't. Why would a cosmic being need a social security number? We'll just note that as a barrier to employment and work on getting you one. And your birth date?"

"As you measure time, April 18, 14 billion B.C., give or take an eon."

"Uh huh. I get it, the whole birth of the universe, big bang thing. Fascinating actually, I'd love to pursue this but we do have to move on. For gender, we'll put 'male'."

"Historically, men have portrayed me as masculine. Perhaps a 'non-specific' category would be more accurate."

"So, you're like, transgender?"

"Not really. Look it's too complicated for your puny human brain. Just mark me as 'male' and be done with it."

"Sure. Why don't we leave 'race' blank for the time being."

"Excellent idea! Trust me, it's not on your form."

Ignoring his client's sarcasm, Whiff continues, "Let's see, you probably don't have a phone—"

"—Actually, I have an android phone, the Galaxy S4." He pulls out the device and shows it to Whiff. After providing the number, he goes on to explain, "Being an older person, I don't really understand all its functions and, honestly, nobody ever calls just to chat."

"Awww, I'm sorry."

"All I ever get is wrong numbers and scammers for vacation condos, prize winnings obtainable for a fee or work at home schemes. Of course, for those scumbags, that's the last phone call they ever make."

"I see. Can't say as I blame you. Anyway, moving on. Who referred you to The Job Ensemble?

"My fellow horsemen: Famine, Bloody War and Conquering Power. Your agency was able to find them jobs. If I remember correctly they were placed as Public Assistance Payments workers at the Agency for Services to Humans—or maybe it was the phone company..."

"Sure, I'll just note that here. Now, about your marital status?"

"Single."

Migg, in a mordant mood and unable to resist, observes, "Hard to believe with a handsome, personable fellow like yourself.

Perhaps, if you got rid of the scythe, bought yourself a nice suit, put on a little weight, wear a pair of those classic Oakley X-Metal Mars shades, you might be able to...you know, get a date. Ah, never mind, not going to happen. So I suppose you have no children?"

"On the contrary, I have innumerable offspring: Hate, Jealousy, Intolerance, Greed, Weapons of Mass Destruction, to name a few."

"I understand but that's not what I had in mind. There are no biological children, correct?"

"Correct."

"What is your annual income?"

"I have no income." With tenebrous humor, "You know what they say: You can't take it with you!"

"Ha, ha, ha, especially in your case! Oh, Grim, you just kill me." Despite his cynicism, he is compelled to hastily add, "Whoa, wait a minute, just kidding—it's not that funny. Don't get any ideas here. Sooo, moving along, are any of the following factors barriers to getting a job? Are you a U.S. citizen?"

"No, for some reason Immigration Services doesn't seem very interested in my becoming a citizen. I don't know why, I'm a good person...um, being...don't you think?"

"Yes indeed, a very nice...being; we'll check that one. Do you have a criminal record?"

"Absolutely not! I don't drink or do drugs. I never park in the 'Handicapped Only' space. I do not litter. I am the most law-abiding creature you will ever find. All I do, all I've ever done, is bring eternal rest to billions of human beings."

"Uh huh. So, probation or parole are not a problem. Do you have a driver's license?"

"No. I ride a pale green horse named Pestilence. I left it outside the building."

Whiff, just to get through the intake, was willing to go along with the craziest, longest, thinnest man in existence carrying an honest-to-god scythe, in a black robe and wearing the best (or worst, depending upon your point of view) mask in the history of cosplay.

However, his patience was wearing thin, so he couldn't help rolling his eyes at the idea of a pale green horse standing in the parking lot tied to some hitching post like it was outside a saloon in the Old West.

Looking at his computer screen, sighing disbelief and wondering how in the world he was ever going to get this nutcase a job, he said, "Whatever. Let's keep going. Do you have any pending legal proceedings that could be a barrier to your employment?"

"I have had a number of individuals try to sue me for damages to loved ones. Interestingly, virtually all of them are Americans and they all seem to have a terrible accident and die shortly after filing their lawsuit. I'm sure it's just a coincidence."

"How convenient. Speech is fine, but we will have to get rid of the whole *basso profondo*, echoing, reverb thing when you go to interviews. Hearing and vision are fine despite your seeming lack of eyeballs and ears. Any dental problems that would be a hindrance to employment?"

"No."

"The next factor is mental health. I was thinking a professional assessment. We would do the works: MMPI-2, WAIS-R, MCMI-III, Rorschach, etc. I mean, considering..." Migg's explanation trails off as his eyes travel to the scythe, then the robe and finally to the hidden face of the figure seated in front of him.

At a momentary loss—assigning clients to mental health assessment or substance abuse testing is probably the most difficult part of his job--he finally decides, as his justification, "...This business with the pale green horse."

The Grim Reaper inquires, with all the coldness of interstellar space, "Do you desire, nay, do you require proof?"

"Of what?"

"Pestilence," orders the Specter, "show yourself!"

Outside the Magritte Works! office, invisible to mortal sight, stands a large and powerful horse patiently chewing on some chicory when it hears its Master's voice. The horse, with a loud slurping sound, winks into full view. It is nearly the same shade as the chicory it's been eating. Pestilence, a defiant and strong-willed steed, often interprets its Master's commands in unexpected ways.

It canters to the picture window to the left of the entrance door to the Magritte Works! Agency office, rears up and smashes out the glass with its front hooves. Stepping daintily over the low sill, it walks into the lobby. After tossing its head and blowing from its dilated nostrils, the magnificent creature crunches its way through the lobby and over to its Master, whereupon it lifts its lime-colored tail.

"That is not the proof I had in mind!" Black Death hastens to explain to his incorrigible mount, then commands, "Pestilence, leave!"

The stallion of pastel verdancy lowers its tail, eyes the Angel of Death and a trembling Whiff, whinnies at them, shakes its jade mane, then departs in full dignity to retrace its step to the chicory patch. With a sucking sound, it disappears from sight and goes back to eating the weeds.

Whiff looks at the Grim Reaper, turns his head to gaze at the space where a green (well, yes, pale green) horse had been standing then turns back to stare again at his client. At last, he truly perceives what is seated in front of him. He clears his throat, hesitates, finally, declares, "You're the real deal, not just some lunatic dressed up in a Halloween costume."

"That is very perspicacious of you, Whiff Migg."

This is further corroboration for the workforce development professional as he immediately thinks: *Nut jobs don't use words like 'perspicacious'; he, it, whatever, is the genuine article. I'm going to die!*

The Ferryman assures the worker, "I'm not here to take you to the other side. If I were, we wouldn't be having this conversation. Besides, it's not your time. Now, back to business. I believe all other employment barriers become meaningless when compared to the barrier of being who I am: Death itself."

When nervous, Whiff likes to make jokes of dubious quality so he examines his form and tells his client, "Agreed, and you know what? I don't see a category under Employment Barriers for 'Death Itself'. I guess we'll have to add that one."

Migg's giggling meets with ponderous silence and quickly subsides. He clears his throat again, "I guess we can just skip all these other categories and finish this up quickly. I notice for Work History you wrote 'extinction'. Um, have you ever had any other jobs?"

"No, that has always been my task."

"OK. Moving right along. You left Education blank. Does this mean you have had no formal schooling?"

"I must admit this is entirely correct, despite my four full years of coursework completed at the University of Michigan."

"Oh, I'm so sorry!"

"No need to apologize. It was my decision."

"Are you working with any other agencies?"

"No."

"That brings us to your Individualized Plan. What is your employment goal, Mr. Reaper?"

"I would like a full-time job with excellent benefits and pay but involves very little effort. Perhaps I should run for Congress?"

"Well, in terms of campaigning for office, you're tall and thin, which is good...but I'm not seeing the requisite skills in prevarication and dissembling."

"I see your point. What about a job with the state?"

"Yes, I think you're on to something, but we'll need a resume. Do you have one?"

Grim Death, with cowl flapping, shakes his head no.

"I didn't think so. No problem. We have a workshop for that and other job searching skills."

Whiff Migg finishes the intake by giving the Reaper a job hunter's workbook and a schedule for several workshops such as Resume Writing, Identifying the Job Market, Networking and Job Interview Skills. His client leaves silently and the case manager releases a huge exhalation of relief while thinking: *How am I ever going to be able to get him a job?*

The Specter made it to all the scheduled workshops and did all the assignments, including a resume using regular ink. He job searched diligently every day Monday through Friday for several hours by reading help wanted ads, making phone calls and combing employment web-sites. His favorite site, of course, was Monster.com.

After a month of this job hunting activity Death was still unemployed so he decided to try his (skeletal) hand at motivational speaking. Bookings, needless to say, were not forthcoming so he switched to selling life insurance door-to-door.

This too did not go well. People refused to answer the door whenever he knocked or rang the doorbell. In fact, as he stood on their front porch fully prepared with his killer sales pitch, they were so frightened they phoned the police. After a few of these calls, the cops suggested to Death he find another line of work.

Accordingly, he tried grief counseling. People weren't dying, but folks were still getting divorced and pet parents were losing their beloved dogs and cats. Again, this occupation was less than successful. Death seemed to lack, his supervisor explained when he was letting him go, the necessary empathy and compassion.

Out of desperation, Whiff Migg decided to place his least employable client in a paid, ninety-day On-the-Job Training to allow him to gain new work skills. In what proved to be a stroke of genius, the Job Navigator chose a placement at Bug Out Pest Services as an exterminator. It was perfect match. Death is as happy as can be in his new role. The employer was so thrilled with the Reaper's efficiency and professionalism, he hired him on as a full-time, permanent worker after only two weeks.

The new hire is a great help to the company's bottom line because he can eliminate any and all bugs or critters without resorting to those expensive pesticides or poisons all of the other exterminators have to use.

M. Kelly Peach is a long-time bureaucrat with the State of Michigan and a husband, a father, and a grandfather. He enjoys reading and collecting books, hiking, camping, hunting, and writing. His work has been published in diverse markets such as: *Punchkin's, Mad Scientist Journal, In Medias Res: Stories of the In-Between, Alternate Hilarities I-III, Woods-N-Water News, Unsung Stories, The Graveyard*, and *Cheapjack Pulp*. His Tumblr blog is: peachmme.tumblr.com.

Save or Die

By C.D. Gallant-King

In a land of ancient gods, warlords and kings, where being kidnapped and eaten by goblins was a real, ever-present danger, and being burned to death by the breath of a dragon was an accepted occupational hazard for peasants, four would-be heroes set out to make names for themselves and become... well... heroes. That's what made them "would-be heroes," after all.

They left the village of Willy-upon-Lilly at dawn, laden with weapons, armor, tents, bedrolls, pack-sacks, mirrors, shovels, climbing ropes, pitons, rations sealed in iron containers, candles, torches, lanterns, bottles of ink, rolls of parchment, several sticks of chalk, a dozen candles, spare cloaks, boots and tunics, a dozen quivers of arrows, a ten-foot pole and a donkey named Steve. The donkey carried several empty sacks across its back, sacks the heroes envisioned would be laden with treasure on their return home.

"Why do we need all this... stuff?" asked Glorien Gravehall, Guardian of the Golden God, as he struggled under a backpack filled with no less than ten two-gallon waterskins. He was a priest, a holy man, who could heal you with one hand and crush your head with a hammer in his other. Truly, he was but a mere acolyte, but being able to both smite foes with a weapon and cast protective magic were traits well desired by any party of heroes.

"You never know what you will need on one of these quests." Jerald Blackblade was carrying significantly less gear than his fellows. He was the group's resident trap-finder, lock-pick, and general trouble-shooter. Most civilized people would call him a "thief," but never to his face, unless they wanted their throats cut and money stolen. He insisted on travelling lightly because he claimed encumbrance interfered with his sneakery.

"I don't think we needed cooking pots and pans." The wizard Bathsheba could barely stay upright under the weight of cookery strapped to her back. Between that and her mammoth magical tomes, she looked like a peddler, wandering into town to sell trinkets to the housewives and sneak off into the woods with their children. "The cave is only a few miles away. I thought the plan was to check it out and be back by supper time."

"Again, you must be prepared!" Jerald's eyebrows bobbed up and down with insistence. "This cave could lead to a deeper complex of dungeons and underground tunnels. We could be down here for days!"

"Or, we could just turn around and go home at supper time," said Bathsheba.

"Quiet!" growled Bob. He was a fighting man, dressed in heavy steel armor, and carrying gear and weapons that outweighed Bathsheba and Jerald combined. He wasn't even breaking a sweat, and he probably could have carried Steve, too. "I think I hear foes approaching."

It was mid-morning. They were travelling through the forests of King Slapappy, a verdant, sylvan wood full of magical creatures and elves and such. They stopped beside a bend in the narrow, rough trail, unable to see what lay ahead. "Bathsheba." Bob's voice was but a whisper. "Does your magic tell us what sort of evil waits beyond yonder turn?"

"Sorry." The wizard dropped her rattling pack and stretched her aching shoulders. "I'm really not much more than an apprentice. I can only remember one spell at a time, and that's not the one I memorized this morning."

"Why did we take her along again?" groaned Glorien.

A group of short, filthy humanoids appeared down the path. Grey-skinned, with tattered clothes, mismatched pieces of armor and rusty weapons, they could have belonged to any of a dozen evil fantasy races, but goblins seemed most likely. The adventurers were quite inexperienced, after all, so goblins would be appropriate for them to encounter.

"You shall not pass!" One of the beasties snarled and waved a bent sword that was almost as tall as it was.

"Do you think we can take them?" Glorien whispered to Bob, strapping on his shield.

"They outnumber us." The fighter counted the goblins and reached a total of six. He had to use both hands. "It would be dangerous. Bathsheba, can you burn them up with a fireball or something?"

"Sorry, I don't know a fireball spell."

"Or perhaps you would rather just leave your weapons and your money and run away like the snivelling little maggots you are?" The lead monster shook its sword at them and cackled.

"Oh, come on, we can't let goblins laugh at us." Bathsheba was insulted. She pulled out her only weapon, a four-inch long dagger.

Bob glared at her and shook his head. "Just stand in the back and try not to stab yourself."

"Of course," said the goblin, as they continued to approach slowly down the path. "We could propose another option? Say, a game of riddles?"

"Oh, I like riddles," said Bob.

"They're afraid." Glorien nodded. "They might be able to take us, but they would suffer heavy casualties, too."

"That's surprisingly intelligent tactics for a goblin," said Bathsheba. "And where did Jerald go?"

"Oh, I like riddles," repeated Bob. "We accept your challenge!"

"Wait!" Glorien held up a hand. "It might be a trap. We should at least work out the terms..."

"Excellent!" The lead goblin didn't hear anything after "challenge." "I shall go first! What sings but has no voice, sleeps but feels no weariness, runs but has no legggrrAAGH!"

The goblin spit up a mouthful of blood.

"What?" asked Bob. "What's a legggrrAAGH?"

"To arms, my fellows!" Jerald pulled his blade out of the goblin's throat. He had crept up behind the creature through the trees, and none of them had even noticed. The goblins still outnumbered them five-to-four, but at least he could count the number of enemies on one hand, so Bob thought that was reasonable odds.

The fighter rushed forward, swinging his two-handed great sword like a reaper harvesting wheat. A goblin's head leapt from its body, chased by an arcing spray of blood. Glorien rushed another humanoid, driving it back with his shield before caving in its chest with his warhammer. Bathsheba began casting her one and only spell, making arcane gestures with her hands while muttering strange words under her breath.

The goblins, having already lost half of their number, fought back feebly. Their rusty weapons were no match for Bob's steel armor and Glorien's heavy shield. Bathsheba completed her incantation and a blast of sparkling silver light leapt from her fingers and caught another goblin square in the chest, knocking it off its feet into the dirt. It curled up and moved no more.

The remaining two monsters, wanting none of this, turned and fled. "We should let them go," intoned Glorien solemnly. "The Golden God teaches that mercy..."

"Screw that." Bob chased the small fleeing cowards. He split one of them from neck to groin with a mighty swing of his blade, though the sixth and final one managed to escape into the trees.

A lull of quiet and uneasy peace fell upon the forest. The party looked at each other with a newfound respect and comradery. They had faced their first threat as one and triumphed. It was a momentous occasion for any fellowship, a sure sign that their venture would be destined for greatness and immortalization in the future songs of bards.

And then in unison and without a word, the four adventurers descended upon the bodies of the fallen like vultures.

"Is this sword worth anything, do you think?"

"This gorget won't fit me."

"I can probably get a few coins from a hobbit for these drawers."

"Oh, look, this one has eight copper pennies!"

Once the corpses were picked over to satisfaction, and the adventurers exchanged a few cheers and high-fives at having survived their first encounter with deadly foes, their discussion returned to the task at hand.

"I need to camp," said Bathsheba.

"Wait, what?" asked Glorien. "We just left town less than an hour ago."

"Yeah, well, you saw that neat spell I cast back there, that made that goblin wish it had never been born?"

"Yes, that was pretty impressive. What of it?"

"That was it. I used up all my magical resources. I blew my wad. I need to rest so that I can recharge and relearn my spell."

"But we only left town an *hour* ago. To camp now would be foolishness..."

"You yourself must pray every morning to regain your magic," the mage reminded the priest. "Surely you can't fault me for doing something similar."

"But at least when I run out of magic, I can still crush things with my hammer!" Glorien hefted his weapon, for emphasis.

Bathsheba raised her shoulders and held up her hands, palms open. She was either trying to cast a spell or give the international symbol for "Whaddaya gonna do?"

"I say we do what the wizard wants." Jerald was making a final pass on the corpses to make sure they didn't miss anything. "We need everyone at full strength when we reach the caves."

"Bathsheba is smarter than I," Bob grunted. "I defer to her wisdom."

"Oh, for the sake of the Golden God..." Glorien sat down petulantly and waited for the wizard to take a nap.

They camped for eight hours, while Bathsheba dozed, then studied her thick dusty tome intently. Bob killed time by sharpening his sword and polishing his armor. Jerald left them for a while, claiming he was "scouting," though everyone knew he was looking for something to steal. Glorien just prayed. Mostly for patience.

When the wizard was ready, their shadows were growing long, and dusk was approaching. "Hup, hup," cheered Bathsheba as she hefted her pack and started back along the trail. "We'd better hurry if we want to make it before dark."

Glorien ground his teeth as they set out once again.

Just as the sun was setting, they came upon a grotto with a beautiful pool of water. Their approach disturbed some sleeping animals, and a few butterflies and birds flew past them in the gloom. Near the pool, half-buried in a small mossy hill and nearly concealed by ivy, was a rusted metal door.

"Hark, I see the entrance!" Glorien took a step forward.

Jerald clutched at his arm. "Be careful, good brother priest." The treasure hunter pointed at something hidden in the undergrowth just a few feet away: a human-looking skull, half-covered in moss and dirt. The party glanced around and discovered a half-dozen more skulls and skeletons, revealing a terrifying secret to the outwardly-beautiful scene.

"By the Golden God!" Glorien began to recite a prayer under his breath.

"What do we do?" said Bob. "I am useless against a foe I cannot cleave in twain."

"Allow me." Jerald smiled and rolled up his sleeves. He withdrew the long pole from Bob's pack. The rogue approached the door, cautiously tapping the ground with the pole, looking for traps or pits, presumably. He stopped every few feet to listen, knelt down occasionally to smell the ground, and eventually, as the sun was completing its descent, he reached the door. "A little light, please?"

Jerald asked, and Bob struck a torch to give his companion illumination as he proceeded to systematically search every inch of the door. First, he tapped with his pole at a distance, then he scanned it closely with his eyes, then he poked and prodded it gingerly with his fingertips. Glorien thought he even saw the damn fool lick it.

"Well?" Bathsheba asked. "Is it safe?"

"Indeed." Jerald nodded, pleased with himself. "I have determined that there are no traps upon this door."

"Great," said Bob, drawing his stupidly-huge sword, eager to behead something. "I shall go first!"

"No, no." Jerald held up a hand. "I will open the door. My razor-sharp senses will alert me if anything goes awry, and I can react faster to the unexpected than the rest of you."

The rest of them shrugged. The assumed he just wanted to go first so he could steal whatever was on the other side, but if he wanted to be the first into the dark and creepy doorway of evil, then hey, more power to him.

Jerald smiled, cracked his knuckles, put his hand on the large brass ring in the middle of the door, and died.

Disturbing the ring triggered the pressure plate beneath his feet. Before, when Jerald had touched the ring with his pole he had been standing far away. Now, his weight activated the trigger buried in front of the door, and two bear trap-like blades shot up out of the ground in the blink of an eye, catching Jerald right across the waist. One blade passed inside the other, and they vanished back into the ground just as quickly as they had appeared.

Jerald's torso and arms fell to the right. His legs and ass fell to the left.

The other three adventurers stood, frozen with shock and horror.

This was the moment that separated heroes from normal men. Normal men would have promptly turned around and rushed back to town and would have been well within their rights to do so. Real heroes, however, when faced with the brutal and nightmarish death of their companion, sucked it up and kept pressing on. After all, if the traps were this bad, there was bound to be good treasure inside.

"Why are we here again?" Bathsheba gasped for breath.

"Princess. Kidnapped by ogres. Big reward." Glorien was having trouble forming sentences.

"How big?"

"Pretty big."

"What are we going to do without a skilled expert to check for traps and sneak about silently?" Bob asked.

Bathsheba contemplated that for a moment. "Checking for traps and sneaking about didn't seem to do much good for Jerald."

"Perhaps we should take a moment, and pray on it." Glorien mostly just wanted to sit down so his knees would stop shaking.

"Indeed," said Bob. "We should take the time to honor Jerald's memory, anyway." He was quiet for only a moment before he added, "Do you think his boots would fit me?"

They had started to pick over the body when a stranger approached in the darkness. He was a crafty one, sneaking up right behind them without a sound.

"Who are you?" demanded Bob, whipping out his sword.

The stranger lifted his hands, palms outward, to show that he was unarmed. "I am called Harold. I am looking for my brother, Jerald. I heard he had come this way."

"You just missed him," said Bathsheba.

Harold's gaze fell upon the corpse at his feet. "My brother! What happened?"

"He got chopped in half," Bathsheba replied as if that wasn't the most obvious question anyone had ever asked.

"I must avenge him!" Harold croaked, kneeling beside his brother.

"Avenge him? He got lopped in half by a door." Bathsheba looked at him sideways. "The only thing you could venge against would be your parents' poor genes for making your brother too stupid to enter a less dangerous profession."

"No, this is the fault of the foul monsters that set this trap! I will slay them all! Let me come with you. Jerald taught me everything he knew; I can help you against the beasts in this dungeon."

"Um, sure." Bathsheba shrugged.

"Wait!" Glorien tried to be the voice of reason. "Is it safe to let some random stranger come along with us?"

Bathsheba shrugged again. "I didn't know any of you until we met in a tavern yesterday. And I mean, he looks just like Jerald."

"I will settle this." Bob put on his best, knightly voice. He raised his sword and pointed it at Harold. "Do you, Harold brother of Jerald, swear to be an honorable man, and on the spirit of your deceased sibling, swear to avenge his death?"

"Yes, that's what I just said."

Bob sheathed his sword. "Good enough for me. Now let's get this show on the road." The fighting man stepped forward and reached for the door ring. There was a "swoosh" and a "scrulsh" and a "thump." Then another "thump" as the top half hit the ground.

"To hell with this," said Bathsheba. "I'm going home."

Bathsheba did not, ultimately, go home. It did not take much convincing for her to stay. There *had* to be some good swag inside that cave/dungeon/tunnel thing. As an added benefit, they had not even finished burying the bodies before they found a replacement for their dead fighter, Bob.

"I am Bob the Second." The large man announced himself as he entered the grotto. The other three men looked at him strangely. "What?"

"The resemblance is uncanny." Glorien squinted in the gloom.

"You knew my father?"

"Your father?" Bathsheba was incredulous. "I didn't think Bob was old enough to have a son your age... apparently the exact same age as your father."

"Bob the First looked much younger than he was." The big man was dressed in plate armor and had a huge battle-axe hung across his back. "And I look older than I am. It runs in the family. If you look closely, you can see my father has more wrinkles."

They peered carefully at the corpse. Harold nodded. "Oh, yes, look at that."

"Wait, you said 'knew' your father," said Glorien. "How did you know he was dead?"

"I live in the village. His ghost came to me and told me that I must go avenge him."

"He only died an hour ago."

"Ghosts move fast."

Glorien sighed. "Well, you look like you can handle yourself in a fight."

"My father taught me everything he knew. I can be of great assistance to you. And as I said, I must avenge his death."

"At the rate we're going this is going to turn into a dedicated mission of vengeful relatives." Bathsheba groaned.

"Can we get inside without someone else dying?" asked Glorien.

"I've seen the trap work," said Harold. "I should be able to disarm it now." The trap-breaker proceeded to earn his due and disarmed the trap through a series of agile motions. "It's done."

They all looked at the door and realized no one wanted to be the one to test it.

Finally, Harold sighed, stepped forward and pulled the ring... and nothing happened.

"See?" said the rogue. "Nothing to worry about."

It was at that moment that a short, grey-skinned humanoid leapt out of the darkness and stabbed him in the back.

"Godsdamn it!" cried Harold as the weight of the beast drove him face-first into the ground.

Bob II quickly jumped forward and dispatched the goblin, splattering it with a blow from his axe.

"This is turning out to be a dangerous excursion." Glorien watched the thief bleed at his feet.

"You realize we're not even in the dungeon yet, right?" said Bathsheba.

Harold moaned. "I'm not dead."

"Oh, okay." Glorien put down his hammer and cracked his knuckles. "I can handle this." The priest knelt by the wounded man's side, held his hands over the bloody hole in his lower back, and whispered the words to a sacred prayer. There was a glow of golden light as the power of Glorien's god travelled through his mortal form and into Harold's body, invigorating him. The wound closed in a moment.

"I am healed!" Harold exclaimed.

"By the grace of the Golden God, yes." Glorien wiped his hands. "You have been restored to life, so that you may fight another day and rid the world of further evil, the likes of which..."

"What are you talking about?" asked Bathsheba. She and Bob II were kneeling over the body of the goblin.

"Oh, I forgot the corpse!" Glorien joined the looting party. They were able to find six copper pennies and a rusty short sword on this particular goblin.

Finally, the would-be-heroes stepped into the dark tunnel beyond the door, guided by the light of Bob's flickering torch. They proceeded with extreme caution, not taking a single step until Harold checked the floors, walls, and ceilings for traps and other dangers. The corridor was made from even-cut stones, and within the first thirty feet, the treasure hunter found and helped them avoid two hidden pits and a poison dart trap. Unfortunately, he missed the trigger for the falling portcullis.

The adventurers leapt out of the way of the rusty iron gate as it crashed down upon them. Three of them jumped clear, but Bathsheba was a heartbeat too slow. One of the spikes pierced her calf, pinning her to the stone floor and causing the wizard to scream and twist in agony.

Bob grabbed the iron portcullis, but it seemed to have locked into the floor. "I cannot move that." He shook his head.

"I'll cut her out." Harold drew a long knife.

"The hell you will!" Bathsheba screamed in agony. "You stay away from me!"

"Look, we can't leave you here," said Harold. "We can't move the gate, so we have to remove your leg from the gate."

"You're not removing my leg!"

"I don't have to cut off the *whole* leg, just about this much flesh and muscle." He held his fingers a few inches apart.

Bathsheba grew pale, and her eyes became unfocussed. "Can't you do anything, priest?"

"Nope, I used my only spell," said the cleric.

"Dammit, that's why you need to camp and relearn your spells!" The wizard moaned.

"Really?" asked Bob II. "There is nothing you can do to ease her pain?"

Glorien shrugged, then bopped Bathsheba atop the head with the handle of his hammer. The wizard went limp. "What?" He looked into the faces of companions. "Like you weren't all wishing she would shut up, too."

Somewhere in the darkness ahead of them, they heard the scrape of claws against the stone tile, and the growl of some huge, primordial beast.

Bob II took a few steps forward, his torch thrust ahead of him, trying to get a look at what was coming. On his third step, he yelped and vanished.

Glorien threw up his hands. "Another trap door."

The torchlight could still be clearly seen, just below the floor.

"The pit's not very deep!" Bob called out. "And I can see other tunnels and doors. Maybe you should all come down here!"

Harold looked at the gate behind them, then turned back and listened to the approaching growls in the other direction. He didn't really see any other options. With two quick swipes of his blade he opened up Bathsheba's calf and then leapt down the hole after the fighting man.

The wizard woke up screaming. Glorien gave her a kick with his foot, rolling her down into the pit as well. "Oh, shut up." He jumped in himself.

When they gathered their senses, Bob was pushing the trap door closed above their heads, and they realized they were in a ten foot by ten-foot cage with iron bars.

"What the hell?" Harold demanded. "You told us to come down here!"

Bob closed the trap door above their heads, and it locked into place with a snap. "I did. It's better than being up there trapped by a monster with our backs against the wall."

Harold was livid. "And what happens with the monster steps on the trap door and *falls into the pit with us*?"

Bob II cocked his head. "I hadn't thought of that."

"Get us out! Get us out!" Bathsheba clutched her bleeding leg. Glorien was trying to bind it, but the wizard wouldn't stop flailing like a sobbing baby.

Harold rushed to the door of the rusted cage and fiddled with the lock. He only tried for a few seconds before shaking his head in frustration. "It's corroded too much, I can't pick it!"

"Allow me." Bob elbowed the thief out of the way. He cracked his knuckles, popped his shoulders, then grabbed the gate with his big beefy hands and pulled.

And pulled.

He groaned and grunted, the metal hinges whined, and a vein nearly burst in the warrior's forehead, but the gate did not move. After a moment, Bob II collapsed, spent, against the iron bars.

"I can't do it." He gasped for breath. "I'm sorry, my friends."

"Can I try?" asked Harold.

Bob wanted to laugh, but he was too winded to do much but step aside. The scrawny man, less than half the fighter's size, got a short run at the door and heaved his shoulder into it. It popped open with a crack.

"What the hell?" Bob II was incredulous.

"You weakened it?" Harold was obviously confused himself. "That doesn't make any sense."

"Um, I'm a master of unlocking, so I know just the way to hit it?"

They shrugged. They had to get out of here before the monster found its way through the trap door.

It found its way through just moments later, and suddenly a two-hundred-pound rat was lying in the empty cage. The four adventurers were outside, tying the busted door shut with a rope from Harold's pack. Glorien had put a crude bandage on Bathsheba's leg, and the wizard was leaning heavily on her staff, watching the beast in horror.

"What is that?" she asked.

"It's a giant rat," said Bob, to his credit not a hint of sarcasm in his voice.

The beast rolled over and lunged at them through the bars. It could not get through the rusted iron, but the ropes groaned and twisted ominously.

"Allow me." Harold drew his short sword with a flourish. He thrust his blade through the bars and stabbed the monster right in the neck, a wound that should kill just about any creature.

The rat didn't seem to notice.

"Well, crap." The thief sheathed his blade.

"Perhaps magic?" Bathsheba weaved a spell. A blast of blinding light shot from her fingers and hit the beast square between the eyes. It staggered back, stunned momentarily and obviously hurt, but the wound closed in seconds while they watched.

"Does anyone have any silver weapons?" asked Glorien.

The others were about to ask why when they discovered the answer for themselves. The rat twisted and transformed, its forelegs lengthening to arms, its claws widening to fingers. Within a moment there was a man sitting in the cage before them, human-looking enough, though with slightly rodent-like features.

"Please," the man begged through buck-teeth. "I am cursed! Please help me, do not leave me here in this cage."

"Not bloody likely." Harold went back to his pack once again. He pulled out two flasks and tossed them into the cage. They shattered at the man's feet, soaking his hairy legs with thick, viscous oil.

"What are you doing?" Glorien was horrified, but before the priest could act Harold grabbed Bob's torch and threw it into the cage. The rat man went up in flames.

Bathsheba gasped. Bob II whistled, impressed. Glorien took the Golden God's name in vain. The man tried to turn back into a rat, but he was already on fire, his fur burned just as readily as his flesh. He tried to extinguish the flames but rolling in the oil only spread it further over his body. His cries were excruciating.

"Why would you do that?" The priest shook Harold by the shoulder.

"You would rather we leave the lycanthrope here, to come after us once it broke free?"

"But this is a monstrous way to die." Glorien's face was pale, his nose wrinkled at the smell of burning flesh. And the screams... "Surely we could have been more merciful."

"If we had a magic sword or a silver dagger, perhaps." Harold shrugged. "I would rather have done it cleaner—this is only going to attract more monsters—but it had to be done. Him or us, right?"

"I had no idea a little bit of lamp oil could do that." Bathsheba looked like she was going to be sick.

"We should get going before this attracts more creatures," said Bob II, echoing his companion's thoughts. They watched it for a few more moments until its agonized screams turned to dying whimpers and the smell became too overwhelming to bear. Glorien considered for a minute whether or not to say a prayer, but in the end he just crossed himself and hurried after the others.

They took the nearest corridor out of the dark room, lit another torch, and followed it until they came to a door on their left. The tunnel also continued. After several long agonizing minutes searching for traps, they opened the old, swollen wooden door and found a tiny, completely featureless ten-by-ten-foot room. After noting how odd this was, and questioning whether someone had forgotten to put something in there, they settled down to rest while Harold pinned the door closed with metal spikes driven through the floor.

They camped to allow Glorien time to rest and regain his healing spell.

After he cast it to heal Bathsheba's leg, they rested another day so he could regain it again.

"Do we have enough food?" asked Bathsheba.

"I cut myself again." Bob had spent most of his time sharpening his axe. In the dark.

Finally, when they were well rested, and spells were regained, and the princess they were looking for must surely have been dead, they opened the door and set out again. The smell of burnt flesh was only a hint now – something had probably dragged the carcass off in the dark. They didn't bother to check – they headed off down the tunnel, continuing the way they had the day before.

It was not long before they found another door, this one blocking their advance. Another long and careful search for traps revealed no deadly spikes, pits or blades, but the door was locked and did require another few minutes for picking.

It swung open to reveal a pile of glittering gold coins.

"Score!" Harold cheered.

Beyond the pile of coins was a young woman in a tattered dress, bound and gagged.

Bob II's eyes widened in surprise. "Holy crap, she's still alive."

"Wait a minute," said Bathsheba. "So, we just camped in an empty room for two days while the girl and the treasure were only twenty feet away?"

They entered the room slowly, cautiously. It was a large cavern, mostly natural by the look of the stalactites, though some corners and tunnels had definitely been carved and hollowed out. The girl saw them and started yelling at them through her gag. She was a pretty thing, though her blond hair was dirty and she had a panicked look in her eyes.

"Look, she seems so excited to see us," said Glorien.

They were stuffing the coins into their packs for several moments before anyone thought to actually go check on the girl. It was Glorien who went first and knelt beside the struggling woman.

"There, there, my lady, you are safe now." The priest smiled and removed her gag.

"What is wrong with you?" she screamed. "Look out!"

They all turned just in time to see the ogre that was creeping up on them, a ten-foot tall brute wielding a club the size of man with arms as big around as trees. A single swing of his massive cudgel shattered Harold's head like a melon, spraying Bathsheba, Bob and the treasure with blood and brains.

The ogre roared in anger.

A moment later, a familiar-looking man rushed out from behind a stalagmite and headed straight for the body of the smashed thief. He was untying ropes from his hands as he ran. "Brother Harold! You came so far to find me, and just when you were about to rescue me, all was lost! But fear not, I will avenge you!" He picked up Harold's sword.

Bathsheba looked confused. "Who the hell are you?"

"I am Harold's brother, Farald!" He leapt out the way as the ogre took a swing at him. Bob II came up behind the ogre and smashed it in the hip with his axe. The blow drew a line of blood, but it only seemed to make the beast angrier.

Glorien shook Bathsheba. "Blast it with your magic!"

"Um, okay." The wizard waved her hands, muttered some arcane words, and a glowing orb of comforting yellow light appeared above her hand. It gave the chamber a cheery glow.

"What are you doing?" Glorien shook with fear and rage. "Use the other one! The killy spell!"

"I told you, I can only memorize one per day. I thought we might need more light."

"Stupid godsdamn wizard!" Glorien took a swing at the ogre with his hammer.

Farald lunged forward, stabbing the creature in the foot. The ogre grunted and grabbed the man's arm, flinging him away like a rag doll. The arm stayed in the ogre's massive hand. The rest of the body shattered against the wall.

"Wait for it..." muttered Bathsheba.

Another man appeared, once again familiar, but this one had freckles and red hair.

"Another brother?" asked the wizard.

"Cousin. I'm Morald." The new thief-looking man, who apparently had also been held captive somewhere in the ogre's lair, pulled out a bow and started firing arrows at the ogre. Bob continued to hack at the beast's legs with his axe. The ogre hit the fighter with a glancing blow and drove him to his knees, but Glorien quickly jumped in and performed his healing prayer, restoring Bob II to health so that the huge man could stand again. With all of his strength, he swung his axe in a powerful upward arc that caught the ogre under his loin cloth.

The monstrous humanoid gurgled, groaned, and died.

After a moment to catch their breath and make introductions to Morald, the party of heroes returned once again to their pile of treasure to divvy out the spoils.

"Look out!" The princess, still bound in the corner, warned the heroes a few seconds too late. As they rummaged through the treasure, a cloud of greenish smoke rose up from the between the coins right in the party's midst. Bob II caught a whiff of it first and keeled over with a rattling clang of armor against coins.

"Poison gas?" Bathsheba gasped, and inhaled a lungful of the venomous mist.

The wizard hadn't even hit the floor before Glorien and Morald leapt clear, diving into the far reaches of the cavern and holding their breath as the gas dissipated. Glorien held his breath for as long as he could until black spots floated in front of his eyes and he was on the verge of passing out. Praying to the Golden God in his head, he finally opened his mouth and took a breath.

He heard Morald do the same, and both men lay still for a few moments until they were sure they weren't going to die. A quick scan of the room revealed their warrior and wizard companions had not been so lucky. Neither was the princess, who had also succumbed to the gas.

Morald kicked some coins in disgust. "What a piss-off! Do you think we'll still get a reward for bringing back her body?" He looked at the cleric and froze.

"Glorien? Glorien what's wrong with you?"

"I don't know," said Glorien, but something was certainly not right. "I feel faint."

His stomach churned and lurched. His head was foggy, his vision cloudy. Morald watched in horrid fascination as the holy man started to vanish before his eyes. Glorien called out to the Golden God, but no sound escaped his lips. Was this an effect of the gas? Or some sorcery they had missed? He was winking from existence. Their mission was a failure, his entire life pointless. Would he see the Golden God in the next world? Or was it his lord who was destroying him now on a whim?

Within seconds Glorien was gone, and Morald stood alone and confused among the scattered bodies.

"What a load of crap!" Lisa slammed her hand down on the table, upsetting Jay's leaning tower of dice. "A gas trap in the treasure room? Seriously?"

Pete, half-concealed behind his cardboard wall decorated with dragons and heroes, shrugged and tried to look apologetic. He couldn't entirely hide his smile. "You always gotta check for traps! It's Adventuring One-Oh-One!"

"Sorry guys, I didn't think he would pull that." Jay looked under the table for his displaced dice. "I died three damn times tonight! I thought we had to be in the clear for sure!"

"You're never in the clear." Dave spat tortilla chip crumbs as he spoke. "You know Pete always tries to screw us out of the treasure in the end. It's too bad. I was really starting to get into Bob II.

Especially after he critted that ogre in the balls. André, what are you doing?"

Across the table, André was frantically erasing his character sheet. "I hate playing stupid clerics!" he grumbled. "All I ever do is heal you jerks. I never get to do anything cool!"

"Glorien's awesome!" Lisa laughed.

"Well, he's gone now!" André blew away the eraser bits with aplomb. "I'm playing a ranger next time. What the hell was the good anyway if everyone else was dead?"

Jay slammed his dice back on the table. "I'm still alive! Do I still get experience points for the ogre?"

C.D. Gallant-King is a writer, tabletop gamer, pro-wrestling aficionado, proud father and happy husband. Unapologetically Canadian, he was born and raised on the cold, rocky island of Newfoundland, was fine-tuned in the artsy streets of Toronto, and now sits on his butt in Ottawa. He writes stories about un-heroic people doing odd and sometimes hilarious things in strange worlds, including the novels *Ten Thousand Days* and *Hell Comes to Hogtown*.

What a Boatload

By Jason Lairamore

All was well in the immortal realm of Abideu, until King Miles O'Crafee's prized Unicorn died.

The roaring fire that had consumed the body of the magical beast had gone to ash, and Ninhib Gesdin, or 'Pick', as the people of Abideu called him, stood poking the remains with a stick.

"What are you, five years old?" asked Tobetha Fatun. "Show some respect. That was a unicorn, rarest creature in the realm." He pointed to the still smoldering pit. "That may well have been the last one of its kind for all we know."

Tobetha was older than Pick and liked to act like he knew a thing or two that Pick didn't. For his part, Pick let Tobe think what he liked. It wasn't like he wanted to hurt the guy's feelings. Tobe was his work partner at the King's stables, after all. He had to see the man every day.

"I hear you," Pick answered. "But did you see poor Uni's bones? They're the color of the rainbow." Pick poked at the unicorn's skull with his stick to prove his point.

"Aye," Tobe said. "I seen em'. And I don't want to again. Magical creatures keep their counsel and I keep mine."

"But he's dead, Tobe."

Pick had heard Tobe's argument too many times to count. Tobe, like Pick himself, had won the King's lottery for a life of ease taking care of Uni. The position had come with a royal title, complete with money, prestige, and security.

"Dead don't change a thing!" Tobe proclaimed, jabbing a thick finger into Pick's bony chest. "Why'd he die in the first place? We've been his caretakers near five hundred years without a problem and then bang-dead, just like that. It ain't natural!"

Pick nodded. It wasn't worth mentioning that the unicorn was magical, and so, by definition, its very existence wasn't natural. They had no clue why Uni had died. They had no clue why he had lived, either. They didn't even know how King O'Crafee had come by one in the first place.

"Wonder what is going to happen now?" he asked. His and Tobe's life had revolved around Uni for so long, it was hard to imagine a day without him.

It had been a boring life though. Being a unicorn caretaker might have sounded exciting to the regular folk outside the castle wall, but Pick knew the truth. Caring for a unicorn was about as interesting as watching grass grow.

Sure, Uni had kept the people of Abideu immortal all these years. That was great and all. But, for Pick and Tobe, the past five hundred years had dragged. Unicorns, for all their mysteriousness and unknown powers, could not be more boring. They were boring beyond words, boring beyond belief.

Uni might well have died of his own uninteresting dullness.

Why, the beast had hardly eaten or drunk anything since the first time Pick had seen it. It had pissed only once every five years or so and was known to go more than a decade between passing a single dropping.

"What happens now?" Tobe repeated Pick's question. Incredulity dripped on his every word. "We're done. The reason that kept us here is dead." He pointed to the rainbow bones smoldering in the graying ash. "We've done our last duty by burning it. It's time to move out of the royal residence, if you ask me."

"Leave the castle?" Pick muttered. The thought hadn't even occurred to him.

"You bet," Tobe said. "Five hundred years of being a pampered stable hand is long enough for me. I'm ready for something different."

Pick nodded, but didn't trust himself to speak. He'd rarely ventured much outside the castle walls. For one, the King required them to have a personal guard any time they left. The pageant-like affair of such a thing always made Pick uncomfortable. For another, people outside the walls tended to look at him strangely, like he was part unicorn or something just because he saw the thing on a daily basis.

Heavy footsteps came from the cobbled path at their back. They turned and saw Gecul running toward them. His big body bounced up and down with every step. His cheeks were as red as summer apples. His eyes were wide in what appeared to be horror. The 'O' of his mouth only added to his look of terror.

Upon reaching them, he fell down. If not for the quick action of Tobe to stop the man's progress, Gecul would surely have rolled right into the smoldering pit to roast alongside Uni's colorful bones.

Pick glanced at Tobe, but for once Tobe didn't have anything pointing to say. He just shook his head and waited for the big man to get himself under control.

It took a while. The wheezing calmed down first. With the relative return to silence Pick picked up a strange noise. It sounded like the buzzing of angry bees.

"Do you hear that?" he asked.

Gecul clawed his way to his feet. He eyed them each in turn. A stark, wide-eyed, look of incredulous disbelief was stamped upon his features.

"I'm out of breath," he proclaimed, as if they'd not just seen him almost pass out at their feet.

Gecul eyed each of them again. "Everything hurts—my knees, my back, my feet." He grabbed Tobe by his tunic and drew him close. "You would not believe how bad my feet hurt."

"Well yeah," Tobe replied, gentle pushing Gecul away. "Uni's dead, no more perfect health." He patted the tubby castle runner's gut. "Gonna have to stay away from the kitchens is all; not the end of the world."

Gecul looked stricken, like maybe the world really had come to an end.

"What's that noise?" Pick asked. The angry bee sound had picked up in pitch.

Gecul jerked out of his personal angst and nodded. "Oh, right, the King wants to see you. He said come fast."

Tobe smiled at Pick. "Our walking papers, I bet." He collected Pick with a push and they were off.

"Thanks, Gecul," Pick called over his shoulder.

"Yeah," the big man replied. "Go ahead. I'm just going to rest here a bit."

They ran back the way Gecul had come. It really wasn't that far. Uni's stables had been set apart from those of the regular animals. The unicorn's accommodations were just to the side of the entrance to the keep, built up against the inner curtain wall.

As they entered the main hall, a page told them that the King awaited them atop the upper parapet.

"Blood-hungry dragons," Tobe muttered. "Walking papers or no, I'm taking my time with those steep steps. Gecul ain't the only one with aching joints."

So they took their time with the tall stone steps that led to the highest point of the castle. And, quite proud of himself, Pick wasn't heaving like Gecul had when they reached the pinnacle. His legs did feel like wet pasta, though.

"Hold a bit," Tobe whispered harshly at the topmost step. They had stopped in the shadow of the open door that led out onto the parapet. "Let my legs catch up. It won't do to fall to my death over the rail when I walk out there."

"Mine too," Pick agreed and edged closer to the opening. The buzzing was at its loudest up here. As he gaze out upon the magnificence of the whitewashed buildings of the city proper he saw what was making all the noise.

An enormous crowd had gathered. People were shoulder to shoulder all the way from the drawbridge out to the lists, and even beyond the stockades and into the streets.

"Get out here you two!" The King called unceremoniously from somewhere unseen around the curve of the parapet.

Pick raised an eyebrow at Tobe, who joined him to look at the gathering mob.

"What the... " Tobe said.

"At once!" the King said. Pick and Tobe wasted no more time in walking out on the parapet.

King Miles O'Crafee was smiling and waving like a madman to the growling crowd as they came to stand beside him.

"Took you long enough," the King said. "This mob is about to storm the castle."

"Your grace," Pick said with a bow.

"Just stand there and look pretty," the King said. He made a motion with his hand, and the noise from the crowd slowly quieted.

"People of Abideu," the King began loudly. "All was perfect. Our waters ran clean. Our gardens produced in plenty. We ate without worry. No problem befell a single citizen."

"But no longer," a voice yelled from the crowd. "Our unicorn is dead."

The King gave Pick and Tobe a wicked grin that made the hairs on Pick's neck raise up.

"But our luck is not lost!" the King proclaimed. He turned his open hands to where Pick and Tobe stood dumbfounded. "Out lottery winners are here! They have been at the unicorn's side all these long years."

A great and unexpected cheer rang out, as loud and as deafening as any fabled dragon roar might have been.

Pick's hands went to his ears as his jaw fell open.

"What do they expect?" Tobe yelled over the din.

"They expect magic, my boy," the King replied. He once again motioned for the crowd to quiet.

"They leave now on their quest to reclaim our serenity," the King sang out. "They mustn't dally a single moment!"

Another rip-roaring applause beat at them from atop the keep's pinnacle. The King pushed them to the opening and back onto the stairs as the crowd continued its racket.

"That will keep them for the nonce," the King said once they'd started down the steep stairs.

Pick's legs burnt like fire. "But, your majesty," he said, "Tobe and I aren't magical."

His majesty was huffing loud enough that Pick thought the King might not live to see the bottom step.

"You can bet your eyeteeth you're magical," the King said between ragged breaths. "You two are the best kind of magic." He gave a short bark of laughter. "The type I can control."

"Looks like he lost his wits when he lost his horned horse," Tobe said quietly to Pick.

"Mind your tongue, Tobetha Fatun," the King said. "I really only need one of you to accomplish my plans, and I like Pick more."

They reached the bottom step. Tobe bowed to the King. "Well then, your majesty, since I am no longer needed I will gladly take my leave."

"Ha!" The King retorted. "Go right ahead." He pointed to the raised drawbridge. "I will have the guards lower the bridge and you can stroll right on out the front. Have fun explaining what you are doing to the throng out there."

Tobe's face went at once pale, but quickly changed to red.

"You set us up to take the fall," Tobe said through clenched teeth. "You knew the unicorn would die eventually, so you worked out a way to keep the people from blaming you when it happened."

"Guards!" the King said.

Pick took a step back to gain some distance should it come to blows. He knew what Tobe said was true. He could read the writing on the wall as good as the next guy.

Tobe also took a step back. He even unclenched his fists and held up his hands as a show of surrender.

"As you were," the King ordered the approaching guard.

"Let's walk, my lucky two," he continued.

They left the keep and made their slow way across the bailey.

"I did not set you up as fall men," the King said. "I figured the unicorn would die one day, and when it did, I wanted to be as ready as I could. That's why I engineered the lottery."

"You were looking for luck," Pick said.

"That's right," said the King. "It was luck that got me that unicorn in the first place and I knew it'd take luck to get another when the time came."

This was the first time Pick had ever heard the King mention how he'd come by the magical creature.

"And how did you get Uni?" he asked.

The King glanced at Tobe, who continued to fume silently beside him. "In a moment. First, let's clear the air before Mr. Fatun's head explodes."

"Explain away," Tobe growled. "How exactly is this not a set-up? The whole realm thinks we are somehow going to deliver them a fresh unicorn while you sit idly by and point fingers."

"I got the two luckiest people in the realm. And I kept them near the most magical creature known to us," the King said.

"So," Tobe interrupted. "You were lucky enough to get Uni. You could do so again. Why dupe us into doing your dirty work?"

The King smiled. "Do you think that mob out front would let me up and leave on a journey to reclaim our immortality?" He shook his head. "I'm collateral, Mr. Fatun. I cannot leave."

He eyed first Pick and then Tobe, letting the seriousness of his gaze settle in before continuing. "If you and Pick fail, what do you think the good people of Abideu will do to me?"

"Ha!" Tobe laughed. "Fool me once, shame on you. It won't happen again."

The King looked hurt for all of a heartbeat then a crooked smile appeared. "Very good, Mr. Fatun. You caught me." He patted Tobe on the shoulder.

Pick was amazed. It had only taken the King a few sentences to completely erase Tobe's angst.

"It is true that I cannot leave, but you are right," the King said. "If you do not return in a timely manner I will simply disappear in the night."

"I don't want to have to do that though," the King added. "I do rather like being the King."

"Yeah, I bet you do," Tobe said with a snicker.

"What's keeping us from disappearing once we are on this quest you mentioned?" Pick asked.

"Well, immortality, of course, my good man Pick," the King said. "If you do manage to find a unicorn, only I know how to use it properly so that it grants us all eternal health once again."

That was good enough for Pick. The King got to keep being King and they got to keep living without worry of death.

"But no more stables," Tobe said. "I want out of the castle and lands of my own."

"Deal," said the King.

At the far end of the bailey, they entered a turret. The King produced a small crank from his robes and stuck the receiving end into a small crack between the stones. A few turns later, a small opening was revealed.

"In we go," the King said. "It's all secret stuff from here on."

After closing back the hidden door, the King led them down a maze of narrow stone corridors. Meager light filtered from above, enough to light their way. The King never paused as he took one turn after another. Every so often, they ran into steps which took them deeper down.

"Where are we going?" Tobe asked. It was getting darker and darker the farther they went.

Then Pick heard it, the sound of the surf hitting the beach.

"The sea," he answered before the King could answer.

"Aye," the King said. "You're going on a little ship ride."

"But I get seasick," Tobe said.

"Of course you do," retorted the King.

Their dark travels ended at the mouth of a small cave not a dozen paces from the beach. A single sailor stood on the black sands. Beside him was a rowboat. Farther out to sea was a small longboat rigged for sailing.

Tobe moaned at the sight.

"The sailor will take you where you need to go," the King said. "On board, you will find a chest with enough gold to buy a fleet of fishing boats."

That much wealth entrusted to their care made Pick nervous.

"What do we do with the money?" Pick asked.

The King smiled at him. "'First Pick', that's what they used to call you before shortening it to just 'Pick'." He shook his head. "You won the first lottery, out of all the thousands who entered."

"That's right," Pick replied.

"Well, I hope you are feeling that luck again today. You are going to need it."

"How, sir?"

"You are going to a secret gambling establishment in a wharf on the coast of Felordor. That is where I won the unicorn over five hundred years ago."

"It is still there?" asked Tobe.

"Sure it is," replied the King, "why wouldn't it be?"

Pick raised a few eyebrows at Tobe, who shook his head. Five hundred years was a long time ago.

"Let's get this over with," Tobe said.

"One more thing," the King said. He pulled out Uni's horn from his robes and handed it to Pick. "Just in case," he said. "Keep it with you at all times."

"Just in case of what?" Pick asked incredulously, eyeing the horn.

The King huffed. "If I knew that, I wouldn't have said 'just in case'. Now be gone." He made a shooing gesture with his hand.

Pick bowed, mostly by reflex, as the King turned back toward the cave mouth.

Tobe had already made it to the waiting sailor by the time Pick found a place to secure the horn. He'd torn a piece of his tunic long enough to use as a necklace. The horn now rested under his shirt on his chest. The weight of the thing was deceptive. It wouldn't be long before the thong of fabric began to eat into the back of his neck.

"How long must I suffer that Kraken-spawned contraption?" Tobe asked, pointing to the gently rocking longboat.

The sailor, a clean shaven man of middle years, stuck his thumb in this mouth, then pulled it out to test the wind.

"Wind holds, I'll have you there afore afternoon tea."

Tobe glanced over at Pick. "Well at least now I know how long I will be puking over the side."

Pick nodded. "Let's go." The weight of Uni's horn around his neck really bothered him. He had a bad feeling about this.

Tobe was true to his word. As soon as he was aboard the ship, he puked over the side. "If man were meant to stand on the waves, he would have been born with the ability."

The sailor looked at Tobe askew as he adjusted the rigging. "That's what boats are for," he said.

"Unnatural, I say," Tobe retorted, puking once more over the side.

Pick waited patiently until Tobe looked to be mostly done with his grisly task.

"Our gambling funds are probably below in the cargo hold," he said.

Tobe perked up at Pick's words. "I'd all but forgotten." He collected a bucket from the deck before he headed below.

"Just in case," he said, brandishing the bucket in one hand while his other rested on his belly.

Pick stayed up top as Tobe handled their gold. Pick was to money as Tobe was to magical beasts. It kept its counsel and he kept his. In his experience, having money led to nothing but trouble.

Trouble—to think, they were sailing through unknown waters with a stranger for a guide, with more money than Pick even wanted to think about.

"What's your business in Felorder?" the sailor asked from the tiller.

Pick didn't know how to answer, but he couldn't out and out ignore the man either.

"King's business," he said.

The sailor smiled from his resting position by the tiller. "King's business is it? Nicely put. Most would tell me to just mind my own."

Pick stared out over the water, not trusting himself to look at the sailor lest his anxiety be too evident upon his features.

"King's business," the sailor said with a chuckle. "Well, not to worry. That bloke with the fancy robes paid me well for this little excursion."

Pick nodded and promised himself that he'd not say another word to the man.

Luckily, Tobe picked that moment to return from below. He grunted with each step. The stairs groaned as he climbed and his pockets clinked with every jarring motion. Once atop the deck, he leaned heavily upon the rail. Pick thought that Tobe was about to vomit once more, but such was not the case. Tobe took deep wracking breaths.

"Now I know how Gecul felt," he said with a moan.

Pick noticed how the fabric at Tobe's shoulders stretched with strain, and how the pockets of his pants hung low on his hips.

"I'm carrying all that I can and your share besides," he said. "It's your turn to go down and get what you can from that great treasure chest down below. There is no way we are going to be able to lift it up those steps."

Pick had no plans to do any such thing. "The King got the gold down there in the first place; why can't we get it out as he put it in?" he asked in a harsh whisper.

Tobe raised a set of bushy eyebrows. "I don't know how the King got it down there. He probably used a dozen strong men, one loading after another. It doesn't matter, anyway. Go get what you can use to gamble with."

Pick shook his head. Tobe made to protest, but stopped short. "That's right. I forgot about you and money."

Pick grabbed hold of the horn on his chest. "I've a bad feeling," he said.

Tobe shrugged. "Saying so doesn't make it go away. We'll just make sure the sailor stays in port and then come and get more treasure if the need arises."

Pick liked that plan.

The rest of the trip was made in silence. It was so quiet upon the sea that Pick heard the noise from the approaching wharf before he saw it. A great rising and falling of voices ricocheted off the water. People screamed out their wares, others just laughed in uproar, some were not human noises at all, but instead sounded like wild beasts.

"Sounds like the place," Tobe said.

"Welcome to Felorder," the sailor said.

The little longboat rounded a soft curve and the wharf came into view. Gray planking stretched for nearly as far as they could see. The entire sea bank was covered with decking lifted high off the ground by great pillars to accommodate for the tide. On the decking were masses of people and animals, colorful tents. and brightly painted permanent buildings. Boats of all shapes and sizes filled up nearly every slip.

"Now for the hard part," the sailor said.

Tobe moaned. "I'd say," he agreed, pointing.

It was low tide. They would have to use a ladder in order to gain the decking.

"I was talking about finding an open slip," the sailor corrected.

They did finally find an open place to tie off and brace their boat. As soon as they were set, a man from the decking above lowered a ladder to them. He hooked its curved upper ends over one of the deck support beams.

"Land ho!" he called in greeting and walked on before they could thank him.

Tobe looked at the ladder. "I'm going to need help," he said flatly.

Pick patted his back. "I'll push you along from below."

Tobe stepped up to the lowest rung and grabbed hold.

"Watch the boat," he said to the sailor. "We will return before dark."

The sailor nodded. "I will stay with the boat."

Tobe nodded and began up the ladder. It took every ounce of strength Pick had to help get the big man up those rungs, but finally it was done. They stood with hands on knees and sucked on the scented air wafting from the various shops.

"I'm not doing that again," Tobe said.

"I'll not let you," Pick agreed.

After a few more agonizing moments, they slowly regained enough composure to stand upright.

"Shall we explore?" Pick asked.

"I can't see us just going up to the nearest vendor and asking to buy a unicorn."

So, they walked the crowed pier until they hit the sea bank and the more permanent structures of the wharf.

"You know," Tobe said. "Any of these establishments might be the one we're looking for. How are we to know?"

Pick smiled. "We use our luck."

Tobe scoffed. "Yeah, our luck."

Pick started to turn a circle to scan the entire area, but stopped only halfway around.

Eyes wide, he pointed.

"Wha.." Tobe began, but did not finish.

From where they stood high above the current sea level, they had a good vantage point of its bluish-green waters. On those waters, sailing merrily from the pier, was the boat and their treasure.

"Stop!" Tobe screamed as he took off at a lumbering run. The heavy gold in his pockets made his going difficult.

The immediate area became alert at Tobe's declaration. Everybody, including Pick, just stared at the spectacle of Tobe's odd, clinking run.

Then Tobe fell.

It was an explosion of gold coins followed by a gasp from the onlookers. In a blink, everyone leaped for the treasure. Tobe disappeared under the mass of bodies. Pick joined the struggle.

"Tobe?" He pulled person after person from his friend. Everyone was fighting for a coin or two. As soon as they had what they could, they disappeared along the wharf.

Pick's worry lessened when he heard Tobe's growled curses from deeper in the pile. He redoubled his efforts to free Tobe from the grunting, money-hungry crowd.

As fast as it had started, it ended. Pick pulled Tobe from the ground and helped him arrange his torn clothes. The crowd of people that'd surrounded them now walked by as if nothing had ever happened.

"Robbed blind," Tobe said. "No boat and no gold. How's that for luck?"

Only one person remained close to where they stood collecting themselves. He was a short man with a greasy beard and clothes that smelled of barnyard. His eyes held an uncomfortable blue intensity that fixated on Pick.

"Is that a … a … unicorn horn?" he asked, pointing to Pick's chest.

Pick clutched the horn where it rested against his chest. His tunic had been torn in the fuss and the top of the horn stuck from the tear.

"I heard you," the man continued. "Your boat is gone. You can have mine." He pointed to a large, run down, cargo vessel with rotting planks and ratty looking sails. "Just give me the horn."

"I don't think so," Tobe said.

The man pulled out a dagger. "I'm trying to be nice. I will have that horn."

Pick looked around. There were people all around, but none of them were paying them any mind. If he yelled for help he'd probably not get it, and the man with the knife would probably cut him for his trouble.

"It's all we got," Pick said.

"That and our breath," Tobe added.

Pick got his meaning. He could see the crazy in the man's eyes as easily as Tobe. He pulled the horn from his neck and handed it over.

The man handled it like a newborn babe. His eyes widened as he brought the horn close to his face.

"Go," he said. "Get on your new boat. I'll not be a thief. It's bad for the blood."

He waved his knife at them for emphasis. Pick glanced at Tobe, who sighed and turned to do as bid.

Once on the boat, the stink of manure was worse even than the man with the knife.

"Like I told ye," the man said from the pier. "I'm a man of my word. You have your boat."

"Little good it does us when we don't know how to sail," Tobe replied.

The man looked confused for a second. "Well, where is it you are wanting to go?"

"Abideu," Tobe said.

The crazy man smiled, which made him look even crazier. He gripped the horn with both hands and stared at it. "Done. See you gents!"

Then he took off in the air like a shot, holding the horn over his head like its point led the way.

They gawked at the sight, then about fell down when the boat lurched away from the pier and began plowing through the waves back the way they had come.

"What is going on?" Tobe asked.

"That old man knew something about Uni's horn that we didn't," Pick said.

"Do you think?"

"Maybe he was a Wizard?"

Tobe scoffed. "You're talking fairy tales. There are no such things as Wizards."

But the guy had flown away. How had he done that?

"Come over here and look at this," Tobe said.

Tobe had lifted the hatch on the main deck. Pick peered inside.

"Is that what it looks like?"

"Yes," Tobe answered. "That is manure."

"The entire hold is full of manure?"

Tobe shut the hatch. "We leave with a mountain of gold and come back with a ship full of this."

"I wonder what the King will say?"

"How about you tell him."

"Why me?"

Tobe rubbed his hands on his torn shirt. "You're first pick and all."

The trip back took less time than the trip there. The boat, under whatever magic the greasy man had placed on it, slipped through the water like a child pulling a toy boat on a string. It wasn't even time for supper when their boat slipped into the little harbor that was Abideu's only port to the sea.

The Harbormaster approached as Pick was tying up the lines.

"Pick?" the Harbormaster said.

"Get the King," Tobe said from the main deck. "And tell no one. We don't need a crowd here."

"Your quest?" the Harbormaster asked. "You have succeeded so quickly?"

"Get the King," Tobe repeated.

The Harbormaster bobbed his head. "Right away. Just stay there. I will be right back."

As he ran away Tobe turned to Pick. "Have fun showing the King our prize," he said. "I'm going to just sit right here and watch."

"Okay, okay," Pick said. The King wasn't going to like this.

The King arrived a short time later. He was alone except for the Harbormaster, and he sent him away quickly.

"My lucky two!" the King said once he was on deck. "Back so soon. Is our new unicorn in the hold below? If so, it smells like it needs a bath."

The King looked first to Tobe because he was the one who usually did the talking. But Tobe only smiled.

"Let me show you what we got sir," Pick said and opened the cargo hold.

The King looked at their endless supply of dung for a long time. Then he looked at first Tobe and then Pick. He gave them both very shrewd looks.

He picked up a single dropping and put it in his pocket.

"Come," he said. "I will see you back to the castle."

"That's it?" Tobe asked as they climbed from the ship.

"Until morning it is," he said.

After informing the Harbormaster to post a guard on the boat and to let no one on board, they made their way back to the castle. A plain unmarked coach awaited them. They climbed in and the driver took off at a gallop.

"What happens in the morning?" Pick asked.

"We shall see how lucky you are," the King responded.

"Pah!" Tobe said rudely. "Keep your half-speak for the crowds. Either tell us true or don't say anything."

The King shrugged. "I won't know until the morning."

They arrived back at the castle without any aplomb. The King bade them good day, and they went to find their supper.

"Well, that was a waste," Tobe said once they'd returned to their residence.

"It really was," Pick agreed. "A whole boat full of it."

"Ha! How in the world did that happen?"

"I don't know. Lucky I guess."

Tobe shook his head. "I'll see you in the morning."

After a good night's sleep Pick felt much better. He ate a hearty breakfast and walked down to the fire pit to see if Uni's bones were still there. As he figured, nobody had touched them. Uni was completely Pick's and Tobe's responsibility. It didn't matter if he was alive or not.

He got his hands dirty pulling Uni's rainbow remains from the pit, but didn't mind. As he was searching for any bones that he might have missed in the ash, Tobe joined him.

"Well, any word?" Tobe asked.

"None that I've heard," he answered. He finished collecting Uni's bones as Tobe watched.

Gecul came at a trot as he was about to head to storage for a wheelbarrow.

"King wants a word," the big man said.

Pick and Tobe exchanged glances.

"Why aren't you breathing hard?" Tobe asked.

"Because you guys succeeded. You are heroes," he said. "I feel great again. Don't act like you don't know."

"Let's go," Tobe said with a grunt. They took off at a run. What Gecul said was true. Pick did feel better. Running wasn't hard at all.

The King was waiting for them in the main hall. Once he saw them, a smile split his face nearly in half.

"Come, come," he said. He led them from the hall into his private chambers. When the door was fully closed, he turned back to face them.

"I can tell by your faces that you two have no idea what you have done."

"We brought you a boatload of crap," Tobe answered immediately.

The King clapped his hands. "Yes you did. But more importantly, it is unicorn crap."

"That whole cargo hold was unicorn crap?" Pick asked. He'd never seen that much unicorn crap in his entire long life. Uni had only dropped about one dropping every ten years.

"It looks like," the King answered. "But, more importantly, it is the crap that has kept us immortal all these years."

"What?" Tobe asked with a shake of his head.

The King nodded. His exuberance was radiant. "Yes! I drop one dropping every decade into the city well, and we are granted immortality for another decade."

Pick's eyes widened. "With all that in the boat—"

"That's right," the King said. "We are set for millennia, thanks to you two."

Pick chuckled as the King patted Tobe on the back.

Tobe shook his head again. "Unicorn poop saved the day, really?"

The King nodded. "You two are heroes."

Tobe sighed. "I will never understand magic."

Jason Lairamore is a writer of science fiction, fantasy, and horror who lives in Oklahoma with his beautiful wife and their three monstrously marvelous children. He is a published finalist of the 2012 SQ Mag annual contest, the winner of the 2013 *Planetary Stories* flash fiction contest, a third place winner of the 2015 *SQ Mag* annual contest, and a recent Semi-Finalist in the first quarter of *Writers of the Future* Volume 33. His work is both featured and forthcoming in over 65 publications to include *Perihelion Science Fiction*, *Stupefying Stories* and *Third Flatiron* publications, to name a few.

You can connect with Jason at:
https://www.facebook.com/jason.lairamore

Mr. V's Cleaner

By Christopher Powers

Vlad took his father's hand in his and squeezed it with gentle affection. He knew time was against them by the way the old man's fingers trembled like sausages on a skillet. Soon he would be gone; becoming little more than a pile of grey ash.

"I have just two requests," the old man rasped. He tried to wriggle into a more comfortable position but the sides of the coffin offered little maneuverability. "Lean in close, boy, don't make me raise my voice."

Vlad leaned in close. The stench of death, so much like rotting garlic, permeated from his father's mouth in thick billows. The twin pointed fangs still loomed out from under his pale pink lips, but now they looked less frightful and almost delicate hanging down from his drawn jaws like melting icicles.

"I've lived a long life," the old man croaked, and Vlad was pained to see how much the effort to speak diluted his father's eyes. He could recall how yellow they once looked, so full of furious glee and a burning hunger which was hard to satiate. The frail skeleton lying before him now was not the man who had brought him into this world, not the same man who had taught him how to prowl the night and catch cattle which walked on two legs. This was an imposter, because surely the man Vlad had loved so dearly and feared so strongly in equal measure could not be the same decrepit creature writhing out the last ounces of his life in the bowels of a castle he himself had helped build brick by brick during those dark days of 1066.

"Everything belongs to you now. This castle and everything within its walls."

"Thank you," Vlad whispered.

"Including Mrs. Jansen."

Vlad nodded. "Of course. Whatever you ask of me now I promise to honor."

"Good..." The old vampire wheezed a string of violent coughs. When it was over, he rasped, "Mrs. Jansen and her family have long held residence here. They took great care of me when your mother was killed. If it hadn't been for them, this whole castle would probably have fallen into ruin by now. And you might not have lived very long at all."

"Yes," Vlad said. This story had been recounted to him many times down the years.

"Mrs. Jansen has earned her place within these walls, just as her mother and her mother's mother earned their place before her. Although she is older now, I want no harm to come to her. No matter what happens, no matter how hungry or angry you might become, Mrs. Jansen is not to be touched under any circumstances."

Vlad saw that familiar glint in his father's dying eyes and knew he was serious.

"Leave me now. My time draws near."

Vlad left the room.

Later that day, when the sun was high in a slate grey expanse of sky, he returned to the dark antechamber and found a pile of dusty ashes on the silken bed of his father's coffin.

Many hours later below a full and bloodless moon, Vlad returned to the castle with a belly full from feasting on the humans who lived in the nearby town. It was always easier to hunt for prey on weekends because so many people came outside of their warm, well-lit homes to play merry into the early hours – just when Vlad was at his most virile.

He wandered through the castle halls, still partly in awe that he now owned everything inside its cavernous walls; from the coats of armor to the expensive paintings, it was all his and his alone.

"Welcome home, Mr. V. Did you have fun tonight?"

Mrs. Jansen was standing on a stood, her svelte frame reaching high into one corner of the room while she swatted cobwebs with a feather duster.

"It was...eventful," Vlad replied. He wondered how Mrs. Jansen felt about working for a family who survived by killing and eating her own kind.

"Well, that's OK then." She swung her arm along the ceiling and a tangled web of dust fluttered to the ground. "I made some chicken earlier, in case you weren't successful during your hunt."

"Thank you. How is my father?"

Mrs. Jansen stopped cleaning and looked over her shoulder, floral dress whipping up round her thighs as she did so. "I thought you knew, dear." She climbed unsteadily from the stool and hobbled towards him. Vlad could see tears filling her eyes. "Your father has expired."

And before Vlad could speak, she had both arms wrapped tightly around his waist, squeezing color into his pale face. "It'll be all right," she cooed. "It'll be just fine. Everything will be fine." She began rocking him back and forth as though he was a small child.

"I know he's dead, Mrs. Jansen," Vlad said, his voice muffled by the floral blouse bunching into his mouth. "I mean, how are the remains? I didn't have time to collect them up earlier. I thought we'd pour him into one of those nice vases in the west wing."

Mrs. Jansen stepped back. "Remains? I didn't see any remains," she replied. As if to double stamp her point, she propped her thick-rimmed triple lens spectacles back onto the bridge of her nose.

"They were there when I left," Vlad pressed. "Perhaps you just missed them."

"Uh-uh. I cleaned the whole room, from top to bottom and there wasn't a thing in that old coffin except for some dust."

"Dust?"

"Yes, a big pile of it. Stacked up in Master Olaf's coffin. You wouldn't believe the smell. Like rotten vegetables it was."

"That wasn't dust," Vlad said. "Those were ashes."

Mrs. Jansen waved a dismissive hand in his direction. "Dust, ash, it's all the same."

"My *father's* ashes."

Mrs. Jansen had returned to her place atop the stool, whistling a tune to herself.

"What did you do with them?"

"With what?"

"The *ashes*!"

"Oh, that pile of old dust. I vacuumed it up."

The color Mrs. Jansen had squeezed into Vlad's face drained.

"Where's the vacuum now?"

Mrs. Jansen was still humming her tune. "The cupboard under the stairs."

"Which floor?"

"Third. No, second! What am I thinking? Must be going senile in my old age. It's on the ground level."

Vlad rushed from the room, taking the stairs two at a time and stumbled into the cupboard. He spotted the vacuum cleaner propped against the near wall and tore it out, quickly ripping open the bag and sending dust into the air in a puff of grey cloud.

Vlad dug with both hands, seeking out the ashes but realizing quickly how futile the job was. One piece of dust looked like another. He would never find his father's remains this way.

Vlad hurried into the hallway and came back holding an electric-blue vase which he placed on the ground before hefting the vacuum's bag over its opening and pouring the contents inside. He noticed an old candy wrapper tumble out, probably Mrs. Jansen's because vampires did not eat sweets as a rule (they tended to get lodged in the fangs), but did not retrieve it from the vase. When he was done, Vlad returned the vase to its place on the shelf. It would have to do for now, he thought.

He stormed back upstairs, a tenacious rage bubbling just beneath the surface of his bloodless veins. Mrs. Jansen was down on hands and knees, her rear end stuck up in the air while she scrubbed at a stain on the carpet. Vlad had a sudden urge to run forward and bury his size fourteen boot in the seat of her floral dress, but his father's words halted him. He would not—*could* not—disobey the man's dying wishes.

"I got the ashes back," Vlad said through pursed lips. "Now my father can rest in peace, alongside all the candy wrappers and dust bunnies."

"That's good, Mr. V," Mrs. Jansen replied cheerily. "Let me just finish up here and then I'll go make a start on dinner."

"I've already eaten, remember?"

"Growing lad like you, I'll bet there's still some room left for a little home cooking."

"I'm 76 years old," Vlad muttered.

"Well, I'm 87," Mrs. Jansen shot back in that same cheery voice. "And I still like a good old-fashioned home cooked meal."

Vlad groaned. "Fine. Make whatever you want. I'll be in my study. I do not expect to be disturbed."

"Very good, Mr. V. I'll call when dinner's ready."

Vlad's study was a large room in the castle's west wing which overlooked the courtyard and part of town. From here he was able to look down at the people middling around below. He imagined these people as being like those lobsters you saw in restaurants which floated in their tanks while fat, greedy eyes peered in at them and prodded the glass as they selected which one deserved to die for their gluttonous pleasure. To Vlad, keeping any animal enslaved in such a way made him sick; if you wanted to kill something, then kill it quick and move on.

He wasn't looking out the window now, but sat back in his father's (now his) reclining chair listening to the castle's heavy silence. It was something he liked to do, especially when no one else was home.

From outside he could hear faint voices, but during the day those curtains remained pulled. He glared at the bright yellow shaft of light which burned just below the curtain's hem. Though he had never seen anyone die by Light Burn before, he knew enough about the damage it caused to stay clear.

Vlad was just beginning to close his eyes when Mrs. Jansen's voice carried along the hallway and into his ears. "Dinner's ready, Mr. V!"

"I said I wasn't hungry," he grumbled under his breath, but rose and headed downstairs just as she was calling him again. "Hurry up or it'll get cold!"

He sat at the table and awaited Mrs. Jansen's arrival with the food.

She hobbled into the room carrying a large silver serving dish. Sweet, aromatic smells wafted out from beneath its domed lid. As she placed it down before him, Vlad asked with a resigned sigh, "What have you cooked for us?"

"Ah, it's one of my favorites," Mrs. Jansen said with a swell of pride. "It's an old family recipe."

"Well let's have it then," Vlad said impatiently, although he had to admit he was actually feeling a little peckish now.

Mrs. Jansen raised the dome lid and a familiar smell rushed out. "*Voilà!*"

Vlad's eyes sprung wide as he threw himself back against the chair, tilting it all the way back and crashing down onto the stone floor with a clout. He crawled along the floor, his nostrils flaring, eyes reddening and watering profusely. He tried to crawl away but the smell followed, its wispy tendrils reaching his mouth and crawling inside, setting his tongue on fire and his fangs a-chattering.

"Close the lid!" he stammered. "Close the lid!"

Mrs. Jansen shook her head. "Honestly, you try cooking something with a little bit of spice and he throws a tantrum. OK, I'll take it away."

She replaced the lid. "It's funny," she said more to herself than Vlad, "your father couldn't tolerate me making garlic, either. Perhaps you're allergic." She hobbled towards the kitchen, humming a tune as she did so.

Vlad climbed to his feet and rushed to the bathroom, splashing his face vigorously with cold water. The crazy old coot had almost killed him! If he'd been any slower the garlic might have gotten into his lungs, and then...The thought was too awful to consider and he brushed it away.

First the ashes, and now this. *Was Mrs. Jansen trying to kill him?* he wondered. It seemed ridiculous, of course. She was an old woman, an old woman who had lived and worked in this castle her entire adult life. To her, Vlad was like a son. She always treated him well.

Then she's going senile, he concluded. A senile old woman living in my castle.

Vlad thought the possibility of her being out to kill him sounded more pleasant.

Several days had passed since Mrs. Jansen's unfortunate cooking fiasco and Vlad was feeling better about things. When he had spoken with her she seemed normal, even spritely, and she displayed no signs of her previous odd behavior.

Must have been something she ate, Vlad considered as he sat in his gloomy study and listened to the sounds of his prey as they talked and laughed and lived their mundane cattle lives just beyond the high stone walls of his home.

Perhaps whatever was wrong has now passed completely and she will be fit as a fiddle again.

Vlad knew that must be it. He looked at the watch on his wrist and saw it was just coming up to noon. If he was to make a successful hunt tonight, then he needed some rest. He headed down into the castle's lowest level and entered the same room in which his father had passed less than a week ago. His old coffin was still there, only now it stood against the back wall. Vlad considered sleeping in the coffin; it was much roomier than his and the linen bedding was to die for, but he decided to leave it be.

He climbed into his own coffin and pulled down the lid, before swiftly opening it again moments later and climbing out. His whole body was itching from head to toe!

"Mrs. Jansen!" he boomed.

A moment later she hobbled into the room. "Yes, Mr. V?"

"What the hell have you done to my bed?"

"I haven't done anything to it," she said in that sweet motherly voice.

Vlad looked from the coffin to Mrs. Jansen and then back to the coffin again. "Nothing? As in you haven't been near it?"

"Nothing as in nothing," Mrs. Jansen replied.

"Well it itches something rotten."

"That'll be the new washing powder," Mrs. Jansen said.

Vlad gaped at her. "You didn't wash the linen? My *toile* linen?"

"It looked dirty." She nodded to his father's coffin. "After I saw all that – what did you call it Mr. V? *Ash* – I decided the whole place could do with a spring clean."

"It's October."

"So I took the linen from your little coffin there and ran it through the washer a couple times."

Vlad swayed. "Do you know how delicate this linen is?"

"It did feel quite antique," Mrs. Jansen admitted, "but I thought that was just because it needed a good old wash down."

Vlad did not reply. He climbed back into the coffin, still scratching at the rough itches along his back, and closed the lid. For the rest of the day he lay there, itching and scratching and cursing the old woman's name.

He was awoken some time later by a sharp grumbling in his tummy. He rose from the coffin and stepped to the window. Full dark seeped beneath the curtains.

"I'm headed out," he called to Mrs. Jansen. "Be back in a few hours."

"Righto Mr. V," came her jolly reply.

"Do you need anything while I'm gone?" he asked, and although she always said no, he still liked to ask.

"No, dear, you go on now."

"Are you sure you'll be OK?" he called back.

"Of course," came the reply.

Vlad dived from the window, quickly transforming into a bat, and soared around the town for a while. It wasn't a good night to feast and very few people were on the streets, but he made do with what was available.

He returned full and satisfied, but also tired.

He considered calling to Mrs. Jansen and telling her he'd be sleeping through the day, but then decided to leave her alone. She was probably already asleep herself.

He climbed back into the coffin and, despite the itching, fell asleep almost immediately.

It was the warm glow on his skin which woke Vlad. He stirred in the confines of his coffin, and then raised the lid.

Bright streaming sunlight poured into the room, covering everything in its warm yellow hue.

Vlad dropped onto his back, suddenly terrified. The curtains were never open down here, never. "Mrs. Jansen!" he called. "Mrs. Jansen!"

She hobbled into the room. "What is it, Mr. V?" she asked.

"The light!" he screamed. "Turn off the light!"

"I can't turn it off," she replied gently, "It's daytime."

"Pull the curtains then!" he demanded. "For God's sake, woman, pull the damn curtains!"

"I can't," she replied.

"Why not!"

"They're in the washing machine."

"*What?*"

"Should be done shortly."

"What am I supposed to do until then? Just lie on this itchy linen and wait for nightfall?"

"Now don't be grouchy," Mrs. Jansen said, her voice stern. "You managed to sleep yesterday afternoon just fine. Now put your lid back on and try to get some rest."

"I could've been killed!" he screamed.

"Oh get off, that little bit of sun won't hurt you."

Vlad had to bite his tongue in order to keep from exploding on the old woman. He slammed the lid down and lay in the darkness.

"I'll come get you when the curtains have finished their cycle."

Vlad had a sudden urge to spring out of the coffin and sink his fangs into the hag's wrinkled old neck, but once again his father's voice echoed through his mind and stayed his hand.

"Just get those curtains back in here *now!*"

"All right, all right, you're the master of the house. I'll go get them."

"Thank you."

Vlad waited in the darkness for Mrs. Jansen to return. After several minutes, he heard the door open and then Mrs. Jansen hobbling across the room.

"Are they up?" Vlad asked tensely.

"Yes," she replied. "They're wet and they're droopy but they're up."

"Thank you," Vlad said again and threw back the coffin lid. Darkness had blissfully returned to the room.

"I don't want this happening again. Ever. Do you understand me?"

"Well, all right then. But don't come complaining to me when this place is so dust-covered you can make handprints on the windows."

"I won't."

Mrs. Jansen suddenly brightened. "You know, I really enjoyed working for your father. But some of his rules, they were so petty."

Vlad smiled in spite of himself. "In what way were they petty?" he asked.

"Oh, you know. It was just the little things which bothered him so much. I remember he used to make me go around the castle pulling the curtains every morning, which made sense of course. And now I also remember why he wouldn't let me cook garlic." She gave Vlad a frail smile. "And why you didn't like my garlic the other night. But then, while I was looking through my drawers, I came across something which I completely forgot I owned." She patted her chest just below the neck. "I never used to take it off, but your father was adamant I not wear it in the grounds. Especially not while you or your mother were around."

"What was it?" Vlad asked.

"What was what, dear?"

"What was the thing you found that my father didn't want you to wear?"

"Oh, oh yes. This." She reached down the front of her blouse and pulled out a gold chain. Something dangled on the end of it and when Vlad moved in for a closer look, Mrs. Jansen uncurled her fist and revealed a gold crucifix resting in her open palm.

The pain was immediate. Vlad let out a howl and staggered backwards.

"That's the same reaction your father had," Mrs. Jansen mused. She turned towards the door. "Well I can't be hanging around here jaw-jacking all day; I've things to be getting on with."

Vlad was still moving backwards, his vision momentarily blurred by the reflection of that gold artifact. He groped out and snared the curtain. It felt moist in his hands, but he didn't care. He wiped his face and the blindness began to clear.

He took a step forward, not realizing the curtains had created a splurging soapy puddle on the ground, and slipped. In his sudden panic he reached out for purchase and snared the curtains, which pinged from their clips and ruffled to the floor along with him.

Sunlight poured in, drenching the grimy old room.

With his father's words still clattering around his head, Vlad screamed out the first thing he could think of to relieve the fresh wave of rage growing inside of him.

"I hope all your rabbits die and you can't sell the hutch!"

And with that the curtain came down on Vlad's brief time as head vampire, snuffed out by a heavy dose of Light Burn and one infuriating senile old woman. He just about heard the faint reply of "But I don't own any rabbits," before the world blinked out.

Christopher Powers lives in Essex, United Kingdom, with his wife and son, and works full-time as a content copywriter. He's been writing scary stories for many years, and loves to scour market stalls and thrift stores for horror paperbacks. His previous works can be found at *DeadLights Magazine* and *Deadman's Tome*. He can be contacted at powers1902@yahoo.co.uk and Twitter @Powers1902.

Split

By Marc Sorondo

There was an old, rusted spring in the couch that squeaked every time Chaz's weight shifted. He ignored it, focusing on the girl with her tongue in his mouth. Her name was Susie or Lucy or something like that, and she was making things easy for him. He ran his fingers through her long, blonde hair. He ran the tips of those fingers down her neck and then lingered over her breasts before he cupped them with both hands.

"Chaz, you're an animal," she moaned.

Chaz pulled away and flashed a devious smile. "You have no idea."

She smiled as he leaned back in and nuzzled at her throat. "This whole night has been... unreal."

"Only gets more interesting," he said, his lips brushing against her collarbone.

"Your roommate isn't going to come home, right?" She pulled away just enough to still feel his breath on her skin.

He smiled again. "Could be home any minute. Who cares? I'll tell him to take a walk." He opened two buttons at the top of her shirt, better exposing the swells of her cleavage and the edge of a scarlet bra.

She let him open another button. "Is he going to be mad if he gets home and we're... you know, doing stuff on the couch?"

Chaz smiled at her again, but there was something sharp in his eyes, something that could have been mischief or something worse. "Are we going talk all night or are we going to do this?"

She smiled at him like a little girl whose just been chided by a teacher. "Sorry." She pouted at him and unbuttoned her shirt the rest of the way.

He drew his sharp gaze across her exposed body. "You are gorgeous." He leaned in and kissed her again.

He reached down, started to work at the button at the top of her jeans, when the door to the apartment swung open.

Walt strode in, too lost in his own thoughts at first to recognize what was going on in his living room. It was the flash of movement as the girl snapped her shirt closed over her naked abdomen that roused him out of his thoughts.

"Oh, shit, I'm sorry," he said. He turned away from them and held up an open hand, as if to block the site of them from the eye in the back of his head.

Chaz closed his eyes and exhaled. "Cock-block."

"Sorry, sorry," Walt muttered, still facing away. "Let me just grab a few things, and I'll get out of here." He headed towards the kitchen, careful to keep his gaze averted.

"I'm sorry," the girl said. "We didn't realize..."

"Hey, don't worry about it. I'm the one who interrupted." He grabbed keys off the kitchen table. "And now I'll be out of your hair."

Charlie's brow furrowed, and he looked at the girl. There was nothing sharp about his gaze now, and there was no recognition in his eyes. He smiled at her, but it was without its devilish charm. "Uh... hold on one sec, Walt," he said over his shoulder. He held up his extended index finger, meeting the girl's eyes for only an instant before looking away, and said, "I'll be right back. Give me one second."

She set to work buttoning up her shirt as he rocked back, the old couch spring squeaking in protest, and stood.

Walt lingered in the kitchen, looking out the small window over the sink full of dishes. "What's up?" He asked without looking Charlie's way.

Charlie got close and whispered, "I don't know who this chick is or how she got here."

Walt peeked into the living room, where the blonde was nearly done covering herself up. There was still just a bit of scarlet peeking out from the open top of her blouse and a generous view of her remained. "Sure you don't, you dog," Walt said. He grinned and held out a closed fist.

"Yeah," Charlie said, smacking his palm against Walt's knuckles. "Something like that."

Walt looked down at Charlie's hand folded over his fist, and then up at Charlie's face. "Hey, no worries man. She's hot. Like out of your league hot. What are you stressing about?"

"You've got to help me get rid of her."

"Seriously, don't worry man. I'll take off. You're good... but stay out of my bedroom. No messes like last time, you freaking dirt bag." Walt shook his head and took a step towards the door.

Charlie grabbed his arm and pulled him back. "Seriously, I need her out."

"But... but... she's so hot."

"Great, so take her out. She's all yours."

Walt's eyes widened. His grin fell away for just an instant, then returned. "You turning gay on me? Or, oh my god, does she have syphilis or something?"

"Shut up. We really need to get rid of her."

Walt patted Charlie on the shoulder. "I see. I know what this is. Are we suffering from a little performance anxiety, big guy?"

"Oh, go fuck yourself."

"Well you sure can't do it, limp dick." Walt chuckled to himself.

"Keep talking shit, werewolf hunter, you freaking psycho." Charlie shook his head. "Forget I said anything. Get out of here and I'll see you later."

"I'm not a psycho. I have pictures to prove it."

Charlie's brow furrowed again. "BS. Prove it."

"Fine. I'll be right back." He walked back through the living room—shooting the girl his most winning smile as he passed—and into his bedroom.

Charlie followed as far as the middle of the living room. He stood there, a coffee table between him and the girl. "Hey... uh, Susie."

"It's Lucy, asshole."

"I know, I'm... just kidding. Listen to this. My roommate here fancies himself a werewolf hunter, and he claims to have pictures proving that there's a werewolf around here.

Lucy laughed. "You're a weird one."

"I'm weird? He sees hairy monsters."

"Apparently you're both weird."

Walt came out and threw a stack of pictures down on the coffee table.

"Wow... you actually printed them out?" Charlie said as he reached down to pick a few up.

Lucy took one and gasped. "These actually look real."

"They are real. And I'm going to kill it and really prove it. Pictures and a body... I'm going to be famous."

"How'd you get these, man?" Charlie asked. He picked up a few more.

"I saw it run past here last night so I followed it. I wanted you to come and see it, but I guess you slipped out a little before I saw it. I keep telling you it's around here... it's here all the time. I think its human form lives around here or something."

Charlie shook his head. "No way. If it's around here so much, how come I've never seen it?"

Walt shrugged. "You never seem to be around when I see it." Walt grinned. "Hey, Clark Kent, maybe you're really Superman." He laughed and looked at Lucy. "He'd make such a gay werewolf."

"Werewolves aren't real, you nut-job," Charlie said. "That's why I haven't seen it."

"Come on, man. Look at the proof." Walt took the pictures from Charlie, flipped through them, and handed one back. It was zoomed in, a close up shot of hunched, hirsute shoulders, a long, canine snout, and eyes that glowed a fiery red.

Lucy dropped the pictures back onto the table and pointed at Walt. "I'm with him. These don't look fake to me."

"I didn't realize you're a photography expert," Charlie said.

"I didn't realize your friend was a special effects expert," Lucy said. She stood. "Maybe I should just leave."

"There is no such thing as..." Charlie doubled over and groaned. He squeezed his eyes shut, ground his teeth.

"Oh my God," Lucy said. She stepped around the table strewn with photos and placed a hand on his shoulder.

"Hey, bud, you all right?" Walt asked.

"I'll be back," Charlie groaned. "I have to go." He half stood and shuffled back towards the door to his bedroom. Once inside, he slammed the door.

"Is he going to be okay?" Lucy asked.

"I don't know. Did you guys meet at a Mexican restaurant, by any chance?"

Lucy grimaced and shook her head.

A grunt came from Charlie's room. There was a clatter, as if he'd pushed all the crap off the top of his dresser and let it crash down to the floor.

"Come on, man... keep it together," Walt shook his head. "You're on a date here."

"Oh, God help me," Charlie said through clenched teeth.

Lucy looked at the door, but backed away from it a step.

"So," Walt said. After a beat of awkward silence he added, "How you doing?"

"Fine... I guess."

"So... how'd you meet Charlie, anyway?"

Lucy smiled and her gaze drifted toward the ceiling. "I'm at this bar, and Chaz walks in and immediately comes over and steps between me and the guy I'm talking to and asks me if I want a drink. The other guy got mad... really mad, and he was huge... like body builder huge. But Chaz didn't even acknowledge him. Finally the big guy gets so mad that he grabs Chaz's shirt, and Chaz just went nuts."

Walt shook his head. "That doesn't sound like Charlie at all. And what's this Chaz crap? And why would you go home with a psycho like that?"

"It's short for Charles, right? It's not like he lied."

"He did lie. His name's not Chaz... it's Charlie."

Lucy shrugged. "I don't know."

"God," Walt said, shaking his head again. "He must be more drunk than I thought. Why the hell would you go home with a guy like that?"

She shrugged again. "No guy's ever fought for me before."

"Talk about asking for trouble," Walt muttered.

Charlie groaned again and then growled through his teeth. The growl went on and on, its timbre dropping.

"Charlie?" Walt knocked on the door. He tried the knob and found it locked. "Charlie?"

Charlie fell silent for just an instant. Then, a booming howl erupted from behind the door.

"Charlie!" Walt yelled, throwing his shoulder into the door. "Charlie?" He slammed his shoulder into it again.

He looked back at Lucy, her eyes wide, her mouth a tense line, and yelled, "It's here! It's here!"

He took a step back and then lunged forward, kicking the door just above the knob. It flew open, scattering splinters across the floor as it ripped out the back of the jamb.

"Oh my God! The werewolf ate Charlie!" Walt screamed as he stumbled backwards.

The beast appeared in the doorway, its hand up, palm sides out. "It's okay," the thing growled.

Walt stumbled all the way back to the wall and then slid over until he could reach the aluminum baseball bat they kept leaning, perpetually unused, against the TV stand.

"A bat? Some werewolf hunter! Don't you need silver or something?" Lucy said.

"You ate my friend, you bastard!" Walt screamed as he ran at the wolf.

He swung, and the beast dodged.

"I didn't eat anyone," the wolf growled. "I didn't."

"Bullshit, you monster!" Walt swung again and caught the wolf in the arm.

"Ow, dick!" the wolf growled. He punched Walt in the shoulder.

"If you're still hungry, eat the girl... not me," Walt said, holding the bat up between himself and the wolf like a sword.

Lucy rolled her eyes. "My hero."

"Both of you, shut up," the wolf growled. "I'm not going to eat either of you."

Walt and Lucy were silent.

"Walt, it's me," the beast growled. "I'm the wolf."

"No shit, you're the wolf. I can see that."

"Dumbass, it's me. Charlie."

"Liar!"

"If I'm not me, and I'm some monster who broke in and ate me, where's all the blood?"

"He's got a point," Lucy said.

"Stay out of this, you weirdo," Walt snapped.

"I'm the weirdo? Me? The werewolf hunter and his hairy roommate and I'm the weirdo?"

"The werewolf never came here until you showed up!"

"The werewolf is your roommate!"

Charlie took a step towards them, his hands up as if to silence them. Instinctively, they both took a step back.

"You came home with him even when he was acting crazy... if it really is Charlie."

"It is me," Charlie growled.

"All right, if you're really Charlie, what's my middle name?"

The wolf laughed, a sound like distant thunder. "Gertrude... after your mother."

Walt's shoulders sagged. He looked down at the floor. "How could you be a werewolf?"

"I don't know. It's only been like this for a few months. I didn't get bitten by a wolf or anything... except that freaky girl I brought home from that bar the one night, you remember her? She bit me something fierce, but I think she was just kinky."

Lucy turned to Walt, and shook her head as she admitted, "You know what, you were right. This is what I get for going home with some random psycho who beats up a guy to try to get me in bed."

Walt shook his head. "But... Charlie?"

The wolf growled and looked from Walt to Lucy and back again. "Actually, I prefer Chaz." He rushed forward and grabbed Walt, his clawed hands wrapping around his arms and squeezing. He tossed Walt against the wall with ease and turned to face Lucy.

"This just gets better and better," Lucy muttered as she backed towards the door.

"You still want to fool around?" Charlie growled.

She reached into her pocket, her progress toward the door uninterrupted. "Do I look like I want puppies?"

"Come on. I take doggy style to a whole new level," Charlie growled. He took a step toward her, fumbling with his pants, his clawed fingers unable to grasp the button.

Lucy pulled out a small cylinder of pepper spray, flicked the cap off with her thumb, and sprayed it into the wolf's face. She held it on, the spray continuous until sputtering out and squirting a final weak stream onto the wolf's snout.

The wolf sneezed twice and then chuckled. "You think pepper spray's going to do anything?"

From behind the wolf, Walt swung the aluminum bat like a golf club, smashing it into the wolf's crotch.

Charlie fell to the ground, whining like a dog and holding himself. "Cheap shot," he said. "You fight like a girl."

"Want another?" Walt asked.

The wolf half sat up and punched Walt in the groin.

Walt dropped the bat and fell to his knees.

"Okay," Lucy said, heading for the door again. "It looks like you two have some issues to figure out, so I'm going to go. Don't get up. I'll let myself out."

"Wait," Walt said. He got to one knee. "I'm coming too."

"Hang on. You guys can't leave me like this. I need your help," Charlie said.

"Sorry, Chaz, you're on your own," Walt said. He stood, but still cupped his manhood in his right hand.

"It's me. It's Charlie."

Lucy shook her head. "I'm out of here. You guys figure this shit out. It has nothing to do with me."

"You can't, like, change yourself back?" Walt asked. "It'd be easier to trust you that way."

"If I could control it, you really think I'd still be like this? You think I'd have changed in the first place?"

"There's that werewolf hunter knowledge," Lucy said.

Walt sighed and pointed at Lucy. "Why did you have to bring this girl home? There weren't a bunch of other nut-job girls you could have had here for this?"

"Listen, Van Helsing. It's not my fault you're the most screwed up people in the entire world."

"Van Helsing hunted vampires!" Walt yelled.

"Listen to you, you psycho," Lucy said.

"I'm not a psycho; there *is* a damn werewolf lying on the floor!"

Charlie stood up. "Can we please focus for a second? I need to get rid of this. I can't live the rest of my life never knowing whether or not I'll turn into a monster."

Lucy threw her hands up in exasperation. "How exactly would we help with this little problem of yours? I don't think a thorough waxing job is going to do it."

"The weird kinky chick," Walt said. "It must have been her."

"You think so?" Charlie asked.

Lucy sighed. "I hate to say it, but psycho-boy is probably right. How often do you get bitten? She's probably the only time, unless you're even weirder than I already know you are."

"So what do we do?" Charlie asked.

"Find her and kill her," Walt said.

Lucy snickered. "Ooh... the hunter strikes again."

"You know what, you can just go home. You're annoying me anyway," Walt snapped.

"Good," Lucy said. "I'll just leave you alone with the split personality horror flick over there, and when he pulls another one-eighty, he can eat you."

"Walt," Charlie said, "I think we need her, man."

"And why, exactly, do we need her for anything?"

"You really want to be alone with me right now?"

"What makes you think I want to stay?" Lucy asked.

"I'm counting on the fact that you're a good person and want to help," Charlie growled.

"Well... what if I'm not a good person?"

"You know she's not," Walt said. "She had the hots for..." He smirked and said in sing-song, "Chaz."

"Please, Lucy," Charlie said. "We can't do this without you."

"You don't have some other friends you can call?"

"No," Charlie and Walt said in unison.

Lucy sighed. "Why am I not surprised? Lucky for you guys, I couldn't resist something like this."

"Thank you, Lucy," Charlie said.

She nodded but didn't say anything.

"What do we do until you change back?" Walt asked.

"Tie him up," Lucy said.

Charlie was tied up, a nylon rope around his hirsute upper arms and then around his wrists. He sat on the middle couch cushion, his taloned feet up on the coffee table, the nylon rope around his ankles.

Lucy and Walt sat on either side of him. The TV was on in front of them, but no one was actually watching it.

"This sucks," Walt said. You could've told me the truth instead of calling me crazy when you knew I wasn't."

"You got all weird, saying you were going to kill the werewolf and all that. I didn't know if you'd try to kill me."

"Come on, man. You know I wouldn't try to kill you... unless you tried to kill me first."

Lucy shook her head. "This is very touching and everything, boys, but shouldn't we be trying to figure out what we're going to do about this?"

"I think we should find that other girl and kill her," Walt said.

"What is with you and wanting to kill everyone? Why is that your answer for everything?" Lucy asked.

Walt shrugged. "I'm just saying, the chick's a werewolf, and she's biting people when she has sex with them. Who knows how many horny werewolves are running around all because they had sex with some monster slut?"

"Hopefully it won't be that much of a problem. I'm still me when I change. My mind is still mine," Charlie said.

Lucy frowned at that. "Lucky us, we have Chaz to deal with."

"What are the odds she's bitten someone else with that sort of condition? The others will all be normal," Charlie said. "If they change, they'll probably just panic and hide. They won't attack anyone."

"And if they do?" Walt asked.

"Why don't we kill them too, huh, Walt?" Lucy said.

"Lay off," Walt said. "I was just asking."

Charlie squirmed against the ropes holding him. "Wait, wait, quiet down a second."

"What?" Walt asked. "What's the matter?"

"This commercial is hysterical. Watch this."

For a minute they're all quiet. Then Charlie and Walt erupt into laughter in unison.

"No matter how many times I watch it," Charlie said, "that guy getting hit in the nuts with the baseball will always be funny."

Lucy shook her head. "I sort of liked Chaz when he wasn't all wolf-like. No offense, Charlie, but you're sort of a dork."

"You would like Chaz," Walt said.

"God, you are just pissing me off, you know that," Lucy said, shaking a finger at Walt.

"Whatever. Seriously, Charlie, we need to discuss your taste in girls. First you bring home a werewolf, then this one."

"What's the matter, Walt? Before, you said she was hot," Charlie growled.

Lucy grinned. "Did you really?"

"Yeah," Charlie growled. "Called me gay for not trying to get rid of him to be alone with you."

Walt sighed. "Was all that information really necessary for us to deal with the problem at hand?"

Lucy smiled. "You got a little thing for me, huh, Walt?"

"This is such bullshit." It was Walt's turn to shake an extended finger. "That was before I knew you were such a pain in the ass. Besides, I also asked him if you had a venereal disease, so that should balance things out."

"Shut up," she said. "No you didn't." She looked to the wolf sitting between them.

Charlie nodded. "He did."

"Do I really look like that kind of girl to you?"

"Yeah," Charlie and Walt said in unison.

"Such assholes."

"Whatever," Walt said. "Look at how you're dressed. And your whole reason for going home with Chaz was 'No guy's ever fought for me before.' What kind of girl does that make you?"

"I'm still a good person."

"Women!" Walt said. "You just don't make sense most of the time."

"Your situation makes sense?"

Walt smiled. "*Touché.*"

"Whatever kind of person you are," Charlie growled," After this is all over, we'll owe you... a lot. If you ever want to see us again, that is."

"You will owe me, and I'll stick around just for that... and for Walt's charm, of course."

Walt shook his head. "Anyway... Charlie, I just thought of something. What the hell makes you change? There's no full moon tonight."

Charlie shrugged. "I've been trying to find a pattern to it, some sort of trigger, but I haven't figured it out yet."

"And what makes you change from Charlie to Chaz?" Lucy asked.

Charlie shrugged again.

"Wonderful," Lucy said.

Walt, Charlie, and Lucy were slumped together on the couch. Walt's head hung back and he snored mightily. Charlie, human and still restrained, slouched forward. Lucy's head rested on Charlie's shoulder. She too snored, though the sound of it was all but lost in the cacophony Walt made when he slept.

Charlie awoke with a start, shaking his head and pulling at the rope around his wrists. His movements disturbed Lucy, who looked around groggily as if she'd expected to have dreamt the whole thing, and Walt, who continued snoring for a beat after he'd regained consciousness.

"Hey," Charlie said. "I'm back to normal. Untie me."

"Oh, yeah," Walt said groggily. "Hold on a second, Chaz."

"Chaz?"

"Just testing," Walt said as he set to work untying Charlie.

Lucy shook her head. "So what's the plan exactly?"

"We get cleaned up, rest up, and then tonight we go to the bar where I picked up that girl. If we don't find her there, we'll go to another bar. We'll keep looking until we find her. Then I'll get her to come back here where you two meet me a few minutes later. Then we can do whatever we need to."

"What makes you think you can pick her up again?" Lucy asked.

"Why wouldn't I?"

"I hate to break this to you, but if it was Chaz that she went for last time, she isn't going to be coming home with the real you tonight."

"You don't think I can do it?"

"I'm sure you can't."

"No worries," Walt said. "I've got a plan."

Lucy laughed. "Let's hear it."

Walt grinned and nodded. "Act like Chaz. Be Chaz... but without actually being Chaz."

Charlie laughed nervously and shook his head. "I don't think I can."

"I know you can," Walt said. "You have it in there somewhere. You just divided yourself up, so that one part of you is all badass, and the other part is... you know, you. But we're desperate, so you're just going to have to take your balls out of that other pair of pants and act like Chaz tonight if you want get this freak to come home with you."

Charlie shook his head again. "I don't know."

"Is there another way?" Lucy asked.

"I guess not." Charlie sighed.

Walt grabbed Charlie by the shoulders. He nodded, his maniacal grin overwide on his face. "Be badass."

"The real me can't get a girl... that blows."

Lucy patted Charlie on the shoulder. "I'm sure you could get a girl, just not that kind of girl."

"You don't want that kind of girl anyway," Walt said.

"Hey!" Lucy reached past Charlie and smacked Walt on the arm.

"I didn't mean you. I meant the werewolf chick." Walt smiled. "You already know I think you're hot."

"Awww... Walter." She reached over again and pinched his cheek.

Charlie shook his head. "I'm doomed."

Charlie entered the apartment, and a beautiful girl followed. Her hair was black, as were her dress and her nails.

He went to the kitchen, while the girl made herself comfortable on the couch. Crouched behind the fridge door, Charlie checked his phone. He had no messages.

"You know, Chaz, I never expected to see you again. When you walked into that bar and knocked out that biker... it was like a dream."

"I've been looking for you. The last time you were here was... weird."

"What do you mean?"

"Ever since, I've felt strange... better."

"You know, don't you?"

"Of course I know. You made me into a monster."

"You can't tell me you don't like it, Chaz. I knew the moment I met you that you could handle the power, that you'd love becoming the beast."

"I'm not even Chaz. He's the beast, already was before I met you and things got worse."

The raven-haired girl crossed her arms but remained seated on the couch. "If that's the way you feel, then why invite..."

Walt burst through the door and Lucy ran in behind him.

"I can't believe you kicked that dude's ass!"

"Focus, Walter!" Lucy scolded.

The girl stood. "What's this? What do you have planned?"

Walt's eyes narrowed. "We're going to kill you."

Lucy rolled her eyes. "You've been dying to say something like that, haven't you?"

"Did I overdo it? I was trying really hard not to."

Lucy made a face. "Maybe just a little."

"What makes you think you could kill me?" The dark girl took a step toward Walt. The fingers of her right hand had become too long, the nails at the tips of her fingers lengthened into claws.

Walt grinned boyishly. "Because we're werewolf hunters, bitch!"

"Ooh, sorry, Van Helsing, that's the stupidest thing I've ever heard."

Walt's eyes went wide. "Van Helsing? Damnit! Don't you read? Van Helsing hunted vampires. What is it with you girls?"

The girl shook her head. "You talk too much. You're going to die first." She strode towards Walt. Her jaw pushed outward, forming a short snout, as her teeth slid out, digging into her lips.

Walt backed toward the door, pushing Lucy behind him.

Lucy grabbed his arm. "You had to get all pissy about the Van Helsing thing."

"That should be common knowledge. You shouldn't be able to get out of school without knowing that."

Charlie scanned the room and grabbed the first object that seemed useful. He ran up behind the transforming beast and bashed her over the head with a potted plant. The pot exploded into a mess of dry dirt and pottery shards.

She turned and scowled at Charlie with yellow eyes. She grabbed him by the throat and lifted him off the ground, her talons cutting into the side of his neck. "This is a three-hundred-dollar shirt, you piece of shit." She threw him across the room.

Walt winced. "Charlie, you okay, man?"

Charlie groaned. "I guess."

"Leave the hunting to the pros, man."

Lucy clicked her tongue. "You're not a pro."

"In a minute, you're going to be a piece of food stuck between my teeth." Her arms lengthened; her shoulders broadened until they strained the fabric of her shirt.

"Could you really eat that much?" Walt asked.

"And not put on weight?" Lucy added.

"Another benefit of the transformation." She looked Lucy up and down. Black fur sprouted on her arms and lupine face, tufted up from the collar of her shirt. "You might want to consider it... looking a bit thick yourself."

Lucy reached into her pocket and pulled out another cylinder of pepper spray. She popped the top and stepped past Walt. "How does this look, bitch?" She sprayed the aerosol into the wolf's face.

The wolf sneezed.

Charlie slapped himself on the forehead. "You got more pepper spray? Because it worked so well on me?"

"It's just a distraction," Lucy said, rolling her eyes.

Walt dove at the wolf from behind Lucy and plunged a silver letter opener into her abdomen.

The wolf stumbled back. Her wide eyes went from yellow to light brown, and the black fur receded into her skin. "You've got to be kidding me? The idiot's the one who kills me?" Her snout shortened and her claws retracted back into her overlong fingers.

"Damn straight! I told you I was a werewolf hunter!" Walt gave the dark girl the finger and then threw an arm over Lucy's shoulder.

She looked at him, seemingly both annoyed and amused at once, and pushed his arm from her shoulder.

"Bullshit," the wolf said. She coughed up a mouthful of blood that spilled from her now-human mouth. She reached down and took the handle of the letter opener with completely human hands but seemed not to have the strength to pull it out.

The others watched as the girl fell to her knees. She turned her head to look at Charlie and moved her mouth, as if to say one last thing to him, but another gush of blood came from her mouth. Then she fell forward.

For a moment, they stared at her still form as a crimson puddle spread out from under her body.

Finally, Walt looked to Charlie and asked, "Feel any different?"

Charlie shrugged and then shook his head. "But I didn't feel any different after she bit me either."

"So how do we know if it worked?" Lucy asked.

"I guess I just wait and see what happens," Charlie said.

"Wow." Walt shook his head. "I'm moving out."

Charlie nodded and then pointed to the body of the dark girl on the floor. "What the hell do we do with her?"

"You know, I hadn't thought about that part before," Lucy said.

"How the hell are we going to get a body out of the apartment with no one seeing it?" Charlie asked.

Walt shrugged. "Fuck it. Burn the apartment and then it'll be done with."

"They would find the body all burnt up, Van Helsing. What then?" Lucy said.

"We tell the firemen that our friend got trapped in the apartment. Then they'll think the fire killed her," Walt said.

"That's a terrible plan," Lucy said.

"It is... besides, I need somewhere safe to stay until I'm sure I won't change anymore," Charlie said.

"And I need to stay somewhere else until you're sure you won't change anymore," Walt said. He looked at Lucy and put his arm around her again. "Hey, Lucy, can I stay with you for a while?"

"No... wouldn't want you to get my venereal disease." She pushed his arm away again.

"You're still mad about that? I said you were hot."

She walked away and he followed after her.

"It'll probably only be for a couple of days," Walt continued.

Charlie looked down at the body. Walt's plan was asinine.

"One day, Walter... two max," Lucy said.

Walt guided Lucy into his room.

Charlie shook his head and turned away from the body. He went to the kitchen, got a half-empty bottle of overproof rum from the cabinet and a box of wooden matches from a drawer and headed back to the living room.

He took a big swig off the bottle, and poured the rest of it out onto the girl's body.

It was a terrible plan. He'd almost certainly end up in prison.

"Fuck it," Charlie said to himself. "Hey, Walt," he called. "Grab your shit fast. We've got to get out of here."

He struck a match and dropped it onto the girl's back. The booze lit up in an instant, and the fire rushed out over the puddle of rum.

Walt stuck his head out of his room and his eyes widened at the site of the flames. "I thought you said it was a bad plan? Holy shit... I thought you'd wait a damn minute."

Lucy stepped out and shook her head. "Idiots. The two of you are both idiots."

"I've got it," Charlie said. He turned his head and pointed to the deep gouges on the side of his throat. "You two get out of here. I'm going to stay. Get rescued by the fire department. Tell them we were attacked."

"That plan still sucks," Lucy said.

"Not your problem," Charlie said. "I owe you two." He looked at Walt. "When the cops ask, because you know they will, just tell them you were out and don't know what happened. Hell... go out for a few beers now, and you won't even really have to lie all that much."

"You're crazy, bro. I love you... but you're crazy," Walt said.

Charlie nodded. "Hurry up and get out of here."

The fire spread slowly at first, consuming the rum but failing to spread to the other surfaces. Once the carpet caught, the quality of the flames changed. The fire spread quicker from then on. It made more smoke and seemed to burn hotter, with more intensity.

Chaz sat there, watching the fire devour the evidence of his old life. He held up his left hand. His extended index finger was too long; the nail that tipped it was a claw. He stuck that claw into one of the small wounds on the side of his neck and pulled it down. The skin unzipped at his touch and the blood flowed, but he knew he was too powerful to have any worries. He dragged that nail across his forehead, opening up a long gash.

He didn't fear injuries or flames. He didn't fear anything... except silver... and werewolf hunters.

Marc Sorondo lives with his wife and children in New York. He loves to read, and his interests range from fiction to comic books, physics to history, oceanography to cryptozoology, and just about everything in between. He's a perpetual student and occasional teacher. For more information, go to MarcSorondo.com.

Ghost Train Out

By Alex Azar

Vacation wasn't a word I got to use often in my old line of work. Sure, as a paranormal investigator I had down time, way too much some years if I'm being honest, but with the possibility of a case coming up at virtually any time, an extended vacation seemed like an impracticality at best and an impossibility at worst. Although I never advertised as such, that's another reason I always prefer to travel by train when needed. It gave me some time to myself and think back to when I had gone on vacations with my family.

Over the years, cases took me all over the world, and as often as possible a train was my means of transportation. However, a handful of times, the train was not only the destination, it was the case.

I.

Sleep eludes me despite how long I lay in bed or how much I drink. When work is slow I become restless, and for quite a while now, 'slow' doesn't even begin to cover the business. Financially, the agency is secure from our last few high-profile jobs, but it doesn't create new work when there is none to be had. When working a case, actually doing something and expending energy, I can sleep like a baby through most nights, even when I don't have the time for it. On the other hand, I'm contemplating moonlighting as anything, just so I could sleep. I kid with Sarah, maybe even as a male stripper. She assured me that wouldn't solve my problems. "I love you, James, but a male stripper isn't going to get you any more work."

We share a laugh as she walks out of my office, but stops short with a startle when she opens the door. "Ooh, hello. Welcome to Argus Agency. Do you have an appointment?" She knows damn well we haven't had an appointment all month.

I can't clearly hear whoever she's speaking to, but my name is clear. Sarah answers whatever their question is. "Yes, he's in. Let me see if he is currently available."

Back into my office she walks, now with a little extra hop to her step. She's excited about this prospect, and working with Sarah for so long I've grown to trust her suspicions. "There's a young lady and a gentleman here to see you. They asked for you specifically."

As weird as it is for me to even admit, I've grown a moderate reputation since the whole sea creature incident was aired live on TV. Most clients ask for me upon coming to the office, and even get disappointed if I'm unavailable.

Sarah admits to not fully understanding what the case is about, but assures me, "It's right up your alley, Mr. Peckman." Familiarity goes out the window anytime there's a potential client in the office, no matter how often I tell her to call me James every time.

I don't bother telling her again. "Sounds good, send them in."

In walk two people: a woman, possibly Hispanic, in a well-tailored ash gray skirt suit, and an older Caucasian gentleman in an ill-fitting uniform. I can't place the uniform occupation, but it looks familiar enough that it will bother me until I place it. The blue vest feels like it should be a dead giveaway. She speaks first. "Thank you for seeing us on such short notice. Well, no notice actually."

"You're welcome; please have a seat. I'm Detective James S. Peckman, how may I be of service?" The practiced introduction rolls off my tongue so easily, it no longer has meaning for me, but people that saw me on TV get a kick out of hearing it, and I still agree with what Elizabeth taught me about having a solid introduction to begin all business interactions.

He remains quiet in his seat, letting her do the talking. "My name is Martha Aguilar. I'm a representative for Atlantic Railway Transportation. And this is Adi Meir, one of our conductors."

That's why his uniform looks familiar. I've ridden on their trains more times than I can remember. "I'm familiar with ART; I ride the rails frequently for my job. What seems to be the issue?"

Mrs. Aguilar takes a moment to compose herself. As often as I've dealt with this sort of thing, I'm sure this is all new to her, so I give her the time she needs. "Throughout the year, we have a themed party trip on the third Saturday of every month traveling from Boston to Baltimore. Unfortunately, for the past several months, we've had..."

I like to make a game of predicting how clients will address the subject. She doesn't seem to be the type to swear, perhaps 'odd disturbances'?

"We've had what we'll call odd occurrences." Damn alliteration, I was close. She sees the levity in my eyes, "Is everything okay, Detective?"

I tell her I'm simply curious as to what occurrences they may be experiencing, and ask her to continue. "Well, we'd have to say it would be best described as missing certain blocks of time." She looks at Adi for confirmation.

He nods silently, allowing her to continue steering the conversation. She tells me how the entire staff aboard the party train reports periods of blackouts for just over eleven minutes. "Every trip, it happens for the same length of time as the train travels through Jersey City, New Jersey."

Dealing with the supernatural and paranormal for as long as I have, I know without any calculations that "just over eleven minutes" actually translates to six hundred and sixty six seconds, the biblical number of the beast. It usually doesn't add up to anything more than someone forcing the number to fit a motif. But I am intrigued by the train-wide memory loss. "Is this something only the staff has been reporting, or are the passengers also experiencing this?"

"Passenger reports have been unsurprisingly low concerning this. The demographic of this trip is typically younger than our regular trips, and it is a party atmosphere."

"I understand." A bunch of drunk college kids aren't going to notice a few missing minutes in the midst of a party. "What about video surveillance? Surely there have to be some cameras on the train. What do they show during this blackout?"

Clearly expecting this question, Martha produces a tablet with a video already queued up. "All cameras, including both old and newly installed, as well as cell phone videos, jump the eleven minutes with no footage of anything in the interim. We've even tried video calling during this time, and the line drops, and is unable to make another connection until the time passes."

"Adi, is it safe to assume you've been on the train during one of these occurrences?"

He nods yes, while remaining silent. Looking at Martha, she gives him the okay to speak. "Not just one of them, I've been the conductor for every party trip since Atlantic began them."

"What can you tell me about how you feel before, after, and if possible during these periods?"

Adi chews on his lower lip for a few seconds before starting, "Well, I tell you, how I feel during is an easy enough answer. I don't feel nothing, not a thing. First few times, I didn't even know nothing was amiss or missing." He pauses long enough to chew on his lip again. It's a wonder he hasn't drawn blood yet. "Before 'n after I feel right as rain, no nothing out of sorts. If I wasn't told nothing, I wouldn't know nothing."

He's back to chewing his lip, but my next question is for Martha, "Have anyone else expressed any discomfort or anything significant?"

Shaking her head before she answers: "No, quite the opposite, in fact. Even after experiencing this time loss, most employees ask to remain on this shift. Including Adi himself."

Seemingly ashamed of this, he nods while staring at the floor. "It's true. I was offered to take a different ride, but if nothing's going on other than me forgetting a few minutes and I feel better 'an usual, who 'm I to complain?" He says the other employees feel the same way.

Martha confirms, "We've tried switching out the entire staff for a run, but the majority requested to stay on."

"Adi, how do you feel right now? Are you tired, or find yourself more tired than normal?"

"Detective, I'm damn near seventy years. Ain't no day go by I don't feel tired, but that ain't nothing to do with the train. Nothing weird going on, just something honky with the new tech keeping time. That's all." He goes into a mini-tirade against modern technology, specifically cell phones for a bit. I let him go on, hoping there may be something of note in his rambling. There isn't.

Martha cuts him off. "I assure you, Detective Peckman, it is more than a tech glitch. While I'll admit nothing of harm has happened to our passengers or staff, ART can't in good conscience let this continue for fear of what may happen."

"May I ask, Adi, are you this excited for any of your other shifts?"

He looks confused as he tries to eat his lower lip for the better part of a minute before finally answering, "I reckon not. It's weird but don't mean nothing; ride gets a fun crowd with good music."

A few explanations come to mind, but none fully cover each facet of this:

Demons have been known to feed on souls in small increments to prolong torture, but none of these victims appear to have been tortured in any fashion.

Incubus and succubus feed on others' life forces, but the entire train, especially the staff that have gone through this more than once, should feel excessively tired and have low energy. They shouldn't look forward to taking the trip again.

A mass haunting of a large number of ghosts could account for the blackout and electronics failure; I can't see anyone enjoying that, though.

Djinn are known to create a sense of euphoria, but typically one victim at a time, and for a much longer period than eleven minutes. Once they have you, they typically don't let you go until you die.

A field of mythological lotus would hypothetically be able to render everyone on a train unconscious for a period, but 1) the effect on technology is unexplained, 2) a field that large would affect a greater number of people in the local area, and 3) up to this point, they are in fact mythological. Granted, pretty much everything I've dealt with since becoming a paranormal detective was at one point a myth, but it seems hard to believe an entire field of lotus would appear in the middle of the U.S. with no one becoming aware.

Martha and Adi see me weighing the options in my mind for a moment. I apologize, but explain that I have a few thoughts that may explain what's going on. "I'm going to need a list of all employees that have worked this shift, and if there's any passengers that have ridden this more than once. Also, please compile a list of all complaints from employees and passengers alike."

From her large purse, she produces a file and hands it to me. "This folder contains a full list of employees on the affected trips, along with all available information. Also included are all complaints and reports of the blackout period. If you can provide an email, I'll have all of this sent over to you, along with any information about repeat passengers that I'll have to look into." She ends with a pat on the file as it sits on my desk.

I'm impressed with her thoroughness, and contemplate telling her as much, but decide to refrain. "Thank you. Sarah out front will be able to provide you with our fax number, as well as our standard contract. One last question: if my internal calendar is running right, the next ride is this coming Saturday, correct?"

She looks disappointed with herself at the question. "That is correct; I apologize for the short notice. We at ART had an internal debate whether or not to bring in outside influence, which I was against, no offense, and things weren't decided by the board until early this morning. Will that be a problem?"

I chuckle to myself, because even when big corporations need help, they can't get out of their own way. "No, that won't be a problem."

II.

The past few days have been fruitless for me, and just as futile for Sarah. She is researching the files on all employees and repeat passengers of the party train, and I've been trying to narrow down my list of possibilities.

While Sarah still has a lot of information to sift through, I decide to take a trip. Specifically, I'm taking an ART train that travels the exact route of the party train. This should give me a better insight of the setting, and possibly even solve this four days before the next time phenomenon occurs.

Martha Aguilar insists on accompanying me. I tell her it isn't necessary, but I thank her for the free ticket. "I ride the trains so often, maybe I should have added a stipend to the contract for free rides for life after solving the case."

This may be the first time I hear her laugh. "Well, if you solve the case, perhaps we can discuss a compromise." The way she stresses the word 'if' makes it difficult to tell how serious her doubts are. She's taking me on a tour of the train, and we enter the dining car when one of the attendants offers her a drink. "I'll leave that for our guest to establish the mood."

"I like the way you think, but I'll have to pass while on the job."

She thanks the waitress, and lets her continue her duties. "If this trip is uneventful, perhaps you'll take me up on the offer during our return trip." I can't tell if she's flirting with me or not, and I don't know if I care or not. In any case, I tell her it sounds like a good idea, and we continue the tour.

We enter an ordinary passenger car. Martha informs me that this one is usually swapped out for the party trains. "This is where the entertainment performs. We have musicians and comedians that

216

take turns performing on stage here." She motions to the side of the train currently facing east. "I understand it may be difficult to picture; however, tomorrow I can take you to the station, and show you the car itself. Would that work?" It does, I tell her, and on we go to the next car.

Making our way through, she tells me the next three are more passenger cars, and finally the cargo bay. "We'll continue the tour shortly, but we're entering the zone of the blackout." She's visibly shaken by this, and clearly would like to be anywhere else.

I remove my cellphone from my shirt breast pocket, and ask Sarah on screen if she heard all that? "For the most part, I think the shirt muffled your voices at times, but the line hasn't dropped yet." She questions the need to be on a video call, if she was going to spend the majority in my pocket.

"I didn't want to risk losing the connection when trying to call you back; better to keep it live the whole time." Her response contains no words, but her intention is clear. Her yawn indicates she'd rather be sleeping, and I don't blame her.

Martha intervenes before Sarah can scold me further, "James, we're entering the blackout zone any moment..."

III.

And eleven minutes and six seconds pass with absolutely no effect on us or any other passengers. "Sarah, you still there?"

"Yes, can I go to bed now?" Martha's chuckle is all the response she needs, and she disconnects the line.

"Well, that wasn't how I expected things to go." I ask Martha what she thought, and she says this is exactly what she anticipated. "How do you mean? I thought the whole point of us coming on this trip was to test the theory that..."

"No, no. That was your reasoning, ART has tested this several times in the past. I just thought you may not have taken me, or 'us', at our word." And she's absolutely correct, there's no point in me even trying to protest. Some things a detective needs to learn on his own, and I'm glad she's aware of this. "We run this round trip nine times a day, every weekday, and six on weekends. The only one that has ever been affected to our knowledge is the party train, coming this Saturday."

Of course she had mentioned this when she and Adi first came to me, but it's one of those things that I needed to see firsthand. This trip did help solidify one thing, "I guess we can cross lotus off the list."

"Locus, like from the Bible?" I can see the doubt in her eyes.

I laugh, but playfully so she doesn't think I'm belittling her, "Lotus, with a 't'. As in the mythological plant that if ingested results in a coma-like sleep. It's from the..."

"Odyssey by Homer, I've read it." She's very comfortable cutting me off. I'm not a fan of it, but she's so friendly when she does it, it's hard to be upset by it for long. "Do you think somehow the water supply was..."

I cut off her just to show her how it feels. "Actually no, but in theory a large enough field could theoretically have a similar affect just by smelling the odor."

Martha picks out a few of the words to question, "Theory?" "Theoretically?" She doesn't use a full sentence or really ask a question, but her intention is clear.

"Nearly everything I deal with was at one point a myth or a theory. Some things were proven true ages ago, but still haven't made it to the general public, while others are being discovered today. No one in my... 'circle' has reported ever discovering the mythological lotus, but that could have changed today."

"But wouldn't a field big enough to affect a whole train be noticeable? Especially in Jersey City, so close to New York?"

"It was a long shot. So, how about that drink?"

"Sure, but you're buying. Vodka cran, thanks."

IV.

"James, call on line one. It's..."

Taking the 'Do Not Disturb' fedora off my face, I grumble to Sarah through the comm on my phone. "I thought I asked you to hold all my calls?" I'm not asking to be a dick, I sincerely can't remember one way or the other. I'm sure Sarah could tell the difference, hopefully.

Her pause makes me doubt myself, "You did, but it's Thaddeus on the line."

"Right, right." Haven't spoken to him in a while, and maybe a fresh set of eyes would help me out, even if he's on the West Coast. Oh God, please don't tell me he's here.

"Hey Thad, long time no talk. How're things?" It bothers me that even though it's been years since he and I patched things up, I still feel awkward with him.

Now it's his pause that's making things worse for me when all I wanted was a mid-day nap. "Jimmy Peck, sorry about that, thought someone came into my office. But of course you're the only one with an active case, am I right? The whole country has gone quiet, but you've got a case laid in your lap. Anything juicy?"

I know he already knows all about the case. He and Sarah speak pretty much daily, not that I mind. They were friends before me; he introduced me to her in our old firm. I'm sure if he were still on the East Coast, she'd be working with him still.

"Recurring lapses in memory and complete electronic blackout. Timing adds up to 666 seconds, every month, on a party train as it enters a certain area in Jersey." I could probably be more specific with him, but since he already knows, I choose to save my breath for my first cigarette after the case is closed.

"You've ridden the rail yourself?" He asks this while knowing the answer, something he's always been prone to do. "What's different from the regular ride and the afflicted one?"

"Thank you Thad, but I don't need your help analyzing the case." If only I was as confident as I sound. But if the only difference is the 'party' aspect of the train, then... "Hmm."

My musing must have been audible through the phone. "Glad I can help. Call me once you've wrapped. It'd be nice to hear the details directly from you for a change." And like that he hangs up.

"You smug sonuva-bitch." Even though the line is already dead, I pick up and hang up the receiver with a thud for emphasis.

"Stop letting him get to you James, you know that's his way of trying." Sarah is standing in the door.

I give her as incredulous of a look as I can muster. "Yea, yea. How many times have I asked you not to talk to him about our cases?"

"When you finally mean it, I'll listen." She folds her arms over her chest, waiting for the request she knows is coming.

"Can you give me the bios of all employees that only work on the party train? Thank you."

Sarah returns to my office with a shorter stack of paper than I was expecting. "The only party train exclusive employees are the entertainment. One cover jazz band, and a comedian. He's at the top of my list. His name is Damion, for Chrissake."

"Thank you." Looking into the file, I'm too focused to notice Sarah leave the office. "Thank you!" Did I say that already?

V.

"You think it's the comedian, don't you?" Martha asks. "We vet all of our employees with vigorous background and drug tests."

I laugh, "There's no drug test that will catch whatever's going on here." She doesn't appreciate the laugh.

"So you know what's going on?" Her question was so full of hope. I hate to dash those dreams, but...

"Not quite. I have a few ideas, but it's just as likely that whatever's going on here is something entirely new." Her deflated look is too much. "But this wouldn't be the first time I've investigated the unknown, and come out the other side with answers."

She doesn't look comforted at all. "Drink?"

"Sorry, I'm on duty ma'am. Only water for me." I jiggle the large water bottle I've brought. "But please, don't let that stop you." I motion my hand to the bar, as she leads the way.

She orders a top shelf scotch, neat, and I'm just noticing how attractive she is. I wonder if the two are related. "You've been avoiding talking about your plan. Please tell me you have one. We can't wait another month."

Chuckling, I assure her I have a plan, "I'm going to observe."

...

She's waiting for me to finish, not knowing I have.

...

"Wait, that's it? You're going to watch it all happen. How is that going to happen, when you black out also?" She takes a large gulp of her drink, finishing almost half of it, and I know it's related to her attractiveness.

I never knew a female's drinking habits influenced my tastes so much. "There's more, but I think it's best if I keep that to myself."

"No, that's the kind of thing people say when they don't actually have a plan." In another gulp she finishes her drink, and I think I'm in love.

"I just need to watch everyone for a few hours to get a better understanding of what's at play during all this." I take a swig of my water to rival hers, trying to cool off. "Let's make our way to the entertainment car; I think that's where all the good stuff is going down." She follows wordlessly.

"Ladies and gentlemen, remember to tip your waitresses. And remember, you're not drunk if you can lay on the floor without holding on." Wow, that Dean Martin impersonator looks and sounds just like him.

I whisper to Martha, "I wonder why the Rat Pack cover band calls themselves The Summit."

"They should be on for another fifteen minutes before Damion takes that stage." Ignoring my comment, Martha points to the other stage on the far end of the cart. "Let's get a seat there."

"I want to hear this." And I take a step closer to the Rat Pack. Clearly frustrated, Martha feels the need to remind me that I'm on the clock, and not here for a good time. "Why can't it be both?"

She doesn't like that at all. "Excuse me?"

"I need to observe everyone, including these guys. I'll check the comedian out when he gets on stage." Somehow, she has another scotch in her hand. If I hadn't checked out the bottles beforehand personally, I would suspect the alcohol might be the issue.

The band begins to play, and the entire crowd is enthralled. Then Dean begins singing and everyone's attention triples. "My wife just told me, have I news for you. The doctor's sure, that I'm way overdue. Wait 'til she finds out my girlfriend is, too." The place erupts with laughter. I feel sorry for the comedian who has to follow this.

"Martha, I'm surprised you allow them to smoke on the train."

She has a puppy dog look in her eyes as she continues watching him. "You try telling him he can't do something." I concede her point.

Frank Sinatra joins him on stage, cutting off the song. "Oh you weren't finished? Well your drink is, so I assumed you were on your way to the bar."

Dean looks at his drink, and seems surprised to learn that his glass is in fact empty. Taking the drink from Frank's hand, he licks the rim of the glass before drinking from it. "Thanks." Without missing a beat, he goes right into his song, "When You're Drinking".

The crowd is eating it up, so is Martha, so am I.

With a new drink in hand, Frank gets back on stage, and the two do a duet medley, before Sammy Davis Jr. joins them, and the three close out their set.

"Wow, have you seen them before? Are they always that good?" As entertaining as that was, I need to keep my mind on the case, lest the urge to have a drink beats out my morals and whatnot.

Still cheering and laughing, I'm not sure if Martha even heard me, but she answers: "Every time they keep getting better and better, they always do different songs. I know it's hard to believe, but I think the banter is all ad lib."

It is in fact hard to believe, but if the stories of the original Rat Pack are true, it is very possible the act isn't scripted. "When is their next set?" I ask over my shoulder, as I watch several of the Summit mingle with the females near the stage, while others leave the car.

Apparently Martha can't hear me. "Come on, Damion is about to start. He has a thirty minute set, and then there's about another half hour before the blackout starts." On our way to the stage, she orders a drink at the bar that is delivered in record time. The employees must be afraid of her.

The bartender asks if I would like a drink, "No thanks, I've got my own." I drink from my water to prove my point.

Damion hasn't gotten on stage yet, but Martha is staring intently, waiting for him to make an appearance. Without looking at me she asks, "What do you think he's doing, that you've got him pegged as the source?"

I don't want to tell her exactly what I'm thinking, but I have to give her something. "I have a few theories, but one is feeling more right than the others. Have you ever heard of an incubus?"

She turns, needing her whole body to question the stupidity of my suggestion. "You mean the alt-rock band?"

Thankfully, the comedian is coming onto the stage now, "Never mind." We give Damion our attention.

He forgoes any form of introduction, and simply begins his routine. "If you couldn't tell from my faded Metallica shirt and black military boots, I'm super straight. But where do I go to pick up females? That's right, lesbian bars. I'm telling you, I've never gotten better advice on everything I was doing wrong. For one? This shirt and boots are a big no-no." Damion goes on about all the free drinks he gets, while never scoring. "I once felt these ginormous fake tits of a trans-girl, and they were glorious. My dick was so confused!"

The set finishes with a story of a girl taking him home thinking he himself was a trans, and her disappointment at finding 'little Damion'. Wiping tears of laughter from her eyes, Martha asks what I thought. "Not my typical kind of comedian, but he was funny. Funnier than I was expecting."

"That's great, but I was asking about the case. Do you still think it's him?"

She asks as I'm drinking more of my water. "Oh, sorry no. I haven't thought it was him for a couple hours. I'm pretty sure it's The Summit. They're a creature that feeds on the life force of others.

Something is off because their victims shouldn't enjoy the experience, but there's one way to find out for sure."

Her sour disposition lets me know she's figured out how I mean to prove it. "We're going to wait for the blackout to start?"

"I need to see them in action if I'm going to know for sure and be able to stop them."

"But James, once they start, you'll forget, be frozen, or whatever they do to us." Her confusion is understandable, but I've got a plan, and tell her as much without actually going into detail about it. "Why do I feel like you're keeping secrets from me?"

I take another swig of my water, "I am, but I assure you it's necessary for the way I work. Nothing personal." She doesn't look pleased, but less concerned. I'll take what I can get at this point.

VI.

Martha has been silently, intently, studying her watch and cell phone clock simultaneously for the better part of a minute, until, "Ok, we should be going into blackout in a few..."

It takes me a moment to notice that she hasn't lost her train of thought; she's indeed frozen stiff, as is everyone else in the car. "Why don't you just stay here, huh?" We moved to the rear car, hoping to keep Martha safe during whatever is happening. Working my way through the train to the entertainment car, it's an eerie spectacle traveling through a dozen or so frozen people like walking within a paused movie.

Entering the party car next to the comedian's stage, the setting I find myself in is both expected and unbelievable. Nearly forty people are stuck mid-party, seemingly without a care in the world, and among them are Dean, Frank, and Sammy moving freely from passenger to passenger. They're too engrossed in whatever they're doing to notice me, but I have no idea what that may be. I crawl my way into the bar at the center of the car to get a better look at what they're doing, but it still makes no sense. Through two bottles of rum, I watch as Sammy plunges his hand into the chest of one of the passengers. Slowly removing his hand, I see, gently gripped between his forefinger and thumb, a small glowing ball of energy.

"That's a soul." The whispered words barely escape my lips, and I regret it immediately. Thankfully, Sammy didn't hear me, but Frank is standing right behind me.

He just stands looking at me with a confused look on his face. "Hey fellas, scope this out. This one's still moving."

Dean and Sammy join him in standing at the entrance to the bar, and looking at me confusedly. "Hey buddy, don't look so scared. We're not hurting them."

It takes me a second to regain my bearings. "You're stealing their souls, how is that not hurting them?"

The three exchange worried looks. "How do you..."

"Holy shit! Are you the real Rat Pack?" My excitement gets the better of me.

Dean, takes a drink from his cup, and I notice there isn't ice in it, but a small glowing soul. "We never actually liked that name. We always preferred The Summit. Now our turn for questions."

"How do you know these are souls?" Sammy asks holding up the ball in his fingers.

Frank asks before I have a chance to answer. "And how are you still walking around? We've never had this happen."

"You're demons, the Rat Pack are demons, and you're feeding on the souls of the people on this train." I slosh around the remaining bit of my water in its bottle. "Holy water and blessed vinegar, not the first time I've dealt with demons, but I can honestly say I've never fought any of my musical idols."

"Fight?" Again the three share confused looks, "Why would we fight?"

Now it's my turn for a confused look, "I was hired to stop you. Not sure how I'm going to, but I will."

Sammy offers me a hand to get to my feet. "It was the clockwork of the blackouts, huh? That's what tipped off whoever hired you, isn't it?"

Stepping in front of Sammy, Frank is more to the point. He takes one of the souls from Dean's cup. "Yes, this is a soul. But look at it, look how small it is. We're not taking whole souls, only a small fraction of a soul. The meat bag... sorry human, gets to continue living, and die however they would, and still go to heaven."

"Most likely not." Dean calmly chimes in.

Sammy clarifies, "Wherever they're going, missing a little itty bitty piece of their soul isn't going to change that."

Frank finishes off where he was. "We get enough soul energy, if you will, to continue living on Earth, and these poor people get an experience of a life time, hanging out with Sammy Davis Jr, Dean-fucking-Martin, and Ol' Blue Eyes himself, me." Goddamn, this man is charming.

"So what's the big deal, friend? Why do we need to be stopped?" Dean asks like it's the most normal thing in the world to keep doing what they're doing. "We're all having a good time here. At least we're playing better music than what's coming out now. Am I right?"

I nod involuntarily; he's damned right about that. But I can't let this slide. "What about the employees? Even if taking only a small portion of someone's soul doesn't have a lasting effect, these people may not have anything left."

"Ahh." They huddle football style for a few seconds. "To be honest, we haven't thought that far ahead. But I'm sure we can work something out." Dean holds his hands wide, and what I wouldn't do to be able to agree with him.

Flicking the remaining soul from his cup into a waitress, Dean tries to comfort me. "See, all better now."

"What if that wasn't her soul?"

"Eh, a soul is a soul. And I guarantee that cupcake there isn't going to heaven, no matter how big a soul she has. If you know what I mean." The three share a laugh that I'm not privy to.

Opening the bottle top to my water, I go to toss the remainder at the trio.

"Stop, you can't stop us with that little bit of holy water."

I open my jacket to show Frank a whole bottle of the good stuff.

"Huh, be that as it may, I'm sure we can come to an agreement."

"You're demons that belong in hell; I can't make a deal with you." I want to make a deal with them, but I can't tell them that.

Frank Sinatra locks eyes with me, and those baby blues dig into my heart, "I think you'll like this deal. Hear me out, ok?" Of course I'm going to hear him out, "We'll leave. Right now, never return. Wherever we go, I promise we won't take more than one small piece of anyone's soul. We'll keep moving around, ok?"

"Yeah, we'll go on tour like we never have before. Maybe I'll start my roast again, although racism isn't as funny as it used to be." Dean withdraws within himself at the thought.

Frank finishes the proposition. "But you need to do us one favor. Make sure they keep the party train alive. These people need the escape from their shitty lives. But on one condition, make sure they never get that no-talent, act-stealing hack Michael Bublé. Not even for Christmas."

I go to protest the deal, not because of Michael Bublé...

VII.

... but suddenly they're gone. Everyone around me is moving, and a few are staring at me weirdly. To them, I just appeared out of nowhere. Thankfully I don't have time to try to explain myself, because Martha comes running in. "What happened? How'd you get in here?"

I take the drink from her hand and take a long drink, burning my chest in a way that I miss. "They're gone, and no one is the worse for wear. Well except maybe her," I point towards the waitress Dean was talking about earlier, "but I'm sure she enjoyed it."

"That's it? You say we're good, and I'm supposed to take you for your word?"

"Well, there is one more thing. Are you a fan of Michael Bublé?"

Alex Azar is an award-winning author bred, born, and raised in New Jersey. He had aspirations beyond his humble beginnings: Alex was going to be a superhero. Then, one tragic day, tragedy tragically struck. He remembered he wasn't an orphan and by law would only be able to become a sidekick. Circumstances preventing him from achieving his dream, Alex's mind fractured and he now spends his nights writing about the darkest horrors that plague the recesses of his twisted mind and black heart. His days are filled being the dutiful sidekick the law requires him to be, until he can one day be the hero the world (at least New Jersey) needs.